PENG

THE ASCENDANCE OF EVIL

Abhinav is a Mumbai-based software developer working for a financial-services firm. His debut book *The Sage's Secret* is the first instalment in the Kalki Chronicles. He has since published a second book in the series, *Kali's Retribution*.

You can connect with Abhinav at:

Instagram: http://instagram.com/am_abhinav
Goodreads: http://goodreads.com/am_abhinav

✦ From the **Kalki Chronicles** ✦

THE ASCENDANCE OF
EVIL

ABHINAV

PENGUIN BOOKS

An imprint of Penguin Random House

PENGUIN BOOKS

USA | Canada | UK | Ireland | Australia
New Zealand | India | South Africa | China

Penguin Books is part of the Penguin Random House group of companies
whose addresses can be found at global.penguinrandomhouse.com

Published by Penguin Books India Pvt. Ltd
4th Floor, Capital Tower 1, MG Road,
Gurugram 122 002, Haryana, India

Penguin
Random House
India

First published in Penguin Books by Penguin Random House India 2021

ISBN 9780143454632

Typeset in Adobe Caslon Pro by Manipal Technologies Limited, Manipal
Printed at Replika Press Pvt. Ltd, India

www.penguin.co.in

For Mishka

NOTES FOR THE READER

- This book is third in the Kalki Chronicles trilogy, with *The Sage's Secret* being the first part and *Kali's Retribution* being the second one. As this book follows the events in the previous instalments, I request you to read them first.

- Over the course of the story, I refer to 'Bhoomidevi' as 'Prakriti' as well. While Bhoomidevi represents '(Goddess of) Earth' and Prakriti represents '(Goddess of) Nature', I use them interchangeably since they are both one in my mind. Just like Anirudh/Kalki is a part of Vishnu, Bhoomidevi is a part of the larger entity, Prakriti.

Aham atma gudakesa
Sarva-bhutasaya-sthitah
Aham adis ca madhyam ca
Bhutanam anta eva ca

❦

O Gudakesha (Arjuna)! I am the atman established in the
heart of all beings. It is I who am the origin, the middle and
also the end of all beings.

—Bhagavad Gita, Chapter 10, Verse 20

ONE

Dwarka
Twenty-eight years after the Great War of Kurukshetra

The rain had slowed down to a slight drizzle. The sky was painted a midnight purple, with grey clouds gliding softly across it. The only sounds surrounding the isolated hut in the forest were the muted patter of drops falling on the roof and the leaves outside, and the timid rush of flowing water nearby.

Dweepa ticked off the instructions as he spoke, 'I am supposed to go into hiding. My disciples are to create an influence in the highest places of power, so that the final avatar can make use of it. Kalki's birth will be marked by red lightning in the sky. Twenty years after that event, my disciple-descendant, who will have my name, should head to the land of Tamilakam and meet the final avatar there. Then, I, sorry . . . my descendant must bring him to Dwarka and teach him Sanskrit and train him.'

Dweepa stopped and looked up at his listener. The dark-skinned man was listening to him with closed eyes. Krishna opened his eyes and nodded to the sage with his dimpled smile.

'My lord, you haven't mentioned anything about the second avatar. Shouldn't I train him as well? When will the other Kalki be born?' Dweepa inquired.

'No, Sage Dweepa, you needn't worry about him *or her*. I shall make the necessary arrangements for the other Kalki too.'

Dweepa remained quiet, respectful of his lord's wishes yet curious.

Krishna satisfied the wondering sage by saying, 'Lord Parashurama and the other Immortals will take care of the other incarnation.'

Dweepa gaped. 'The Immortals?'

Krishna nodded. 'Of course, you are aware of Hanuman, Lord Parashurama, Mahabali and the former king of Lanka, Vibhishana, who live beyond the clutches of death. There are a couple more of them, and time will inform you of their identities.'

After a pause, he added, 'That also reminds me—the Immortal beings will be training your descendants as well. After the successor, or Dweepa, has been chosen, he or she should undertake training with the Immortals, to gain knowledge of warfare and statecraft.'

Dweepa bowed and quickly jotted down the Dwarkadeesh's words. After that, the sage waited patiently for the ruler of Dwarka to continue.

But Krishna surprised him by saying, 'I guess that's all, Sage Dweepa . . . That's the least I can do for my successor . . .'

Dweepa looked at the ninth avatar with a mixture of sadness and pride in his eyes. Sadness because the instructions came to an end, and pride because his lord had entrusted this important and secret task to him.

Silence descended on the room as they both sat unmoving. Then, finally, Krishna spoke.

'The rest is all up to the Kalkis themselves; they will decide what to do and how to do it. Mankind's fate lies in their hands now . . .'

Dweepa affirmed it with a brief dip of his head.

'Also, Sage Dweepa, ensure that the palace, my home, is secure after it submerges. Kalki will need it.'

Dweepa noted that last instruction of the night.

As Krishna stood up, Dweepa asked him with concern in his eyes, 'My lord, what about the man who overheard our discussion?'

At this, the lord of Dwarka turned to the windowsill and looked at the stone resting upon it.

Well played, Ashwatthama. You are learning well and fast—a stone that conceals the presence of energy of people from me! Impressive indeed . . . he admired in his mind.

'And why did you let him escape?' the sage asked.

Krishna turned back to the worried sage, and bestowing on him his disarming and mesmerizing smile, the evening-hue-skinned man placed his hand on the former's shoulder and consoled him, 'He cannot harm us in any way, Sage. He knows only a part of our plan, and he doesn't know about the two Kalkis. So that works in our favour. I let him escape because I know he has partial knowledge, and it won't affect us.'

'But shouldn't we change our earlier plans? What if they try to disrupt us?'

The god laughed softly, taking his hand away. 'No, dear Sage, let's not change the plans. They will *expect* us to change our plans, but let's not. When they see that the plans are going exactly as per their knowledge, then it will make them wonder why the plans haven't changed. They will be wary and confused. They will rack their brains trying to figure out why we aren't acting differently, and *that*, Sage Dweepa, is something of a delightful spot to put your enemies in. They will scratch their heads trying to analyse things, fearful of some other contingency plan which they are oblivious to, but which we know are non-existent.'

Dweepa smiled and acknowledged the words with a bow. 'Sometimes, inaction is action as well.'

Krishna nodded with a grin.

'Anything else, my lord?' the old man asked as he started to pack the leaves and the stone pencil.

Krishna looked at him solemnly and said, 'Yes, one last thing, Sage.'

At this, Dweepa readied himself to take down the instructions. But the Dwarkadeesh shook his head, and the sage's hands stilled.

'Do you know that Vyasa Rishi plans to recite the events of my life one day to the people? He will also be talking of many more events related to Kurukshetra, the Pandavas and Kauravas. He will be narrating the entire history of the battle.'

Dweepa's brows furrowed. He was aware of all this, and his answer reflected on his face.

Taking a deep breath, the midnight-hued god said, 'Ummm . . . in all of this history, you will not be mentioned. For your safety, you will be kept out of the picture, Sage Dweepa.'

The sage humbly dipped his head, and said, 'Lord Krishna, I am most happy to be left out of the picture. No one will know of my presence, my existence, and that serves my purpose. There will be no one looking for me, and I can always remain unknown. "Dweepa" is not a name that is of import now.'

Krishna smiled, 'It is not significant to anyone else yet, but it is to us. And it will always remain so. That's why I told you to bestow the name of Dweepa on your descendants. It's not a name per se, it's a title.'

Dweepa bowed in appreciation of the lord's gesture.

And with that, their rendezvous ended. Krishna and Sage Dweepa left the hut. With the clear night sky above their heads, the two inhabitants headed to their own destinations, to set in motion the plans to aid Kalki.

TWO

The beach near Beyt Dwarka, Gujarat
The night of Anirudh's death, 2026 CE

'Hanuman has infiltrated the Kalabakshakas . . . He must be at the stone palace now.'

Parashurama's words shocked everyone standing at the desolate beach, except Kripa.

Parashurama explained to his audience about Maruti's disguise as a Kalabakshaka to penetrate the elusive stone palace and the mysterious order of sorcerers. Meanwhile, Kripa telepathically reached out to his fellow Immortals, Sage Vyasa, Vibhishana and Bali, who were in the Himalayas, waiting to hear about the events unfolding at the beach. They were nervous ever since Parashurama had appeared in their mountain cave, requesting that Kripa accompany him to disengage the impenetrable dome, which Ashwatthama had built around Anirudh and himself. Kripa quickly told them of the tragedy of Anirudh's death and called them to the beach.

'When did this happen?' Avyay asked Parashurama.

'We were counting on the attack today, so we decided to make the best of it and came up with a plan to locate the stone palace. When Kalarakshasa himself entered the battle, Hanuman infiltrated his band of sorcerers and took the place of one of them.'

Avyay nodded.

She looked down at Anirudh's body, lying motionless on a bed of sand.

'So, as soon as Hanuman reaches out to us, do we attack them?' she asked.

'Depends on whether Hanuman wants us to attack then or wait for an opportune moment.'

Avyay turned back to her mentor and said, 'But either way, let's get the soldiers ready for battle.'

'Yes, I will get to it.'

Sage Vyasa, Vibhishana and Bali appeared on the beach next to the others. Their faces wore shocked expressions as they looked at the young boy on the sand.

While the three fabled Immortals paid their respects to Anirudh, Parashurama spoke, addressing Sadhika and Siddharth, 'There is something I want to tell you both, a secret that's been maintained since the age of Krishna. A while back, Anirudh, during his last breaths, told Dweepa to give Asi the Kaustubha locket and his diary to Kalki. And you, Sadhika, even expressed your confusion when you heard those words. I will explain what he meant by that . . .'

The duo looked impatiently at the Immortal, awaiting the unravelling of the secret.

'So there are two Kalkis. One is Anirudh, the other is Avyay,' he said softly.

'What?' Sadhika said, astonished.

'Yeah,' Parashurama confirmed. 'Krishna had intended it to be that way all along. Only the Dweepas and us Immortals know this fact. The two avatars were to work as a team for accomplishing the Kalki avatar, but sadly, we only have Avyay now.'

Everyone looked at Anirudh's corpse on the sand a couple of feet away from them. They turned and met Parashurama's eyes, acknowledging the information he had just given them.

'She will be carrying the mantle of the Kalki avatar from now on.'

After a pause, Parashurama spoke, 'Ummm . . . So we will be attacking the stone palace after we hear from Hanuman.'

Looking at Avyay, he continued, 'But you will not be a part of the attack, Kalki.'

Avyay's eyes widened with surprise. She asked, a bit cheesed off, 'Why not me, Dada?'

Parashurama took a deep breath as he looked around at the people surrounding him. Everyone's eyes were fixed on him.

'All of you, listen to me carefully now,' he spoke. 'Confronting Kalarakshasa is not the most important thing at this moment. The foremost of our tasks is taking Anirudh back to his parents and performing his funeral rites.'

Avyay nodded.

'Secondly, Avyay, you are a secret. So it would be foolish to let you be on the front lines this soon after Anirudh's departure. We don't want to reveal you until we have Kali on the field as well. We don't know when we will hear from Hanuman or when we can pay a visit to the stone palace. However, for the next few days, you have things to take care of regarding Anirudh.'

He turned to the duo and said, 'Sadhika and Siddharth, I hope you will keep Avyay company during these days.'

The man and the woman nodded.

Pausing, Parashurama took a step towards Dweepa and placed a gentle hand on his shoulder, an act of consolation and that of encouragement too.

'Dweepa, I want you to go with them to Anirudh's parents and offer them your condolences. This has happened on our watch and, in a way, we are responsible for this. The least we can do is be there for them.'

The sage bowed in obedience.

'Unfortunately, we Chiranjeevi cannot attend the funeral since we have to keep our identity a secret. As much as we wish to, we have to hold ourselves back. Also, we will need to be available to Hanuman, should he reach out to us,' said Parashurama.

Avyay nodded, saying, 'You are correct, Lord Parashurama.'

She walked to Anirudh lying on the beach. The others followed her.

Getting down on her knees next to him, she cupped his face in her palm gently.

'I will take him home,' she said.

Dweepa also went down on his knees next to Anirudh.

He picked Asi, the divine sword, off the ground and gave it to Avyay.

Avyay took the blade and looked at the glowering steel. She got up and gave the sword to Parashurama. 'I don't have any need for this sword at the moment. I am not under threat, but you all are, or will be once you take on Kalarakshasa at the stone palace. So please accept this sword for your endeavour.'

Surprised, the Immortal replied, 'But this sword belongs to the Kalki, I cannot accept this. It was intended to be used by Kalki.'

With a sad smile, she answered, 'Lord Parashurama, Asi isn't anyone's possession. It is a blade created for the purpose of fighting evil. When it was forged, there was no wielder in mind, but rather the purpose of the wielder. Everyone's purpose on this beach is the same, so anyone here can wield Asi.'

Parashurama nodded appreciatively and graciously accepted the simmering blade.

Latching the sword to his waist, he said, 'We will head to the EOK mansion for now. It is a good place for us Immortals to lay low while waiting for Hanuman. I am guessing you would be curious about the updates, so we will keep you posted on any movements.'

Avyay looked down at Anirudh briefly and then back at the axe-wielder avatar, 'No, that's all right, Dada. I will be occupied with the arrangements for Anirudh and I won't be able to give my best to you.'

Parashurama looked intently at her and said, 'I understand. Nevertheless, if there is something important, I will inform you, or Dweepa.'

'Shall we take our leave then?' Parashurama asked her, referring to himself and the Chiranjeevi.

He patted her gently on the shoulder and gave her a reassuring smile, the best he could offer in that moment.

Soon, the Immortals disappeared into the darkness as they made their way to the mansion.

Avyay looked at Sadhika, Siddharth and Sage Dweepa. They took Anirudh to his home, with Avyay teleporting them to their destination.

THREE

Chennai
A few months ago, 2026 CE

'Yes, slay me a million times . . . But the fear on your face tells me you have realized the truth, Krishna. I cannot be destroyed, ever . . .'

Anirudh's eyes opened with a start. His heart was thudding. The room was enveloped in darkness. He turned to his right and saw Avyay's silhouette—she was fast asleep on her bed.

He got up from the couch and exited the bedroom silently.

As he made his way to the kitchen, he checked the time on his phone.

3.05 a.m.

Very quietly, he started shuffling around in the kitchen. He switched on the light and set some water to boil.

How can I destroy Kali? How does one destroy a soul? his thoughts echoed Krishna's words.

Sleep wouldn't come to him now, such was the effect of the dream he had seen. He thought back and recalled all he had dreamt: the conversation between his preceding avatar, Krishna, with Kali, who was hiding in Duryodhana's body.

'My soul is eternal and indestructible—just like yours. So you cannot stop me "for good" ever, for I will rise again . . .' Recalling the cold voice of Kali and the words he uttered, the thinly veiled malice and threat made a shiver run down Anirudh's spine. It made the hair on his body stand.

Outside the kitchen window, all he saw was darkness. Anirudh turned his attention to the bubbling hot water. With his thoughts still on his nemesis and his challenge to Krishna, he made a large mug of black coffee for himself. After he poured the concoction into a mug, he turned off the light, merging the kitchen with the darkness outside. He sat at the kitchen table and set the coffee mug before him.

'How do I defeat you, Kali?' Anirudh whispered softly, as he took a sip of the hot beverage.

Fifteen minutes later, with an empty coffee mug keeping him company, Anirudh scratched his forehead helplessly. He wasn't any closer to an answer.

He sat back and exhaled forcefully.

'How do I best you at your own game, Kali?'

Then, determinedly, he closed his eyes and inhaled deeply. Calming his mind, he rallied his attention to a single objective.

He instructed himself, 'Play the life of Kalki from the beginning . . . Recall everything you know, Anirudh. There has to be something!'

When he opened his eyes, the darkness in the kitchen had been replaced by the sublime, fiery shade of dawn. And such was the state of his mind as well—his thoughts, a collection of jigsaw pieces, were hinting towards a potential solution. And to reach the solution, he had to unravel the answers to some questions and arrange the pieces of the fragmented puzzle to unveil the true picture . . .

But the efforts to solve the mystery had to wait. For standing before him, with raised eyebrows and a hand on her hip, was Avyay, staring hard at him from the kitchen door.

Before she could ask anything, Anirudh wished her cheerfully, 'Good morning, Hayati.'

The stiff gaze remained. She knew he was trying to be cheerful, but there was something bothering him.

Getting up to make coffee for her, he asked, 'Would you mind talking to me about your "Kalki" life with me? Including the dreams that you may have seen . . .'

Her stern look melted and gave way to a puzzled expression.

FOUR

Chennai
The day after Anirudh's death, 2026 CE

Anirudh's close associates entered Avyay's home, and she closed the door behind them. She looked at the still switched-on lights—she had left a few hours back, in a hurry, to be by Anirudh's side on the beach. Safeed, Siddharth, Sadhika and Dweepa settled in the hall. She sunk into a chair and put her face into her palms. Just a few hours had passed, and her whole world had changed!

They had returned to Anirudh's home and had completed Anirudh's funeral rites. Avyay had ensured that everything was taken care of for the evening, thus allowing his family to mourn in peace.

Sadhika walked to Avyay and placed a hand on her shoulder, squeezing gently. Avyay rested her palm atop Sadhika's, in response. After a moment, she gathered herself and got up.

'I will make coffee for all. It has been a long evening . . .' she said, addressing everyone, and made a move towards the kitchen.

The Ascendance of Evil ✤

Dweepa quickly arose and stopped her. 'You get some rest. I will get the coffee going in the meantime.'

'It's all ri—' Avyay had begun to protest, but the sage persuaded her otherwise.

Standing in front of the locked door, Avyay looked at the circular pendant, now cupped in the centre of her palm. It was pleasant to look at, glowing softly with a shade of whitish pink. She recalled the way the locket lay on Anirudh's chest. Her eyes longed to see the pendant aglow on his dark chest, her cheeks yearned to feel his skin and her body ached for his warm embrace. She suppressed the tears that arose within her, willing herself to be strong. She slid the necklace over her head and tucked the locket inside her tee as she unlocked the door and headed to the kitchen to help Sage Dweepa with the coffee.

Around an hour later, everyone called it a night, hoping to catch at least a couple of hours of rest before daybreak. Dweepa and Safeed slept on mattresses lined in the hall.

A few minutes later, Avyay heard Sadhika's soft breaths as she lay asleep beside her. Siddharth was asleep on the couch in the same room, sound asleep. The Kalki avatar stared at the ceiling, deprived of sleep. She wanted to close her eyes, but her mind was restless.

Where are you, Anirudh?

She had known him to be someone who held a lot of things close to his chest, things which he seldom let out. Despite being close to him, she never got to know his thoughts easily. He would let her on to him only when he was fully convinced of it.

Where are you, Anirudh? she wondered again, wordlessly.

He was cautious of his thoughts so much that guessing his preciously guarded secrets were next to impossible, Avyay muttered inside her head. She was the only one in the entire universe who knew a secret of Anirudh which no one else was privy to.

Her eyes fluttered to welcome the drowsiness enveloping her senses. The strain of the evening's events was finally catching up to her, in the form of sleep. And just one thought arose in her mind. A thought which remained half-formed as her mind succumbed to the blankness of sleep.

Anirudh was looking forward to his death . . .

FIVE

The beach near Beyt Dwarka, Gujarat
The previous evening

When the divine Asi left his side and rushed towards Ashwatthama, Anirudh was surprised.

Wasn't Asi supposed to follow my directions? he wondered.

He looked at his opponent and saw a slight flicker of lightning in his eyes and on the gem on his forehead.

That explains why Asi is heeding Ashwatthama's call . . . Rudra, he thought.

He brought his attention back to the stream of water in front of him and continued to attack Ashwatthama with icy knives.

When the icicles pierced Drauni's body, Anirudh heaved a sigh of relief. His plan had worked, he was able to incapacitate his opponent. A moment later, he saw the sword rushing back towards him.

And then everything slowed down to a standstill.

A couple of feet away from him, Anirudh saw the sword stopping midway on its journey towards him. Suspended in the air, it vibrated vehemently and started glowing with a blinding white light. It exploded into a huge sphere of radiance. When the light receded, a tall and lean man stood in place of the sword. He glowed with the splendour of the moon, his dark skin alight with an ethereal glow.

Anirudh's memory jolted the identity of the person to his lips in the form of a bare gasp. 'Asi . . .'

The divine being bowed to Anirudh and said, 'My lord, it is an honour to meet you. And an even greater honour to serve you. As you identified correctly, I am Asi.'

The avatar was bewildered. He couldn't quite explain to himself the reason for the celestial's presence on the beach. He questioned the being, fumbling to find the correct words to phrase his question, 'Asi . . . What . . . How . . . Why are you here? In your human form . . .'

Asi replied with a smile, 'My Lord, I was created with the explicit purpose of eliminating evil. I have had the fortune of having served Lord Rudra as his weapon. And my ownership has belonged to you, Lord Vishnu, since then. But now, I find myself in battle between the two of you, and this is a great conundrum to my servitude. Lord Rudra has now directed me towards you and I am poised to strike you. I request your permission to deflect myself and return to your hand.'

The great creature of destruction then bowed in reverence, waiting to hear from Anirudh.

Anirudh chuckled. 'Asi,' he pronounced. Hearing his name, the swarthy celestial looked up at Anirudh.

'Please carry on. Strike me and kill me.'

The divine destroyer was aghast. 'My lord . . .' he gasped with horror.

'Asi, there are greater things at play here. My death is welcome, and I am looking forward to it.'

Asi's brows scrunched in doubt and worry.

Seeing the creases on his forehead, the Kalki avatar told him, 'Death is a necessary step in my journey, Asi. One cannot escape fate, and so I won't escape mine. You being sent to attack me is not an act of coincidence, but one of destiny. So please fulfil your purpose, and strike me.'

The avatar's words carried a tone of finality, and Asi obeyed it with a bow. With another burst of white light, the celestial abandoned his human form and took the form of the fabled sword.

Then, the spell of stillness broke. Anirudh could hear the sound of the waves and the rush of the breeze on the beach. And before he could realize it, he gasped and broke his breath. He looked down at the divine sword embedded in his chest. The pain caused tears to escape from his eyes. With the screams of his friends resounding in his ears, he crumbled to the ground.

SIX

He felt his body lying on something soft, yet prickly. The rocking lullaby of the waves, going back and forth, were pleasant to his ears. The breeze accompanying the music lulled him to sleep. He could feel the vibration of the sea running through the ground beneath him. The fragrance of the wet sand filled his nostrils. And then he became aware of the darkness in front of him.

Why is it dark?

Almost immediately, he felt his eyes roll against his closed eyelids.

Before he could soak in anything else, breaking the sound of the soothing waves, he could hear the sound of soft purrs around his head. He opened his eyes and saw a cat take a quick, startled step away from him. He sat up and looked at the black-furred animal. The creature was fluffy and healthy, with a glossy hide. His brows scrunched in doubt as he observed the furry being. It was translucent. He blinked his eyes repeatedly, but the sight remained as is. The furry animal peered at him with its light green eyes, and deciding that it felt safe around this visitor, stepped closer to him.

Curious about the place, the man looked around. The evening sun was glowing in the sky with a serene hue, painting the surroundings in a shade of golden orange. He looked at the translucent foamy waves rushing towards the shore a few feet from him.

He stood up and looked around. The cat had started brushing itself against his leg. He smiled softly and instinctively reached out to pat the feline's head. When his limbs made contact with the round, soft head, he was surprised. He was half-expecting his fingers to go through because of the translucent effect.

Brushing its head affectionately, he gently implored the cat to start walking beside him. He looked around the beach and gasped as he soaked in the surroundings. A few moments ago, all that he had seen was the fiery shade of dusk, but now, it was filled with all sorts of colourful creatures roaming around him. Birds of hues like brown, black, yellow, green soared across the blue sky, illuminating it with their glowing bodies. Fishes jumped and floated around in the ocean, boasting of luminous shades of orange, pink, green, red, and some hues that were too ethereal for him to place. He saw a bear burrowing the sand a few feet away from him; a leopard and gazelle were rollicking around; a lion was taking a stroll around the shore with a dog and a fox; and an elephant was trumpeting as it wrestled against a tree playfully, goaded along by a tiger. He could see the creatures were scattered across the beach, well into the distance. He looked at the trees, they were numerous and dense.

He had noticed something that was common among them all—the creatures, the trees, the birds.

Just then, his mind was diverted by the meowing beside him. He looked down at the animal trying to climb him. He laughed and held out his hands to take its paws.

Picking up the furry being into his arms, which was surprisingly weightless, he looked around him.

'Everything here has one common thing in them—everything is translucent. Almost like ghosts . . .'

He observed the forest surrounding him. He had noticed the translucent trees earlier, but he now noticed the ghostly flowers of various colours, and insects of various shapes and sizes roaming among the brown barks.

Where am I? he asked himself.

'Anirudh?' he heard a voice behind him.

He turned back and saw a woman in a green sari, with fair, glowing skin. A laurel wreath of green leaves decorated her head like a crown.

'Bhoomidevi?' he whispered.

He registered the shock in the otherwise serene blue of her eyes.

'What are you doing here?' she asked him, her voice almost a tearful scream of despair.

SEVEN

Outskirts of Indraprastha,
Twenty-seven years after the Great War of Kurukshetra

The night was still, except for the gentle breeze that blew through the forest. The moon was the only source of light. Krishna looked at the man sitting under a tree a few feet away. Ensuring that there was no one around, the lord of Dwarka approached the cloaked figure under the tree.

'How are you, son of Drona?' asked Krishna as he sat opposite to the hooded man.

The covered head moved slowly upwards to look at the unexpected visitor in the desolate jungle. When he recognized his guest, the man sat up with tremendous effort and pulled back the hood with the same slow pace. Krishna looked at the man in front of him, who was now visible because of the silver radiance. His face was covered in bloody sores and so was his entire body. His eyes were watery, and saliva dribbled from his mouth. The god knew that the mental faculties of this man were down to a minimum. And this caused the man to lose memories of everything except for the few, precious, intimate ones—like his identity, his childhood, bits of his adult life and the identity of his visitor.

'What . . . are . . . you . . . doing . . . here?' Drauni asked, straining to speak the words.

'I came to visit you,' Krishna said, placing a blue-coloured stone on the man's lap.

Ashwatthama peered down at the gem shining with a faint blue hue in the dim surroundings. Moving his weak fingers to the stone, he picked it up. He brought it closer to his eye, to confirm that it was the one he thought it to be. His hands shivered when he recognized the gem.

'How did you . . . get . . . this gem? Bhima had . . . taken it . . . away . . . from me . . .'

With a smile, Krishna replied, 'Yes, he had taken it from you as a punishment for what you did—your bloodthirst to see the end of the Pandava lineage. The stone, which defined you, had been taken instead of your life.'

At these words, Drauni hung his head in shame, and fidgeted with the gem between his trembling fingers.

Krishna continued, 'This isn't the one that Bhima took. I have created this one for you.'

Ashwatthama looked at the dark-skinned god, trying to comprehend his words. 'But . . . my gem . . . It was special.'

'So is this one. It blesses you with the same virtues the other one did—invulnerability against diseases, hunger, poisons, and weapons, too, to a certain extent.'

'I thought . . . all weapons . . . I am invincible . . . against all . . . weapons,' Ashwatthama countered with evident difficulty in stringing words together.

'Not all weapons . . . There are some weapons that can hurt you despite the gem. One such weapon is Asi,' Krishna replied firmly.

Drauni's eyes widened at the revelation. He knew about Asi. His father had possessed it once, before it was passed to his uncle. But he had never touched it, as his father was very protective about it.

Krishna raised an open palm towards the son of Drona and waved it once. The warrior of the great battle felt a new sense of vigour emanate from within his body. The tremors in his hands and body started to calm, and his skin started to heal slowly. He looked down at his hands in amazement.

His brows scrunched in doubt. After a couple of moments, as his curiosity grew, he asked, 'If it was a punishment, then . . . then why are you returning the gem to me? And why are you helping me?'

'Before I answer that, I want you to recall that taking away your gem wasn't your only punishment, Drauni. I gave you a curse as well . . .'

Drauni's eyes met those of Krishna, and he nodded slowly. He ran his fingers over the pus-filled cracks and sores that pockmarked his face—a gift of Krishna's curse. Most of his memories were making their way to the surface of his mind, as he felt the new energy heal him.

He recalled it very clearly, the words still resonating in the depths of his mind—'For 3000 years you shall wander this earth without any company. Alone and without anybody by your side, you shall wander through diverse countries, having no place amid people. The stench of pus and blood shall emanate from you always, and you shall find your abode in moors and forests. You shall walk upon this earth, you sinful soul, with the weight of all diseases on you.'

Krishna had cursed him for he had committed a grave crime of shooting the fatal Brahmastra at the pregnant womb of Uttara, Arjuna's daughter-in-law and Abhimanyu's wife.

He had done this act to kill her child, thus extinguishing the last progeny of the Pandava lineage. However, Krishna revived the foetus with the divine energy of the same weapon that had killed it.

'Your punishment and your curse, do you think they were unjust?' Krishna asked, his peacock feather glistening as he leaned forward.

Ashwatthama shook his head and shrugged his shoulders. 'I don't know—I did what I felt was right in that moment!' he confessed.

Krishna smiled softly. 'There's no denying that your actions were wrong, and thus, you have been punished. Even though you did those acts out of your desire for vengeance against the sons of Pandu for the unjust killings of your father and Duryodhana, that doesn't make the crimes any less forgivable. You are a slayer of children.'

Drauni took a deep breath and looked away into the trees by his side.

'However . . .' Krishna spoke, and Ashwatthama turned back to meet his gaze.

'However, I believe that I can relieve you of your burden slightly.'

The warrior's eyes widened with surprise. But he got over it soon and his eyes squinted in doubt.

'Why so? There is something else on your mind . . . You wouldn't forgive me easily for these heinous crimes. So tell me, Dwarkadeesh, what's the catch?'

Krishna laughed when he heard his words. 'Ohh Ashwatthama . . . I have known, for a long time now, that you are much more than what you seem to be.'

Ashwatthama leaned in closer.

'Well, let me say this first . . .' Krishna spoke, 'Ever since you killed the sons of Pandavas and their army that night, I had realized that there's more to you than meets the eye. That night, you ceased being an ordinary human. I know that you are meant for a greater purpose, thus, I am here to take a bit of the burden of the punishments off your shoulders.'

'Why now, after all these years?' he asked.

'Because now it is time for you to meet your destiny . . . Remember, there is a time for everything . . . everything indeed.'

Ashwatthama continued staring at the avatar curiously.

'I am not here tonight, meeting you in secret, just to unburden you. But I come here seeking your help . . .'

Drauni sat up immediately, alert. His tremors had ceased completely and the years-old fog over his mind and senses had lifted.

'What I am going to ask of you is something that will be expensive and the path will not be easy,' Krishna continued. 'You will be playing against me, and also, more importantly, against every fibre of your being.'

'Playing against you?' Ashwatthama asked.

'Well, not just me. You will face me and Kalki, my next incarnation,' he continued. 'Are you up for it?'

Ashwatthama hid well the surprise that came over him at the mention of the next incarnation, and with a stern demeanour, he studied the lord of Dwarka closely.

His next avatar? The warrior wondered.

Wishing to know more, he replied, 'You know my answer to this—it's a yes. I believe that you are proposing this to me because you know that I am looking to do penance for my crimes.'

'You are not wrong in believing that. But that's not the entire truth. There are a couple of more reasons as to why I am choosing you, which I shall reveal shortly. However, before I do so, let me tell you something else.'

Ashwatthama nodded.

'You must have realized by now, by my presence here and the gem in your hand, that I am here for something really important. Though I am not being too severe with you now, it doesn't mean that I am taking the curse away. Instead, I am modifying it—extending it, is the better term, I believe.'

Ashwatthama gasped in shock.

'Let me ask you this again, Ashwatthama. Do you feel that the curse is a "curse" indeed?'

The son of Drona spoke in a spate, 'Of course it is a curse . . . To roam alone, unable to have anyone accompany me or be social with me, to have to carry this broken skin and broken body . . . All this for 3000 years! I'd rather have death . . .'

'Well, it is supposed to be a punishment. But hear me carefully now: "For 3000 years, you shall wander this earth . . ." Do you realize that by the virtue of this curse, by these words, that nothing can kill you for those many years!?'

His brows rose as he saw the curse in a new light.

'You are an immortal being now, son of Drona!' Krishna said.

Ashwatthama replied without any cheer, 'Again, as I said before, I'd rather die. Immortality without being able to enjoy the simple pleasures of being a human is a curse and is worthless.'

'Hasn't your body healed yet?'

Drauni looked down at his hands, he ran his fingers over his face and flexed his limbs. He nodded in surprise. However, his sense of wariness took a stand again, and he asked, 'But is this temporary? Will it only last till you are here?'

Krishna shook his head. 'It is permanent.'

Before the warrior could react, he continued, 'And I am extending, as well as modifying, the blessing now. You shall be alive on this earth until the end of the Kali Yug. You shall not be alone, for you shall be in the company of people whom you choose to aid you in your purpose of resurrecting Kali. Henceforth, you will be able to mingle with people normally to achieve your objective.'

Having said these words, Krishna raised his palm to complete the invocation of his blessing. Ashwatthama, throughout the benediction, stared at him, blank and stupefied. Too many questions flew around in his mind.

'Ask me your questions,' Krishna said, seeing the confounded expression on his face.

'Why me? And who is Kali?' he asked, for that's all he could manage in that moment. He was still processing the 'blessing' in his mind.

'Ahh . . . Well, see, as I said earlier, I know that you are no longer a mere human. You have the blessings of Rudra himself! He's the one who enabled you to massacre an entire army that night, single-handedly. You know it as well. The other reason is that you are Kali's closest friend. So, I am giving you the responsibility to resurrect him when the time comes.'

These words hit him hard. 'Kali is my closest friend? I don't understand. And how, and why, am I to resurrect him?' he asked, confused.

'Before Duryodhana died, did he tell you to preserve his body?' the lord asked.

The son of Drona, now in complete possession of his mental faculties, recalled the memory vividly.

29

'Yeah, he did . . . but, how did you know about it?' he asked, surprised. Not even his uncle Kripa or Kritavarma were aware of this fact.

'I know a great many things, Ashwatthama. Like the fact that the one who told you to preserve the body wasn't your friend, he was Kali,' Krishna revealed, his face grave.

Krishna proceeded to narrate his experience when he had visited Duryodhana, after he had fallen in the Great War, the very same night that Ashwatthama had butchered the descendants of the Pandavas and their military forces. He also filled him in on the details of Kali, the demon.

By the time the Dwarkadeesh ended his anecdote, his listener's face was pale.

'There is nothing for you to worry about, Ashwatthama. Just do as I say, and it will all be fine,' Krishna consoled him.

Ashwatthama looked at Krishna, pensive. 'And I assume this will be in relation to the "greater purpose", correct?'

Krishna nodded. 'Your purpose is to resurrect Kali when the time comes.'

'And how am I to know when that moment arrives? And how does this all tie in with your next avatar? How will I help by resurrecting the demon?'

Krishna grinned slightly before answering. 'When Kalki retrieves Asi, I want you to launch an attack on him. After that, resurrect Kali.'

Ashwatthama's jaw dropped.

'Asi with the next avatar? And I should attack the Kalki?' he asked the Dwarkadeesh, full of disbelief.

'Yes,' Krishna confirmed his reply to the question.

'But why?' Ashwatthama asked, confounded.

'Tell me this, Drauni. Do you want Kali to be defeated?' the god asked him.

'Of course I do. But you already know so much, and you are aware of the threat he poses, then why don't you vanquish him now? Why resurrect him at all?' he cried, trying to reason with Krishna.

Krishna just stared with a slight, inexplicable smile on his face.

Trying to reason further, Drauni said, 'I know where Duryodhana's remains are hidden. I can cremate the body, and then Kali won't return.'

'Dear Ashwatthama, remember, fate will always have its path. Even though I possess the knowledge and power to turn the path of destiny, I seldom interfere with the flow of things.

'And this whole deal with Kali's resurrection,' Krishna continued, 'It is your destiny, and it is Kalki's destiny to defeat him, forever . . .'

Drauni stared in thought.

The lord of Dwarka cautioned again, 'But do not attack the avatar before he fetches Asi. The sword is your signal!'

'So you want me to play a double game? Act like their man, but in fact, be your guy in the enemy ranks.'

Krishna smiled. 'Not enemy ranks, no. You will be the supreme commander of the enemy, Drauni.'

'I see, yeah. And what if I betray you?' he asked.

'You won't,' Krishna said in a firm, confident tone.

'How can you be so sure? I can really betray you . . . I would seek revenge on you by unleashing Kali into this world,' he argued.

'Son of Drona,' Krishna spoke, his voice cold, 'If I thought you were to betray me some day, then I wouldn't be sitting here talking to you. If I knew you to be a worthless existence, in addition to being a killer of children, then I wouldn't have cursed you to roam for millennia. I wouldn't have spared your life, which was already forfeit by your own actions.'

With a voice that held undertones of impending thunder, the Dwarkadeesh continued, 'You do not know me. If I wanted you relieved of your living, then I would have done so. If I wanted to make your life a replication of hell, then I wouldn't have held back. I wouldn't be here. But here I am.'

Ashwatthama's hands started trembling.

Looking into the petrified eyes of the warrior, the god spoke, 'You do not know Kali, Ashwatthama. But I do. And I know exactly what you are going to do when the demon rises.'

The warrior looked away, his heart melting and beads of sweat breaking on his skin.

'How do I resurrect him, the demon? You know that I lack the knowledge to do so . . .'

'Do you?'

Drona's son looked questioningly at him.

'If you lack that knowledge, then why did you keep your prince's crown safe?'

Ashwatthama's eyes widened. 'How did you . . .' He checked himself, understanding the omniscient being in front of him. 'What does the crown have to do with anything?'

'Time will tell you everything,' Krishna said.

'I just did it instinctively . . . I held on to it because it was my dear friend's crown . . .' Ashwatthama argued.

Krishna raised a palm towards him to calm him, and using the other hand, he conjured a scroll from thin air. He handed it to the warrior.

'What's this?' he asked, as he accepted the scroll.

'You would need to grow much more powerful than you are at the moment in order to survive against Kalki. And also to aid Kali in rising again . . .'

Ashwatthama unrolled the parchment and went through its contents. As he read the list of texts and their locations, he asked, 'What are these texts for?'

'They will help you start your journey, grow your knowledge and guide you as you come into your powers. Like I said, you must be well-prepared before Kali is resurrected. He would fancy an army and power, for sure.'

'And this would help me bring him back?' Drauni asked, pointing to the open scroll.

'The last one is not a book. It is the name of the person who is well-versed in the art of Mrit Sanjeevani,' the god answered.

The forest-dweller's eyes expressed surprise as he took in the information.

'So how do I go about it?' he asked the lord of Dwarka.

Krishna got up and looked at the moon in the sky. 'You can go about it however you want, Ashwatthama. It's your plan . . .'

Looking down at the son of Drona, he continued, 'But start soon. You have plenty of work to do . . .'

Ashwatthama rolled the scroll and looked up at the dark-skinned god.

'I shall start soon, I assure you.'

Krishna smiled and acknowledged him with a nod. 'What's your first step?' he asked.

'Don't you already know that, lord of Dwarka?'

At this, Krishna let his smile widen. 'Yeah, I do. Bhairava . . .'

The son of Drona snapped his finger at the correct response. 'Yes, Bhairava. I have to secure the remains of Duryodhana. He is the only one who knows where it is right now.'

Krishna nodded and took a deep breath. Then, he spoke, 'Well, that concludes our meeting, doesn't it?'

'What about Asi? How will Kalki get it?'

'I have already thought about the arrangements for that . . . So, don't worry about it.'

'So you are helping Kalki as well?'

'Yes, I have to.'

'Well, isn't this nice! You are helping Kalki, and Kali as well . . . It is so twisted.'

There was no response, and Ashwatthama didn't wait for one. 'Well, doesn't matter to me. It's your lookout. I have Kali to deal with.' He waved the scroll to the god.

Then, recalling something, he paused in thought. Krishna observed this but remained silent. He knew what was coming.

'Earlier, you told me that the work, this objective, will be expensive and the path won't be easy. You also told me that I would be acting against myself, so to speak . . . Why did you say that?' asked the warrior.

'You will see for yourself,' said the lord, but with a sense of graveness, and that of finiteness as well.

Ashwatthama got up and said to the god, 'I guess this does conclude our meeting.'

Krishna nodded. 'From this moment onwards, you are to treat me as the enemy.'

The son of Drona smiled. 'I will be a good enemy, Krishna.'

It was Krishna's turn to smile. 'I know that, Drauni.'

EIGHT

Thirty-two years after the Great War of Kurukshetra

Hovering miles above the ocean, Ashwatthama looked down at his creation, which was suspended mid-air, many feet above the tumultuous waters. The structure, made from black stone, glimmered orange in the sunset.

The magnificent stone mansion was a fruit of the knowledge of the esoteric texts he'd consumed over the past few years. The feat was astounding and terrific, and Bhairava, standing beside him, was looking at it breathlessly.

Happy with his creation, he turned to his companion and told him, 'Take the kids inside the mansion, I will meet you there. I will put some protective enchantments around it.'

The aide bowed and disappeared. Their first batch of students was waiting on the shore, orphans from various parts of the country. They also had among them some older men and women, whom they had trained a couple of years back and who were in their service for a long time now. They would be serving as teachers and caretakers to the new child recruits. After his aide disappeared, the sorcerer started muttering charms as he created barriers around the stone structure. After some time, satisfied with the protections placed on the mansion, he made his way inside. When he reached his chamber, he saw that Bhairava was already there, busy stacking books on the shelf.

'All of them settled well?' the son of Drona asked, walking to the desk, his red robes fluttering behind him.

'Yes, they are all fine,' Bhairava replied, with a smile. 'The kids are calling this a "stone palace", given its opulence and stony interiors.'

Ashwatthama laughed. 'Stone palace? I love the sound of that . . . Then, that's what it shall be known as henceforth.'

After settling into his chair behind the desk, he looked at the bound text in front. 'Bhairava? This book . . .'

His aide glanced at it and answered, as he returned to arranging the rest of the books on the shelf, 'Yeah, that's the book you were reading. So I kept it aside.'

Ashwatthama thanked him and flipped through the pages. It was a book containing stories of asuras. As he browsed through the text, his attention was drawn to a section with a drawing on it. It was that of a bull's head. Below it was a word written in Sanskrit, 'Arishta'. The leaves following the sketch contained the story of Krishna's battle, when he was a young boy, against the bull-demon, Arishtasura, who was sent by his uncle, Kamsa, to vanquish him.

Ashwatthama's gaze was held by the animal's face and he didn't bat even an eye. Then, he pointed the image to his aide and asked him, 'What do you think of the bull? Do you think we can make this our emblem?'

Bhairava eyed the animal's head with interest and then looked at his lord. 'Emblem for . . .?'

'Well, for our palace . . . For the staffs that the recruits will be using and for our attire . . . The bull seems frightening. It will make for a great symbol.'

'We can do that, yes,' his aide agreed, slightly less enthusiastic.

'You don't sound very pleased . . . What's wrong, Bhairava?'

'Nothing's wrong, my lord. Just incomplete . . . We don't have a name to go with our emblem yet.'

'Ahh, I see. You are correct! What can I name it?'

'Well, we can keep thinking about it and settle on one soon. We have all the time in the world to think of a name . . .'

Ashwatthama's eyes twinkled when he heard the statement. *All the time in the world, indeed*, he pondered.

'Time . . . *Kaal*,' he thought out aloud.

Then, sitting up excitedly, he spoke, 'We are going to withstand the waves of Time. Through us and our recruits, our legacy of sorcery will survive eons. Time isn't a matter to us any more, we have devoured it, like we did our mortality. Then, our legacy will also be immortal in that sense, devouring time itself. Kalabakshakas—that's what our sorcerers will be called. Devourers of Time!'

That name made Bhairava's eyes twinkle with awe.

'And you will be Kalaguru—their teacher, who teaches them how to live beyond the grasp of Time!' Ashwatthama announced.

Bhairava bowed in deep gratitude, overwhelmed with his title.

After regaining his composure, he asked his master, 'What about your title, my lord?'

'My title?' Ashwatthama asked. 'Of course, Bhairava. We can't use my name.'

Bhairava agreed, and said, 'Yes, we'll have to think of a title for you, something you can use freely. The leader of the Kalabakshakas . . .'

'Well, now that you say it, as the leader of the Kalabakshakas, I believe my name should do justice to our demonic intentions. Well . . . hmmm . . . the Demon of Time . . .'

Bhairava held his breath, awestruck, when he heard his lord utter the name:

'Kalarakshasa.'

NINE

'This is the person you have to bring back to life,' the man in red robes informed the elderly sage who was staring down into the marble coffin.

Shukracharya, with shivering limbs, looked up at Kalarakshasa.

'Who is he?' he asked, his eyes moving between Koka, Kalarakshasa and Vikoka.

Kalarakshasa stared intently at the old man.

Shukracharya, impatient for an answer, asked again, 'Who is he? What is his name?'

He was met only with silence. 'Without knowing his name, I won't be able to revive him.'

At this, the master sorcerer uttered just one word. The name. 'Kali.'

Petrified, the old man stumbled back in fear.

'No . . .' he said as he stepped back. He stumbled as far from the white edifice as he could, and when his back was opposed by the marble wall behind him, he stopped.

'I won't do it . . . no,' he said again, his breath heavy with shock. His body was trembling and his eyes were wide with terror.

'What else do you need to bring him back to life?' Kalarakshasa asked calmly.

'No! I am not bringing him back to life! Do you even know what you are asking of me?' he cried, his gaze roving between the three people in front of him.

'Acharya, you are bringing him back to life,' the red-robed sorcerer asserted in a cold voice. 'There is no argument about it, and you needn't try to escape doing what's asked of you.'

The two men stared at each other, seething.

Mustering up courage and standing upright, the old sage announced, 'No. I'd rather die.'

The twins exchanged a glance and looked at the learned man with amusement. They were eager to see how their master would deal with the deadly threat.

Kalarakshasa took slow steps towards the man, saying, 'I want you to remember this, Shukracharya. You . . . won't . . . die.'

Then, without a warning, the sorcerer waved his hand towards the sage. The old man was pushed against the white marble wall and his body went rigid. It felt like his entire body had frozen, but without a sense of chill. Kalarakshasa walked towards him. Shukracharya suddenly felt a lack of breath in his lungs. He sensed that his breath was just enough to keep him alive. He tried to open his mouth, but they were clenched shut. He tried to take in a deep breath, but his lungs ached when he tried to inhale hard. His body was out of his control. He didn't realize it was possible, but he had accepted it. The man in red robes was feeding him breaths of life, keeping him hanging between life and death.

'I won't let you die, Guruji. But I won't let you live either. So don't think that you are in control of things here . . . You will obey me!'

The acharya wanted to wince in pain, his hands itched to claw at his neck in desperation for more oxygen, his throat yearned to suck in mouthfuls of air, but he was immobile, his lungs aching for more breath. The pain was unbearable. He felt as though his chest and innards were being pricked with needles.

Kalarakshasa tortured the sage for a couple of minutes more and then released him. The wizened teacher fell to the ground with a thud. His hands went to his throat, gasping for breath. After a while, he sat up, trying to regain his composure. The old teacher, wiser now of the situation he was in, looked at his tormentor with fearful eyes.

'I cannot perform the resurrection ritual today. I will need some ingredients, which I must sanctify during the day tomorrow with specific mantras. I will only be able to perform the revivification tomorrow night.'

Seeing that his prisoner was compliant now, and relishing the terror and submission in his eyes, the sorcerer asked, 'We will provide whatever you need for the ritual. Apart from those items, what else do you need for reviving him?'

'Kali . . . He likes gold. Do you have anything made of gold that he once possessed?' the acharya asked in a trembling voice, pointing to the figure lying inside the grave.

TEN

Accompanied by the Guardian, Kalarakshasa entered a dimly lit room. It was illuminated by two yellow torches held in brackets along the walls. He stepped to a side as he let Koka carry on with his work. The Guardian headed straight to the stone wall in front of them and opened a large chest resting in front of it. He pulled out a black marble box from inside.

After sitting down on the floor, he placed the marble box on the floor and restored it to its original size, revealing it to be a chest. Looking up at his lord, the Guardian gestured towards the chest, as he got up and moved away from it. The Demon of Time shuffled to the marble container now in quick strides. He bent down and opened it. The marble chest was quite hollow and was lined with purple velvet. Resting on this fabric, at the bottom, was a scarred crown of gold and a leather-sheathed sword with a green pommel.

Kalarakshasa took the crown out and looked at it. It was his friend Duryodhana's crown. It bore the scratches and marks of a battle-worn helmet, and there were a few dried specks of blood on the golden surface. He took out the leather scabbard and nodded to Koka before walking out of the room. The Guardian quickly closed the box and followed his master.

Hanuman, in the form of Kalarudra, was arranging books on the shelves of the library as Kalarakshasa and Koka walked across the hall. The immortal ape-god had taken the form of the Kalabakshaka after defeating him in the forest earlier, and had occupied his place in the league of sorcerers. The black-robed Maruti quickly stepped behind a bookshelf, ensuring that he was hidden from everyone's view. He then reduced his body to the size of an ant and leapt into the air, flying towards the lord of sorcerers.

Kalarakshasa entered the chamber of Lord Kali. He saw Shukracharya standing at the head of the marble coffin, his eyes transfixed on the figure lying inside it. The sage's eyes were filled with fear and hatred. The sorcerer kept the sheathed sword against the wall next to the door and walked towards the old sage with the gold ornament.

'I hope this will do . . .' he said, interrupting the man's trance, and extended the crown to him.

The acharya looked at the crown held out to him and, involuntarily, took a step back. His eyes were wide with horror. 'Yes, the crown will do . . . *very* well.'

Kalarakshasa narrowed his eyes at those words. The sage gestured to him to place the crown on the body, not willing to touch it himself.

As he placed the crown atop Duryodhana's chest, Kalarakshasa asked, 'Why do you need something that belonged to him? And why does a crown work better than any other possession?'

He was curious to understand the role of the crown; he had retained the crown on instinct, and Krishna wasn't exactly forthcoming about it.

Shukracharya, fidgeting with his trembling fingers, asked in return, 'Kali . . . Why do you want to revive him?'

'Because he wanted to be revived,' the sorcerer answered curtly.

'But why must it be in this body?' the acharya asked, pointing to the one inside the marble casket.

'He used to reside in this body . . . Before he died, he told me to preserve the body and bring him back to life in Kali Yug.'

'I see . . .'

'So what's the rationale behind the crown?' Kalarakshasa asked, looking down at the ornamental headgear lying atop his friend's chest.

'Well . . . you told me he told you to preserve this body. Kali is very fond of gold. He is known to have resided in ornaments of gold, especially crowns, and control the wearer, leading them to their doom. Since the body hasn't been cremated, there is a possibility of some residue of Kali's energy leftover in the crown. That residue will help in inviting Kali to this body, thus reviving him.'

Kalarakshasa nodded. 'Please begin the revivification. How much time will it take you to complete the ritual?'

Witnessing the proceedings inside the white room was a shocked Hanuman, in his miniaturized form of Kalarudra, as he sat atop the marble arch above the chamber's door.

They are resurrecting Kali! he muttered to himself, taking in the gravity of the threat that was about to emerge. *I have to inform Lord Parashurama at once!*

'Around ten minutes to finish the recitation,' he heard the acharya say. 'But after the essence of Kali enters the body, the soul will take some time to adjust to the body and learn all the motor functions.'

'Why would that take time?' Kalarakshasa asked.

'To put it in simple terms, the soul would have to learn about its home anew. When you pour water into a vessel, it conforms itself to the shape of the vessel. It is likewise for the soul entering a new and unfamiliar body.'

'I see . . . And how much time would this conformation take?'

'I don't know, to be honest,' the sage confessed. 'It varies from soul to soul, and I have no experience of such a situation.'

Kalarakshasa nodded and gestured to the acharya to start the ritual.

The ape-faced god leapt off his perch and flew out of the room. He zipped to a window in the main hall. *Time is of the essence, I have to deliver the message as soon as possible*, Hanuman told himself as he reached the window. Looking at the clear night sky outside, he darted towards it.

I hope they are prepared!

ELEVEN

Chennai,
A few months ago, 2026 CE

Avyay was seated at the kitchen table with a coffee mug next to her. She had finished narrating her 'Kalki' life and the dreams that she had seen in the past to Anirudh, who was standing by the kitchen window, the warm sun on his back.

'Why are we having this discussion . . . about my life regarding the avatar?'

Pulling up a chair, Anirudh answered, 'To check if we both had similar experiences, and mainly to confirm if we saw the same dreams . . .'

'And did we—see the same dreams?'

'Yes . . . For the most part.'

'What do you mean by "for the most part"?'

'Well, you didn't dream about Kali . . .'

At this, Avyay's jaw dropped. 'Kali?' she managed a whisper.

Anirudh nodded and described the dream he'd seen a few hours earlier.

'Anirudh . . . How do we defeat Kali?' she asked, concern evident in her voice.

The young man shrugged his shoulders. 'I don't know. My mind is all about the question that Kali posed to Krishna: "How does one destroy a soul?"'

'Soul . . .' he continued. 'It is one of the biggest enigmas of this universe. What is it made of? What makes it indestructible? Why is it not affected by any physical damage?'

With a sigh, Avyay spoke, 'The answers to those questions would help us defeat Kali. But how do we get these answers?'

They looked at each other. To an ordinary person, Anirudh's glance would seem like a casual one. But Avyay, knowing Anirudh very well, saw a soft glint in his eyes.

With a sudden movement, she held his wrist. 'Have you found the answer?'

Anirudh shook his head, but as he did so, a smile appeared on his face, which spoke of knowledge privy only to him.

'Then, do you know how to find it out?' she asked him, shaking his wrist vigorously.

'Possibly . . . I am not sure,' said Anirudh, suppressing his smile.

'Is that what you were thinking of when I walked into the kitchen this morning?'

He nodded. 'Mostly, yeah. At the moment, it's like jigsaw pieces scattered all around. I am trying to arrange them to complete the picture. But the thing is, I guess there are a couple of pieces missing. I need to figure them out . . .'

She rested her other hand protectively on his forearm and asked, 'How can I help?'

'Once I have figured things out, I just need you to support me unquestioningly throughout my plan.'

'Obviously! That goes without saying, Anirudh.'

Anirudh smiled broadly, but this time it didn't hold mystery. It radiated doubt and disbelief.

Avyay noticed this, but before she could say anything, he asked, 'When you were training with the Chiranjeevi, did you happen to learn what "soul" means? What is it defined as?'

Avyay had revealed to him that she had been trained early in her life by the Immortals. She was teleported to and from secret locations for her training, so that the Chiranjeevi could train her in isolation, hidden from the world. Her parents were already anticipating this, since Krishna, through their dreams, had informed them of Parashurama's arrival beforehand.

Considering his question, she shook her head. Anirudh bit his lip in thought. As he got up to take the coffee mugs to the kitchen sink, Avyay caught his arm. 'Anirudh, I want you to know that I will support your plan, to the last word. Trust me on this . . .'

Anirudh just smiled and kissed her forehead. 'I trust you, Avi . . . That's why you will be the only one who'll be aware of my entire plan.'

As he washed the mugs, he turned to her and wondered out loud, 'What do you think happens after death?'

TWELVE

'Why do you want to know what happens after death?' Anirudh didn't answer immediately. He just finished washing the mugs and dried his hands on a towel.

'Do you recall that I told you our dreams match for the most part?' he asked her, going back to his chair.

With narrowed eyes, she nodded her head slowly.

'Well . . . The differences in our dreams, though few, are bugging me,' he told her.

'And they are?'

Raising a hand, he said, 'I will get to that. But before we go further, tell me this . . . have you ever seen Bhoomidevi?'

She shook her head.

'Not even during your training?' he enquired further.

'No . . . I haven't seen her at all. If I had seen her, I would remember it.'

'What about in your dreams?'

She shook her head again. 'Nope, I told you about all of the visions I have had until now.'

Collecting his thoughts and taking a deep breath, Anirudh leaned forward with a sense of certainty.

'As I said before, there are some inconsistencies that are bugging me, four instances to be precise,' he said, in a businesslike tone.

Avyay took a deep breath and leaned closer as Anirudh continued.

'First, how did Krishna speak my name exactly in the first dream I saw, that of him and the ancestor, Dweepa, crafting the Kalki hoax? Second, why, or how, did I happen to dream of Vishnu and Bhoomidevi at Ksheera Sagar? Based on all of your experiences that you've told me, I gather that you haven't seen those dreams, at least not yet.'

She nodded to confirm his words. Anirudh continued, 'Third, how come only I saw Bhoomidevi during the battle between Dweepa and Kalanayaka? Why weren't they able to see her? And fourth, how did I dream of meeting Bhoomidevi outside Sage Dweepa's house, after that duel between Sage Dweepa and Kalanayaka? Of all my dreams, that's the only one that stands out, for it is the only one which happened in the present . . . I mean, most of my dreams were from the past, more like memories, but not this one.'

As an afterthought, he added, 'There are a couple of others as well, which fit the pattern of "non-memory" dreams—the one where I dreamt of meeting Dweepa at Marina beach, and the one where I dreamt of your face.'

Avyay smiled softly. After a few moments of silent pondering, she spoke, 'I guess the first one, Krishna uttering your name, is bothering you because Krishna managed to "hack", for lack of a better term, the dream to mention your name.'

'Exactly,' Anirudh confirmed, tapping the table. 'How did he manage to pull it off?'

'Anirudh . . . He has done it multiple times,' Avyay revealed.

Anirudh scrunched his brows in doubt.

'Not just with you. He told Dweepa about going to Marina beach to meet you, he told your parents about Dweepa's imminent visit, he informed my parents about Lord Parashurama's arrival . . .'

Anirudh's brows unscrunched and his eyes widened.

'You are right!' he exclaimed. 'I had totally forgotten about them . . .'

Avyay squeezed his arm gently, giving him an understanding nod. He looked at her and let a smile appear on his lips. He clasped her palm appreciatively and held it as he closed his eyes. *This information could add some missing pieces to the puzzle . . .*

After a few moments of analysing the information, he opened his eyes.

'How is Krishna able to manipulate our dreams?'

After a pause, she continued, 'About Krishna being able to manipulate dreams in the present, I guess that's because he was a great yogi, wasn't he? He must have been capable of a great many things . . .'

Anirudh's lips parted to reveal a broad smile.

'What?' she asked of him.

'Your words . . .'

'What of them?'

'Krishna *was* a great yogi . . . was. Krishna isn't here any more. Then how do you explain this "phenomenon"?'

Realizing the reason in her words were not valid anymore, Avyay nodded with a sigh. 'I see . . .'

Sitting up with a renewed vigour, Anirudh said, 'Let's park Krishna's powers for a moment. What about the other cases I mentioned? How come I dreamt of Vishnu?'

'Vishnu does exist, Anirudh. So I am not surprised about those dreams. It's a mystical universe out there . . . Filled with secrets that we aren't aware of. We don't know how things function, do we?'

Anirudh considered her words and nodded in agreement. 'What about Bhoomidevi? I dreamt of her in front of Dweepa's house . . . During the battle, only I was able to see her, Kalanayaka or Sage Dweepa weren't able to see her.'

'Well, she is a goddess. So she would be able to demonstrate such feats, wouldn't she?'

'She would, yeah. But these are extraordinary feats, Avi . . . Krishna, Vishnu and Bhoomidevi . . . all three have communicated to me in such a manner, which, while perfectly plausible, is making me wonder how it was done.'

'That's true . . .'

'Krishna has left this world, yet he is able to communicate with us. No one knows where Lord Vishnu is, yet I was able to dream about him. No one knows what Bhoomidevi looks like, nor that she has a human form, yet I have seen her and dreamt of her as well. How can you explain this?'

'The Vishnu bit . . . Couldn't that be just a dream? A vivid imagination based on the information you knew. You were aware of the milk ocean, Ksheera Sagar, right?'

'I would have agreed with you normally, had I not seen Bhoomidevi later. Seeing Bhoomidevi affirmed that my visions about the Ksheera Sagar were more than just dreams.'

'They were actually visions?' Avyay ventured.

Anirudh remained silent, absorbed in thought. He knew that he was close to an answer.

Avyay asked him, 'What are you thinking?'

And then his eyes shone.

'What?'

Sitting upright, excited, he asked her, 'Can we actually confirm that all three of them—Vishnu, Krishna and Bhoomidevi—have physical human forms at the moment?'

Avyay, ticking a list off her fingers, replied, 'Krishna definitely doesn't. Vishnu, we can't confirm. He is depicted to have numerous forms . . . Bhoomidevi, well, this entire planet is her physical form. But she does seem to have a human form, according to your experience.'

'True . . . So consider Krishna. He doesn't have a definite physical form, he is no longer alive. So how is he able to communicate with me, and others, from beyond death? Something that is beyond the bounds of time and space and death . . . Something is definitely beyond the science we know . . .'

Avyay stared at him hard, and then whispered her guess, 'Soul . . .'

THIRTEEN

Unknown location

Anirudh looked around, confused.

'Where am I?' he asked, looking back at Bhoomidevi, awestruck by his surroundings.

Bhoomidevi, her despair still intact, stepped towards him. 'You are in the astral realm,' she said. 'How did you come here?'

The cat reached out its limb and started pawing the boy's chest. Anirudh, stroking the animal's coat, scrunched his brows. 'I don't know . . . I just woke up here.'

Bhoomidevi looked perplexed.

Anirudh, recalling her words, asked her, 'Wait . . . Did you say the "astral realm"?'

She nodded.

'Oh . . . Do people come here after they die?'

'Not all of them. Humans do not come here much. The animals, birds, trees, plants—they enter the astral realm after they die.'

Anirudh nodded and looked around once more. The beach was the same one, the one where Asi had struck him.

After confirming his surroundings, he addressed her query, 'Then it is not a mystery how I came here . . . I died.'

'What?' she shrieked, startling Anirudh.

She stepped closer, aghast.

'How did you die?' she asked, concerned and torn.

Anirudh smiled, and with his casual charm, replied, 'I got killed in battle by the enemy.'

'But how? I mean, I didn't know there was a weapon that could kill you.'

'Asi,' he answered quietly.

'Oh,' she managed, still unable to wrap her head around the events.

'Also, I wanted to die,' he revealed.

'What? Why?'

Moving around the sandy shore, he told her, 'I wanted to understand what a soul is . . . And how to destroy it.'

'Destroy a soul?' she asked, curiosity lacing her voice.

'Yeah. I have to end Kali once and for all.'

Turning his attention to her, he explained, 'During the Krishna avatar, he told me no matter how many times I kill him, he would always return, because a soul is indestructible.'

'That is true, isn't it?'

Anirudh sighed. 'That's what I want to find out. I want to understand the mechanism of a soul . . .'

'I got that . . . But, I am still not able to figure out how death helps you do that.'

'Well, being alive wasn't going to help me with this problem any sooner. It would have probably taken me a tremendous amount of meditation to detach myself from my body.'

Bhoomidevi nodded, motioning Anirudh to keep going.

'So, I thought that I'll just opt for the quicker path to get what I want . . . my soul form. Just the way I am right now . . .'

FOURTEEN

With Bhoomidevi walking beside him, and the jet-black cat trotting along his side, Anirudh asked her, 'So what *is* the astral realm exactly?'

'Well, it is a placc where souls come to. It is a replica of the universe, except that it is populated with souls that have passed on from their physical manifestations.'

'So these used to be actual trees, plants, forests and animal life on Earth?'

'Yeah.'

Anirudh gazed across the length of the beach behind him. The luminous creatures drifted around in play.

'You should know two things about this realm,' Bhoomidevi continued. 'First, this place lies outside the bounds of time. So any time spent here doesn't reflect in the physical world. Second, you can travel around in this realm at the speed of thought. You want to get somewhere, just think about it, and you will be there.'

Anirudh looked at the goddess with astonishment as he took in the information. He nodded and turned away, as his eyes roved around the beach.

Suddenly, he recalled the brutal deaths of the EOK warriors, which had happened on the same beach.

'What about the people who died on this beach?'

Bhoomidevi smiled. 'This realm is only for the animals, plants and birds—the non-humans, if I may use that word.'

'Why so?' Anirudh asked, curious.

'Well, mankind is dominating the entire earth out there. So they don't deserve a separate realm now. But these sentient creatures, they have led lives drowned in fear. Fear of human hunters who wanted to exploit these beings for their own benefit. Even more horrifying were their deaths—killed brutally using knives, spears, guns, steel traps. Some were mutilated even during their last moments—tusks ripped out, skinned alive, feathers pried out. And the non-sentient ones, the trees and plants, they were cut down to make way for civilization.'

Anirudh sighed. He turned and looked down at the four-legged furry creature walking beside him.

Bhoomidevi smiled at the animal and bent towards it. 'Meow!' she cheerfully called out to it. The cat looked at her with its bottle-green eyes and acknowledged her with a meow.

Standing upright, she told Anirudh, 'Meow—that's her name!'

'Ahhh, I see. *Very creative!*' he replied, in a tone of mischievous sarcasm.

She detected the tone in his words, but let it slide.

She looked at the feline being, and a glint of sadness fluttered across her eyes. Anirudh didn't miss it.

'What?' he asked her.

She shook her head with a smile.

Anirudh looked at Meow and back at the goddess.

'Why did you become sad?' he asked her.

'Her death . . .'

'What about it?' Anirudh enquired.

'It wasn't a pleasant one,' she replied. Anirudh waited for her to continue.

'She was, somewhat, stoned to death.'

Anirudh stopped in his tracks, his eyes wide. 'What do you mean?'

Bhoomidevi stopped as well and turned to him.

'There was a huge family picnic a few kilometres away from here. Meow was roaming around in search of food, and the children, noticing her wandering about, pelted her with stones. Some of the rocks were jagged and they pierced and wounded her badly.'

'Why did they do that?' Anirudh asked, a rage unbottling inside him. Meow was bouncing around, chasing a butterfly that had caught her attention.

'Just for fun, to see how she reacts. To hear her squeal . . .' Bhoomidevi replied glumly.

'And where were the parents?' he enquired, the rage rushing to the surface.

'The children were far away from the parents, out of their earshot.'

A shade of red clouded Anirudh's eyes. His anger and sadness changed into tears. He went down on his knees.

Feeling the mood change in his new-found friend, Meow stopped pursuing the butterfly and bounded to Anirudh. Feeling the sadness flooding him, the raven-coloured animal licked the human's face. The avatar laughed through his tears, feeling honoured by the gesture, and kissed the cat on her head.

Bhoomidevi smiled looking at the two of them.

'She is in a better place now,' she said gently.

Anirudh stood up and resumed walking.

'Thank you, Bhoomidevi, for giving all of them this wonderful place,' he said to her with immense gratitude.

Bhoomidevi nodded. 'It is the least I could do.'

'I am glad that humans are not allowed in this realm,' Anirudh said. The red in his eyes was still there, though it was a light cloud now.

Anirudh looked at Meow purring happily beside him. He looked at her smooth fur and then at Bhoomidevi's perfect skin. He raised his fingers to his chest and felt his unbroken skin where the sword had been plunged in.

'Does this realm heal us of our injuries? Meow's fur doesn't have any signs of stone-pelting, your skin isn't cracked or bleeding, and my chest doesn't have the injuries I had sustained during the battle . . .'

Bhoomidevi answered him with a smile. 'Injuries are on your physical body, not on your soul,' she said.

Anirudh nodded in understanding. He looked down at Meow with concern, which didn't escape Bhoomidevi's notice.

'No, Meow doesn't remember anything about the events of her death. None of them here remember the pains they underwent in their physical life.'

Anirudh looked at her curiously.

'I didn't want them to remember their past pains, so I wipe them clean on their death. If they remembered the pain and death that humans delivered unto them, do you really think Meow would have warmed up to you so quickly? Would any one of them even be roaming around freely on this beach after you appeared on it?'

Anirudh shook his head.

'Their entire lives, like I said earlier, were spent in fear of humankind. I didn't want them to be haunted by that fear after their death too.'

Anirudh nodded, understanding her point.

♣ Abhinav

'Sometimes, I wish to end mankind forever,' she confessed with barely concealed distaste.

Anirudh simply stared at her quietly. He knew where she was coming from.

60

FIFTEEN

'How did you know I had arrived in this realm?' Anirudh asked Bhoomidevi.

They were seated on a wooden log overlooking the translucent waters in front of them. Meow was jumping and playing around in the waves, approaching and retreating from her.

'I felt a spike in the energy of this place, so I came to investigate the cause of it, and found it—well, you.'

He stared at her, at a loss.

Bhoomidevi smiled and explained, 'I am aware of anything that happens here. I feel the energy patterns of this realm. Whenever a creature dies, it comes to this realm, and I know of it because it causes a shift in the power here. However, when you appeared, I felt a sudden surge of energy in the environment. And that's a pretty rare thing! I knew something wasn't right, so I came over.'

The young avatar nodded slowly. Meow came back to them and bundled herself on the avatar's lap. With a chuckle, he started stroking the head of the animal as the furry creature fell asleep.

'What will she eat in case she is hungry?'

'Hunger is restricted to physical forms only—not the soul. Your soul has no need for food and water, it experiences no thirst and hunger.'

He acknowledged the words as Meow snuggled into a more comfortable position.

'Do you know how I came here?' the young boy enquired.

'Meaning?'

'I mean, you mentioned that this place is off-limits for humans. Then how did I enter this place?'

'You are not human, are you?'

'Pardon me?'

'You are the creator of this entire universe, so you can be anywhere you want to be.'

'Ummm . . . What?'

'Anirudh, you have created everything. Even this place, though I created it, was done with your help . . .'

He looked at her, unconvinced and unanswered.

'Also, it matters what you were thinking of during your death . . .' she added.

He raised an eyebrow at her. 'I was thinking a lot of things—Kalki, the avatar's purpose ahead . . . Avyay, my parents, the Immortals . . . Plenty of stuff. Which one triggered my presence here?'

Bhoomidevi sighed and shrugged.

'Talking about death . . .' she started, 'Who is going to protect me now that you are here? You had promised to avenge me, do you remember?'

Anirudh looked into her ocean eyes.

'I remember that. You still have people looking out for you . . . Avyay is also Kalki, and she will be the only one henceforth.'

Bhoomidevi threw a questioning glance at him, and he explained Krishna's rationale and intent behind having two Kalkis.

Bhoomidevi considered his words. Meow got up with a jerk, startling both of them. Sniffing the air, she leapt off Anirudh's lap and bounded towards the water. They heard a squeak as she chased a rat that had caught her interest, which made Anirudh and the goddess chuckle.

'A while ago,' Bhoomidevi spoke, 'you told me that during your final moments you were thinking of "the avatar's purpose ahead". So were you thinking about Avyay's purpose?'

'Yeah . . . And mine as well.'

'Ahhh, yes . . . to understand the mechanism of a soul, correct?'

Anirudh smiled, and he explained Kali's challenge to Krishna.

'So do you know the workings of a soul? What is it made of? How can I destroy it?' he asked her.

'I will let someone else answer that because I have to go back to the physical realm now.'

He found himself getting impatient as he asked her immediately, 'Who?'

'Do you recall that I told you how I found your presence in this realm?'

'Yeah, because of the energy surge . . .'

With a grin, the goddess revealed, 'Well, this surge has happened before too, when a divine being left his mortal abode. And that person will answer your queries about the soul, if he wishes to.'

Anirudh was about to ask her the person's identity, when a voice greeted them from behind, 'Hello, Anirudh and Bhoomidevi.'

They stood up and turned around. Their eyes settled on an older self of Anirudh.

Bhoomidevi greeted him in return, and then turned to Anirudh. She leaned in closer and kissed his cheek. 'Take care, Anirudh. I will see you later.'

Too stunned to reply, he just nodded and reciprocated her gesture.

Waving them both goodbye, the goddess vanished.

Anirudh exhaled and turned his attention to his older self.

'Hello, Krishna,' he greeted the figure, who was playing with the peacock feather in his hand.

SIXTEEN

The Stone Palace,
The night of Kali's resurrection, 2026 CE

Hanuman had earlier reconnoitred the whole stone palace and found that the place was covered by a protective dome of energy shield. Thus, telepathy didn't work from inside the palace. The stone structure also had countermeasures against energy tracers, which is what prevented the Immortals from discovering the place by supernatural means. And the shield rendered the structure invisible—to untrained eyes.

To use telepathy, Hanuman had to fly far away from the palace, outside the energy shield. Having soared high enough, he turned and look down at the stone structure. It was a huge mansion, made of black stone, standing alone, far out in the middle of the dark sea. It was suspended a hundred feet above the sea. There were no bridges connecting it to the mainlands of Kerala.

There isn't a need for bridges if you know teleportation, Hanuman mused.

Without wasting time, the ape-god closed his eyes and communicated through his thought, *Lord Parashurama . . . Can you hear me?*

❧

Meanwhile, inside the opulent white chamber, Shukracharya sat on the marble floor in the lotus position. He closed his eyes and started chanting. Kalarakshasa walked to Koka and whispered, 'Tell Kalaguru to ready the soldiers. They are to be assembled with their staffs and helmets. Tell him to organize them in proper formation in the main hall.'

Turning to the body inside the coffin, he continued, 'I suppose Lord Kali would want to see his army.'

Koka bowed and left the chamber.

❧

In the EOK mansion, Parashurama was walking around restlessly, waiting for a word from Hanuman. The other Immortals and Acharya Sreedhar, the head of EOK, were seated around the large dining table, speculating about Hanuman's success, as well as the possible dangers of getting caught.

When Hanuman's voice came through to him, the axe-wielder raised a hand, and the voices fell silent.

Yes, Hanuman, I hear you. What took you so long? he replied telepathically to his fellow Immortal.

I have been doing a bit of exploration and investigation. There's an energy shield around the stone palace that protects it from being traced and keeps it invisible.

Parashurama conveyed this information to the others at the table. Energy tracing, as they all knew, was a technique to send out energy waves in an attempt to encounter what is being sought. If it was sought, the waves would act as a pointer to the source. When Kalanayaka was in the drug-induced state of speaking the truth, they had gained an idea of how the palace looked on the inside. They attempted to trace a physical location which matched the description using energy waves, but the energy waves faded into oblivion. The shield that Kalarakshasa had erected allowed the energy waves to pass as if the stone structure didn't exist in the first place.

Are all of you around? Hanuman asked, in a rush.

Yeah, the Immortals are all here. What's happened? You sound urgent, Parashurama asked, concerned.

I hope you are ready to attack the stone palace . . . now, the ape-god's voice entered his mind.

Koka located Bhairava in the practice hall, overlooking some Kalabakashakas fighting and correcting their forms. Seeing the Guardian, Kalaguru walked towards him. Koka passed on Kalarakshasa's message of gathering the soldiers so that Kali can see his army, and also told him that the resurrection of Lord of Kali had begun. Bhairava acknowledged the message and turned to the sorcerers practising around the hall. He barked at them and instructed them to get into their uniforms and equip themselves with their staffs. He ordered them to assemble in the dining hall in five minutes.

Where is the stone palace? Parashurama asked as he turned to the Immortals. They were all looking at him, waiting to hear from Hanuman. The axe-wielder gestured at them to assemble the EOK warriors.

As soon as they received the instruction, Bali, Kripa and Vibhishana ran out to the hall to gather the troops.

The stone palace is in the middle of the sea, off the coast of Kerala, Hanuman's voice replied.

That's terrific, the avatar replied.

It is, the ape-god affirmed. *Also, no bridges connect it to the shore.*

Parashurama informed the others at the dining table, 'I will be back soon.'

And the Immortal being vanished.

Hanuman looked at the lord hovering next to him. Parashurama nodded and they slowly floated down to the energy shield, which was visible to their divine eyes. Parashurama held his hand over it and closed his eyes. His lips muttered chants while his fingers twitched against the shield.

He opened his eyes and looked at Hanuman. 'There are a couple of defense mechanisms that are not so straightforward to crack. It is not impossible, but time-consuming, yes. However, what worries me is just this one shield. It is easy to break, for it is made for breaking. Upon destruction, the barrier will alert Ashwatthama. We should break it just before breaching, else he will come to know that the shield has broken, and he can put up countermeasures.'

Hanuman nodded. He had recognized Ashwatthama the moment he walked in without his hood and spoke to Bhairava in the library earlier in the evening.

'I suggest we breach immediately. We should not lose time, for there is one important event undergoing inside the palace.'

'What is that, Hanuman?' Parashurama asked.

SEVENTEEN

Having learnt what was happening in the palace, Parashurama returned to the EOK mansion. He walked to the dining hall with quick strides and noted that Bali, Kripa and Vibhishana had returned.

'Are they ready to attack?' he asked, as he started twirling his hands in front of him, producing a blue orb between his palms.

'The only question is "When",' Vibhishana replied.

'Good,' Parashurama acknowledged as he reached the large table, gathering everyone's attention to his hands. 'Because the answer to that is "now".'

Everyone exchanged a curious glance. The axe-wielder spread his arms wide and pushed the blue orb to the centre of the congregation. Everyone stood up as the ball took the holographic shape of a mansion, suspended in air, surrounded by the sea.

'The stone palace, surrounded by sea on all sides, with no bridges to the land,' Parashurama explained.

He leaned in and proceeded to explain the plan, and everyone listened with rapt attention.

'We will have four teams, and we will breach from each direction. The teams will be headed by Hanuman, Kripa, Bali and Vibhishana. We will all arrive at the stone palace and take our positions at each side of the mansion,' said the de-facto leader of the Immortals as he pointed to each side of the palace. 'First, we will teleport the warriors and wait on aerial platforms, since the stone palace is a floating structure. Kripa and I will work on deactivating the defences. Upon breaking the barrier, we will teleport inside the mansion and commence our attack.'

'Kill or subdue?' Vibhishana asked.

'Kill,' the axe-wielding god replied in a grave tone.

'Maharishi Vyasa and Sreedhar will remain here at the EOK mansion,' he instructed.

Everyone nodded.

'Before we leave, there's something else you all should know,' he said.

'Kali is being resurrected as we speak. So this is no mere breach,' said Parashurama as everyone listened with rapt attention. 'Time is of the essence here, and if we attack soon, we can stop the resurrection. If we don't, our objective changes to taking down Kali and all the prominent members of the Kalabakshakas. Given that the revivification of the Lord of Evil himself is happening, I will join Hanuman after breaking the barrier. Kripa, you too must join us after you teleport your team inside the mansion.'

Kripa nodded. Parashurama clapped his hands once, and the blue holographic mansion disappeared.

He brought out Asi, which he carried on his person, and handed it to Vibhishana. The former king of Lanka accepted it with a bow. After that, everyone dispersed, with no time to react to the shocking revelation they had just heard.

∽

Bhairava inspected the rows of Kalabakshakas standing in front of him. Bull horns protruded from their black hoods, and their staffs—with miniature skulls and horns—were held firmly in their hands. Hanuman, in his ant-form, saw this assembly from the window. He quickly flew back to his position in the dark sky and waited.

&

Standing on a platform around fifteen feet above the stone mansion, Parashurama surveyed the situation below him. The fortifications of the structure were disabled by Kripa, except for the one barrier, which was left intact for now since it would alert Ashwatthama upon destruction. There were four teams of EOK elite soldiers, dressed in light-blue robes, standing at the assigned breach points outside the mansion. Hanuman, Vibhishana, Bali and Kripa stood at the front of their teams.

He spoke telepathically to the four leaders, 'Hanuman has noted that all of the Kalabakshakas are assembled in the main hall, so it should be an easy breach. But the main hall is where the battle is going to happen. So guide your teams carefully and let them be forewarned. Bali and Vibhishana's teams breach the main hall, Kripa's team will check around the mansion for stray Kalabakshakas. Hanuman's team will breach the chamber where Kali is being resurrected. Kripa, as soon as we enter, you put up an anti-teleportation shield around the mansion. We don't want anyone to escape.'

After everyone affirmed the plan, Parashurama pulled out his axe.

'On my mark,' he announced.

He jumped off the platform and hurled himself towards the final energy shield below. Wielding his axe for a swing, he started chanting the counter charm to bring down the barrier. His axe started glowing brightly like a star, it shone in the dark night. With a loud clang, he struck his blade on the roof of the invisible energy dome. After a moment, the barrier broke into smithereens and vanished into thin air. Nothing stood between them and the stone mansion.

Suspending himself in the air, Parashurama roared, 'Now!'

Upon hearing the command, the four teams teleported from their positions. Confirming that they had advanced, Parashurama also vanished into thin air, following Hanuman.

The stone palace had been breached.

EIGHTEEN

When he heard the loud clangour shatter the silence of the chamber, Kalarakshasa's reflexes kicked in. Instinctively, he conjured up a barrier, which protected the old sage, the tomb and himself. He saw that the sage was undisturbed and was still chanting. He created a sound barrier around Shukracharya so that the meditating man wouldn't be disturbed. He closed his eyes and discovered that the protective shell around the mansion had been broken. He opened his eyes and looked around furtively, expecting the enemies, the allies of Kalki, to attack any moment.

'How did they know of this palace?!' he asked himself through gritted teeth.

He shook his head, acknowledging that the mystery would have to be ignored for now, given that they were here now. He communicated to Bhairava, Koka and Vikoka telepathically, *The barrier has been breached, the stone palace has been discovered by the Immortals. Koka, save as many people as you can. Rendezvous at Jana's cottage. Bhairava, come to me right now. We are under attack.*

Jana, he said to himself.

He was the only disciple who came to Kalarakshasa's mind at such short notice.

In his mind, he reasoned his choice of that person, *He is a trustworthy Kalabakshaka and has been serving me faithfully for years. Of course, it was under his tutelage that a powerful sorcerer like Kalanayaka had risen. Alas, that student met his end at the hands of Anirudh. However, Jana should be able to give shelter to us for some time.*

As soon as they heard the thunderous gong echo across the main hall, everyone became alert. Bhairava shouted to the hundreds of soldiers in front of him, 'Arm yourselves!'

Koka, too, was on the lookout. Everyone's eyes were darting hither and thither, wary of the deathly silence. And then, the storm arrived. A swarm of blue-robed people appeared in the main hall on either side of it. As soon as they arrived, Kalki's army commenced their attack. They spread themselves quickly and launched fatal projectiles of water and earth towards the enemy soldiers. Some of the excellent warriors of Kalki launched their blades towards the enemy. The bloodthirsty swords kept striking down enemies, moving from one target to the other.

Bali and Vibhishana noticed the two black-robed sorcerers standing at the head of the assembly, countering and neutralizing the EOK soldiers.

As Kalaguru and the Guardian engaged the enemy forces that breached the mansion, their leader's voice appeared in their minds. They exchanged a quick glance.

Kripa and his team arrived in a room lined with beds. He instructed his team to clear the palace and strike down any enemy they came across. After ensuring that the dormitory was empty, the soldiers dispersed in an orderly manner. Kripa closed his eyes and started creating the anti-teleportation barrier around the mansion that Lord Parashurama had tasked him with.

As soon as Hanuman and his team appeared in Kali's chamber, Kalarakshasa extended the protective shield to include Vikoka as well. The intruders started attacking with elemental projectiles, and Hanuman rushed ahead with his mace to strike the red-robed sorcerer. But all of their attacks fell flat against the protective shield that extended to two feet around the red-robed sorcerer. Kalarakshasa telepathically instructed Vikoka to take the sword lying by the door. As he finished directing the Seeker, he saw Parashurama materialize in the room.

In the main hall, the disciplined Kalabakshakas quickly formed two lines, backs against each other and took on the assault. But they had lost the battle even before it had started. They looked around at their fallen comrades, which was half of the total assembly. They tried to defend themselves as much as they could.

Seeing that Bhairava had disappeared from their sight, Vibhishana and Mahabali looked at each other. Bali nodded to Vibhishana, who took the hint and disappeared as well. The sage knew that the black-robed teacher would be headed to the chamber of Kali. Bali appeared in front of Koka, ready to take him on.

❧

Bhairava arrived in the white marble chamber and took down two enemy soldiers with fiery ropes around their necks. He dodged the mace hurled by Hanuman. He threw back a mace made of earth in response. Parashurama, without even looking at it, swung his axe against that weapon and it turned to dust. The avatar's eyes were fixed on the marble grave that was lying open in front of him. His gaze went to the aged man reciting mantras. 'Shukracharya!' Parashurama roared, trying to break the sage's concentration.

Kalarakshasa laughed at the attempt. He yelled at the meditating saint, 'Acharya!'

But the old man didn't budge even a bit. The Vishnu avatar realized that the sorcerer had put some enchantment around the sage. Kalarakshasa telepathically announced to his three followers, *We need to hold them off for two more minutes, the recital will be complete by then.*

He put the protective shield around Bhairava as well. Parashurama swung his axe against the shield, but it was defeated by the barrier. 'It's the same one I had trapped Kalki in, so save your breath!'

Vibhishana appeared in the chamber. Kalarakshasa noticed Asi in his hand.

'You shouldn't be wielding that sword, Vibhishana,' he told the former king.

'You killed the one who's supposed to be wielding it, in your lust for this divine blade,' Vibhishana replied.

These words evoked a twitch in the red-robed sorcerer's brow.

'Your death is written at the end of this sword, so we will carry it against you always,' the former ruler of Lanka grunted.

Kalarakshasa laughed. 'That's just it, O King. It is just a sword in your hands, not Asi . . .'

Vibhishana looked down at the blade in his hand and then back to the sorcerer. This statement of the demon lord also caught the attention of Parashurama and Hanuman.

'What do you mean?' the Lankan asked.

Kalarakshasa was about to reply when he heard Koka's words in his mind.

The Guardian, who had spent the majority of his life protecting treasures, had a few spells handy with him. He protected himself and the sorcerers against the enemy attacks. Bali struck the barrier with his mace, but it was futile. The king of the netherworld smiled and let his mace rest by his side but kept it ready for an attack.

Koka, not wasting time in understanding the mystery behind the smile, ran to the Kalabakshakas. They were safe for now under the protective barrier he had created. It was absorbing the attacks and nullifying them. He looked at his fellow soldiers and marked them.

He closed his eyes, dropped the shields and started to teleport himself and the Kalabakshakas around him to Jana's place, just like his master had instructed.

But he felt a heavy blow on his back and screamed out in pain. He opened his eyes and saw that they were still in the stone palace. A couple of the sorcerers fell down from the attacks launched by the blue-robed sages. He turned and saw Bali taking another swing of his mace at him. Before the mace could strike him, he pushed the Immortal away with a wave of strong wind. The other black-robed warriors did the same to their attackers who had them surrounded.

Koka reconstructed the protective shield around them and himself, and informed Kalarakshasa, *I am unable to teleport out of the palace. Someone has blocked the place . . .*

Kripa, having conjured the anti-teleportation mechanism around the stone mansion, teleported to the marble chamber.

When Kalarakshasa saw the presence of Kripacharya in the chamber, he found the explanation to Koka's inability to teleport. The red-robed sorcerer laughed loudly. 'I see most of the Immortals are here! I am blessed indeed!'

Having got the attention of the intruders, he spoke telepathically to his three followers, *Koka, hold the fort for some time. All of you, listen to my teleportation instructions carefully now. Koka, take the remaining Kalabakshakas with you. Bhairava, take Shukracharya. And Vikoka, take the sword and the coffin with you. When I give the command, teleport from here to Jana's place.*

Vikoka moved towards the coffin and Bhairava stood behind Shukracharya. These movements caught the attention of the Immortals and their soldiers. Kalarakshasa closed his eyes and took in a deep breath.

All of a sudden, a loud thunder roared through the black sky and the dark expanse split open with a huge flash of lightning. The enemy soldiers as well as the Kalabakshakas looked at the ceiling in alarm. The terrible rumbling continued as they heard the rain start pouring. Kripa placed his hand on the translucent shield created by the red-robed sorcerer. Then, when another thunder rolled above, Drauni opened his eyes.

When the followers of Kalki looked at his eyes, they were taken aback. They were sparkling with a shade of electric blue, and the jewel on his forehead shone with a dark blue fire.

Echoing everyone's thoughts, Hanuman gasped, 'Rudra!'

Ashwatthama breathed heavily, feeling the surge of energy coursing through his veins. He stepped outside the protective shield but still maintained it around the others. He roared and pushed Kripa against the wall, binding him against the marble surface. Since Kripa's contact with the shield had been broken, the spell to bring down the barrier was broken too. Hanuman swung his mace at the sorcerer. The other foot soldiers of Kalki too joined the fray and launched attacks on their enemy, sending across blades of steel. As he worked on bringing down the anti-teleportation wall, Kalarakshasa punched the oncoming mace, which fell to the ground. With his eyes ablaze and with tremendous speed in his movements, Kalarakshasa dodged the knives headed towards him. Effortlessly, he turned the shining blades to face their throwers. With a flash, they attacked their owners and killed them. Vibhishana was about to pounce on the leader of the Kalabakshakas when Parashurama signalled him to hold back. Vibhishana noticed that he was saying something under his breath, his axe held tight in his hands. Hanuman, with his fist at the ready, launched himself at the dark-skinned sorcerer. Kalarakshasa quickly side-stepped the punch and holding the wrist of his attacker, tossed him and pounded his heavy body on to the ground.

Suddenly, silence descended on the chamber. The rumbles of thunder could no longer be heard. Everyone was still, not moving an inch. The sound of life had echoed in the room amid the chaos. Kalarakshasa had finished breaking the anti-teleportation shield. Parashurama had finished chanting and his axe was glowing with a dark blue hue, sparks emanating from it. Shukracharya opened his eyes, having finished the recitation. He was taken aback by the crowd in the room.

Then, every pair of eyes in the room turned to the source of the sound they had heard earlier—the marble coffin in the centre of the chamber. And as they looked on in awe, it happened again. The chest rose and fell again, a breath escaping the slightly parted lips. It was accompanied by the beat of the heart. Ironically, the signs of life rendered everyone in the room still.

But the silence was short-lived, as Kalarakshasa saw his window of opportunity amidst every distracted person in the room. He reinforced the protective shield around the coffin, Shukracharya and his two followers. He yelled, 'Nowwww!!' to Bhairava and Vikoka, and telepathically to Koka as well.

Before Bali or the soldiers could react, the Guardian disappeared with his platoon from the main hall.

'He has broken the anti-teleportation shield,' Kripa cried, relieving himself slightly of the sorcerer's clutches.

Kalarakshasa held the shield strong as his followers quickly grabbed Shukracharya and Kali's coffin.

As soon as Kripa warned them, Parashurama flung the blazing axe at Kalarakshasa. Parashurama called out to Vibhishana, pointing towards the sorcerer. Understanding the signal, Vibhishana launched Asi at the red-robed man.

The Kalabakshakas were awestruck by the two weapons charging furiously towards their leader.

'Go!!!' their master yelled at them, with fiery white eyes. And that was the last word they heard from him before he took the two weapons in his chest. When the two blades struck the vessel of Rudra, a loud thunder clapped in the chamber. Kalarakshasa's body was sent flying back, and his body soared past the coffin and his followers. The sorcerer hit the wall with a boom, and the marble shattered under the tremendous impact. The Demon of Time went right through the thick marble wall, the weapons carrying him out into the storm.

Before they teleported, the black-robed sorcerers saw the body of their cherished leader soaring through the air, with his red robes fluttering about in the heavy rain. A loud thunder and lightning highlighted the airborne sorcerer in a nightmarish hue of blue, as he began his descent. In the momentary flash that illuminated his face, the two sorcerers noticed that their leader's eyes were closed, his face was calm. With that final sight, they vanished from the room, carrying out the final instruction of their deceased ruler.

Kalarakshasa's torso, impaled with the two majestic and powerful blades, was drenched in blood and rain. Lashed upon incessantly by the torrential downpour, the muscular frame wrapped in the wet, red cloth, gradually gravitated down, towards the dark, foamy sea. With a splash, he hit the surface of the turbulent sea. The roaring waters, with their fangs glistening with blood and lightning, swallowed Ashwatthama's body whole, devoid of any remorse or prejudice.

NINETEEN

Parashurama stood by the large gap in the white chamber's wall, looking down at the stormy sea under him. Hanuman quickly sat down on the floor and closed his eyes, going into a meditative state. He was trying to trace the movements of the Kalabakshakas via their energy signatures. Vibhishana rushed over to Kripa and freed him.

Parashurama extended his hands over the waters below. He closed his eyes and checked for any signs of life. There were none. He then summoned the two blades. After a few moments, the axe and the sword erupted out of the ocean and flew to the hands of their summoner. He opened his eyes and took control of them as he retreated into the room.

The axe-wielding lord looked down at the two weapons in his hands, the sea had cleansed them of the red life-fluid. He sheathed the glowing Asi and placed the axe on the hook on his back. Vibhishana looked around the magnificent chamber. Walking around the room slowly, studying it, Parashurama reached a majestic chair made of marble. He ran his hands over the white throne. 'Kali had a great throne waiting for him . . .' he commented.

Kripa stated, 'Kali . . . He's back.'

Vibhishana nodded and looked at the axe-bearing Immortal.

The Immortal strode to Kripa, kept a hand on his shoulder and squeezed it gently. 'I am sorry about your nephew, Kripa . . .'

Kripa acknowledged the condolence with a silent nod.

Vibhishana offered his sympathies as well.

At that moment, Hanuman opened his eyes, stepping out of his trance. He was visibly frustrated.

'I am unable to locate them,' he grunted.

Parashurama sighed and spoke, 'I am not surprised.'

After a couple of moments, Vibhishana asked, 'What should our next step be?'

Parashurama turned to the gaping hole in the wall, and then to Kripa, telling him, 'Seal this. No one should be able to enter this chamber or this palace from here. Meet us in the main hall after you are done here.'

Kripa nodded and set himself to work.

Vibhishana offered to take the lifeless remains of the EOK soldiers back to the EOK mansion, to which the leader agreed.

Parashurama, accompanied by Hanuman, walked out from the chamber as the sage disappeared with the bodies of the soldiers.

In the main hall, Bali ordered the warriors to search the mansion for any clues or interesting objects. He told them to be on the lookout for any Kalabakshakas left behind and instructed them to be captured alive, if possible.

'Did we stop Kali's resurrection?' he asked Parashurama, who was walking towards him.

He shook his head and said, 'They teleported Kali from here, along with Shukracharya. Hanuman tried to trace them, but to no avail.'

Hanuman shrugged his shoulders, taking a look around the large hall. The king of the netherworld nodded solemnly, sighing with dejection.

'But,' Parashurama said, 'we got Kalarakshasa.'

Bali's eyes widened with surprise. 'That's great, we can ask him where Kali and the others are headed.'

'He is dead.'

The look of remorse returned to the face. 'How is Kripa taking it?'

Parashurama remained silent.

Bali and the Vishnu avatar walked among the remains of the enemy soldiers, looking for anything that stood out. They also looked into the large practice area, which was visible from the hall. Having found nothing worth their attention, they walked around the hall. Kripa and the EOK soldiers made their way to the antechamber at the same time. One of the soldiers stepped up and gave them a report of the entire mansion. She highlighted two areas of interest—Kalarakshasa's room and a room with a boxful of mystical texts.

After she finished her report and left, Hanuman asked, 'How do we track Kali? We cannot let them get away, can we?'

Parashurama hummed as he let his thoughts wander for a couple of minutes. Everyone looked towards the leader in anticipation.

'Let them be,' he announced finally.

'What?'

'Yes, Kali will eventually find us, so let us conserve our energy now,' said Parashurama, justifying his decision. 'We have to contend with dealing with Kali some other day. Let's keep our resources focused on training our warriors and protecting Kalki now.'

All the Immortals nodded.

Parashurama dispatched Hanuman and Kripa to the room with the texts, telling them to get the texts to the red-robed sorcerer's room. He instructed the warriors to clear the hall of the mortal remains and cremate them with proper respect. Accompanied by Bali, he went to Kalarakshasa's room.

In the room of the leader of the Kalabakshakas, the two Immortals looked around, studying every nook and corner. After ascertaining that there was nothing of importance apart from the large bookcase, they headed towards the shelves of books near the study table.

Bali took out a couple of books and started flipping through the pages. Parashurama scanned the book spines, checking if any of the names interested him. The titles were handwritten on a few of them and the rest were clothbound. One such book, covered with red cloth and set on the top shelf, caught his attention. Parashurama took the book and headed to the desk. Placing it on the wooden table, he started browsing through the yellowed pages.

Kripa entered the room, followed by Hanuman, who was carrying a huge chest full of books. He placed the box under the window and looked around the room. Kripa saw the vermilion book that held Parashurama's attention and asked him, 'What does the book contain?'

The avatar looked up and said, 'Many chants. But there's an interesting one here.'

He passed the book to the acharya, who took it and read the page that was pointed to him.

'The mantra to block the trikalagyanatvam!' he exclaimed, after reading it.

This caught the attention of Bali and Hanuman as well.

'Does this also mention the chant to counteract or dispel the block?'

Parashurama shook his head.

'I must confess, Kripa, your nephew was a collector and he was very powerful indeed.'

'I don't know how he came about these books, but they are advanced in nature and he certainly seemed adept at them,' Bali said.

Hearing this, an intrigued Hanuman took out a book at random from the granite box and started reading it.

'Yeah, from the looks of it, he not only collected these texts but also soaked in their knowledge,' Kripa admired.

'He is a sad loss, Kripa. If he was on our side, then we would have been undefeatable,' Parashurama said solemnly.

'I don't know, Lord Parashurama. I have a feeling that he is not lost yet,' Kripa said.

Hanuman looked up from his book, curious.

'He passed away in front of our eyes, Kripa,' Bali spoke with empathy.

'You may find it impossible, King Bali. But you didn't see him at the peak of his powers today! It was like Lord Rudra himself was in front of us—fighting against us.'

Parashurama contributed, 'I saw him too—it was exactly as Kripa described. Ashwatthama was very powerful.'

'Yeah,' Hanuman ventured, 'At the same time, he was shielding his people, keeping Kripa bound and also removing the anti-teleportation barrier.'

'I wouldn't be surprised if he was also telepathically instructing his followers about the escape plan,' Kripa said with a melancholic smile on his lips.

'He was a genius,' Hanuman said, keeping the book back in the box.

Kripa, looking at the book in his hand, said, 'That's why I find it difficult to accept that he met his end like this . . .'

'He died having fulfilled his mission,' Parashurama said. 'The mission of reviving Kali.'

Kripa gave a grave nod and handed the book back to Parashurama.

He went back to exploring the chamber and walked around the desk. He pulled the drawers out. After glancing through the contents, he closed all of them, except one. It contained a rolled scroll inside it.

'Where did he get these books from? They are really profound and dangerous,' Hanuman said as he replaced another book he had picked up.

'Yeah, I was wondering the same,' Bali said, as he ran his fingers over the book spines on the shelf.

'Krishna gave him some of them,' Kripa said, as he finished reading the scroll.

All of them looked up in surprise. Handing the parchment to Parashurama, he said to them, 'He also informed Ashwatthama about Shukracharya.'

Parashurama ran his eyes down the list.

Bali wondered out loud, 'What was Krishna playing at?'

They all exchanged looks, but none of them had an answer to the question.

Finally, Parashurama said, 'Well, whatever it is, Krishna wouldn't have done anything without some forethought about the consequences.'

Hanuman turned to the violent storm outside the window and said the words running through everyone's minds, 'Krishna himself wanted Kali to return. He practically handed the solution for it to Ashwatthama.'

Then, Parashurama recalled something that Hanuman wasn't aware of yet. He stepped to the ape-god and placed a hand on his shoulder. Hanuman looked at the hand on his shoulder and then up at the axe-wielding avatar. 'What is it, my lord?'

'Hanuman, there is something you should know . . . about Anirudh.'

The leader shared the information of Anirudh's demise and the secret of the second Kalki avatar with his fellow Immortal.

TWENTY

'So, even the Immortals don't have an idea about how a soul can be destroyed . . .' Anirudh sighed, looking at Dweepa seated beside him and at the hologram of Avyay seated on a chair in front of him. They shook their heads in response.

When he was unable to reach a solution to the question that Kali had posed to his predecessor, Kalki turned to seek help from the Immortals, reaching them via Dweepa and Avyay. They had responded saying that there was no way to destroy a soul, and it wasn't designed in that manner.

Anirudh sat back in his chair, his index finger rubbing against his thumb. His foot was tapping restlessly on the floor. His mentor saw this mannerism of his and was familiar with what it meant. His ward was thinking about the design of the soul and racking his brain to see if he was missing something.

'What's the design of a soul anyway?' Anirudh groaned to the two people listening to him.

'Well . . . A soul cannot be created or destroyed, and it cannot be damaged or attacked. It doesn't have a birth or death . . .' Avyay responded.

Anirudh stared at her with an 'I-know-that' expression.

She flashed him a helpless smile in response.

Anirudh sat up and wondered out loud, 'How is that possible? Everything in the world that takes birth has to die . . . Then, how does the soul . . .'

Anirudh broke off, his eyebrows scrunched in thought, his lips pursed.

After a few moments, a twinkle shone in his eyes and a soft smile appeared on his lips. Avyay and Dweepa exchanged a glance and looked back at the wondering avatar intently.

Anirudh muttered to himself, *The soul enters and exits . . .*

TWENTY-ONE

EOK Mansion,
The day before Anirudh's death, 2026 CE

Avyay's eyes stared at him with concern. She had come down to meet him before he left to retrieve Asi. They were seated next to each other on the bed.

'How are you feeling?' she asked.

'Excited, I guess.' He grinned.

'Really? That's strange.'

'Why so? Tomorrow I will finally get to lay my hands on Asi, the most powerful weapon!'

'Ahhh, yeah. That's there . . . But Anirudh . . .' she hesitated.

'What is it, Hayati?' he asked, leaning forward.

Taking a deep breath, she continued, 'Isn't there a danger of Kalarakshasa and his men trying to attack you tomorrow?'

Anirudh smiled and said, 'I am counting on it . . .'

Avyay gasped and asked him, her voice just short of a scream, 'What? What are you saying, Anirudh?'

'I am looking forward to their attack,' Anirudh explained. 'Kalarakshasa, or his men, will give me the doorway to the next part of my journey . . .'

'I don't understand,' Avyay confessed.

'If I asked you to measure the depth of the ocean, how would you do it?'

Parking aside her annoyance at the detour, Avyay answered, 'Ummm . . . Measure it from the surface to the ocean bed.'

'And to do this, you would have to dive into the ocean, right?'

Avyay nodded. Then, she impatiently asked, 'How is this connected to Kalarakshasa and the next part of your journey?'

Anirudh raised his palm, gesturing at her to be patient, and he asked her, 'Do you remember I asked you once: what happens after death?'

Avyay, curious, replied, 'Yeah . . . And you conveniently chose not to answer my repeated questions about it . . .'

Anirudh smiled. 'What is a soul?'

'Oh god, still wandering around with this question!' Avyay complained, exasperated. 'And you are still ignoring the question I asked you earlier . . .'

Anirudh sat up with purpose.

'To measure the ocean, you have to dive into the ocean, right? Similarly, to understand the workings of the soul, I have to dive into it.'

'And how would you "dive" into the soul?'

Anirudh replied with one word—a word that shook her to the core. 'Death.'

TWENTY-TWO

Astral Realm

'How long have you been here?' Anirudh asked his predecessor.

'Not long,' Krishna smiled at the young lad.

Krishna came to the wooden log and they sat down together. The evening sun glimmered over the sands and the waves of the sea.

'I don't have permanent residence here—I just came here a while ago, after I sensed that you had left the earth,' he added, playing with the peacock feather he carried in his hand.

'Ohh . . . I see,' Anirudh managed.

He looked at Meow frolicking on the shore, digging into the sand.

'Did you come here as well, after you died?' he asked.

Krishna nodded. 'I had been here for some time.'

'And then? Where did you go from here?'

The god smiled again, 'Nowhere. I just unmanifested myself.'

'Unmanifested yourself?' Anirudh asked curiously. 'How? And why?'

'Why? Because I was done with the purpose of my avatar. How? You will learn it on your own.'

'If you had unmanifested yourself, how are you here?'

'I manifested myself back, Anirudh.'

The young man looked bewildered.

Krishna explained, 'We can manifest and unmanifest as and when needed.'

'We? Even I can? I didn't know that.'

'Oh, but you do. Else, you wouldn't have been able to come here.'

Anirudh scratched his forehead, trying to wrap his head around Krishna's words.

'I didn't intend come here at all . . .' Anirudh started but trailed off as he pondered over the matter. 'Wait a moment . . . do you know why I am here?'

Krishna let out a grin.

'So you know what souls are made of, and how to destroy them?'

Krishna gave him a brief nod.

'Great!' Anirudh continued. 'So tell me the workings of a soul and how to destroy one, so that I can destroy Kali . . .'

Krishna sat back and took a deep breath. 'No,' he said in a firm tone.

'What?' Anirudh was aghast. 'Why not?'

Krishna tossed the peacock feather up into the sky and it vanished into thin air.

'Because . . .' Krishna answered as he turned to Anirudh, 'You already know the answers you seek.'

'What?' he asked, perplexed. 'I don't!' he cried.

'You do, Anirudh. But you have forgotten it,' Krishna revealed with a smile.

Anirudh looked helplessly at the sea in front of him, his brows scrunched in confusion and annoyance.

'Defeating Kali . . .' Krishna spoke in his characteristic mellifluous voice, 'That's . . . That's your destiny, Anirudh. I have lived my purpose and I have helped you all I could.'

The creases on Anirudh's forehead vanished hearing his predecessor's words.

Krishna continued, 'You have to handle Kali in your own way. If it was up to me, I would have done it during my lifetime. But his destiny is in your hands. So you have to undertake this journey on your own.'

Anirudh nodded to the avatar as he soaked in the words.

He looked around at the flora and fauna inhabiting the realm.

'Bhoomidevi said that this place is outside the bounds of time . . . How does that work? How is this realm not subject to time?'

'What she meant is that there is no concept of time here. To put it plainly, life just goes on here. You are not getting any older or younger.'

Anirudh's face wore a confused expression. 'How can time not exist here?'

'How do you measure time?'

'By looking at the watch . . .' Anirudh said, as he looked down at his wrist, a force of habit. But his wrist was naked.

Krishna smiled. 'Without the watch, how would you determine the time?'

Anirudh looked at the orange sun hovering in the sky.

'Right,' Krishna agreed. 'The sun, yes. Now, ignoring the sun, can you guess how much time has passed since you woke up in this realm?'

'An hour or more, probably . . .'

The lord of Dwarka pointed to the sun and asked the young lad, 'Do you think the sun has moved at all since you opened your eyes on this beach?'

Anirudh thought back to the time he woke up and compared the position of the sun then versus its position in the present moment. He stared open-mouthed at the orange globe of light.

'It has been at the same place all this while!' he whispered to Krishna.

Krishna patted his back. 'And that is by design. So time is constant here, but life goes on.'

'But why is the time "designed" to be dusk? Why not dawn? Or night?'

'From the perspective of humans, time exists as a concept— we have quantified it into hours, days, years and so on . . . But from the view of these animals and plants, time doesn't exist in a quantifiable manner. For them, it is a cycle. Their day starts with the sun and ends with sundown. In the mornings, they roam around in search of food and the end of their attempts to find food is marked by dusk, when the orange sun is setting. Done with the day's activity, they now look forward to the night's rest. It is a sweet spot, to be honest. A feeling stems from the gratification that the day has ended and now rest awaits. It breathes a new life in them. So Bhoomidevi kept this realm in everlasting dusk, so that these creatures could remain in that pleasant feeling as long as they are here.'

'I see,' Anirudh whispered, as he looked at the living beings roaming around the beach.

'How old is your soul?'

'My soul's age? How would I know that?' said Anirudh, surprised at the question. 'Well, if the soul is born when I am born, then I guess my soul is roughly twenty-one years.'

'Ahhh.' Krishna grinned. 'But was your soul born when you were born? And by you, do you mean Anirudh, or Vishnu?'

'I meant me, as in Anirudh. But I see your point. Now that you put it that way, I don't know when my soul was born.'

'If you recall my words to Arjuna, a soul has no birth and . . .'

'No death,' Anirudh completed.

'I see you remember the words,' Krishna mentioned with a chuckle.

Anirudh smiled and bowed his head in acknowledgement.

'Since a soul is eternal,' Krishna continued, 'without life and death, the astral realm is eternal as well. There is no life and death here. There is no sense of time here. The animals and plants enter and exit this place . . . just like entering and exiting a dream.'

'Exit as well!? Why would they want to exit this realm?' Anirudh asked, surprised.

'Well, life goes on, doesn't it? They move on to their next birth, a new life . . .'

Anirudh considered the words. 'You said they would enter and exit this realm like entering and exiting a dream, but it is not exactly like that, is it? Suppose I am in the physical realm. When I dream and when I wake, some time has passed in the physical realm. Then how does the astral realm work?'

'Time wouldn't have passed in the physical realm,' the god answered.

'What?'

'Yes. However much time you spend in this realm, when you go back to the physical realm, you will reach it at the same moment as when you left it. That is why this realm is beyond death.'

TWENTY-THREE

The two avatars were walking along the shore, the gushing waves washing the sand off their feet every once in a while. Meow was bounding alongside them, enjoying the spray of cold water.

'How did you appear in my dream? How did you mention my name, Anirudh, in the dream?' Anirudh asked Krishna.

'Well, the answer to both the questions is that we are connected on a higher level of consciousness. So I was able to enter your dream as if I were visiting you. And so, I was able to learn your name as well. I know everything about you and you know everything about me, even beyond what the texts say about me.'

'I don't think so . . . I don't know you that well, Lord Krishna.'

Krishna laughed when he heard this. 'Firstly, don't address me as "Lord". We are both one.'

Anirudh smiled sheepishly.

'Secondly,' Krishna continued. 'You do know me well.'

Anirudh clicked his tongue, shaking his head.

'I am so glad . . .' Krishna said softly.

The boy looked at his former avatar curiously. He heard a hint of relish in his voice.

Without warning, the dark-skinned man conjured a dagger out of thin air and jabbed it towards Anirudh's chest. Anirudh, his reflexes kicking in, took hold of Krishna's wrist and toppled the lord of Dwarka into the water.

Krishna sat up in the water and slicked back his wet hair, taking a deep breath of air. Anirudh stood over him and extended his hand to help him up.

Krishna looked up at the hand and then at his successor.

'Why?' Krishna asked, pointing a wet finger at the outstretched hand. 'I just tried to stab you.'

Anirudh looked into the dark eyes of Krishna. 'I believe you have a good reason for it.'

'Why do you think so? My reason could have been just a plain one—an intention to harm you.'

'It isn't that, I know it,' Anirudh said firmly.

Krishna licked the water droplets off his lips and looked back at the young avatar.

'How do you know that? Nobody knows what my intentions are until I reveal it to them.'

'Well, I am not some "nobody", am I? I know your intention wasn't to stab me. There was some other motive behind the assault. I also know that you will reveal it to me now.'

Krishna smiled and took Anirudh's hand to help himself up.

'Also,' Anirudh continued, 'I detected a subtle happiness when you said you were glad. It gave me a clue that you were probably up to something. What it was, I didn't know. But I knew enough to beware of something that you were bringing on to me . . .'

'And wasn't it you who, a while back, was saying you don't know me at all? You do know me, Anirudh. Not in your immediate memory or thoughts, but on a subconscious level you know me. That's the way we are. You may not know me like an open book, but you can know me should you want to know me. We are connected.'

The young boy considered the words.

'I believe you have another question for me,' Krishna spoke, mischief evident in his voice.

Anirudh nodded, suppressing a smile. 'You mentioned that you unmanifested yourself sometime after your death. So did you manifest yourself back to enter my dream? How does the re-manisfesting work? How did you enter the physical realm—into my dream? Were you waiting for centuries to pass by before you entered my dream?'

Krishna rubbed his hands in thought. 'Anirudh, you are going to find these answers on your own soon, but I shall tell you one thing: I—even you for that matter—can enter and exit the physical realm upon wish. In fact, we manifest ourselves into an avatar to become a part of the physical realm and aid humankind in whatever form we want to, be it a fish, a tortoise or even something as terrific as a half-man–half-lion. But we are not bound to our physical forms to exist in the physical world. I can, and have, thus entered your dream without the need of any physical form. We are connected, so I can manifest in any form—as a dream or as a thought . . .'

With a smile, Krishna added, 'Or as a memory as well.'

Anirudh turned to look up at Krishna, amazed.

'So the dreams and visions I had about your life . . . Hiding the objects in the underwater cave, hiding Asi in the underwater chamber . . . All that was because of you.'

'Ummm . . . well, no. I didn't make you see those dreams. Since we are a part of the same consciousness, you were able to see them yourself. Our memories are shared.'

Anirudh thought for a couple of moments and asked Krishna, 'I understand that we are connected and so I was able to see your memories. But how did you appear in the dreams of my parents, or that of Sage Dweepa? I am guessing you didn't take any physical form to enter their dreams . . .'

'You guess correctly. They are all connected to the supreme consciousness, and I am connected to it too, so that's how I was able to interact with them.'

'Tell me this, just like you and I are connected, I guess I am connected to Vishnu as well. That's why I could dream about Vishnu and Ksheera Sagar, right?'

Krishna paused in thought for a couple of minutes before answering him.

'Well, not exactly, Anirudh. You dreamt of me because we are connected, yes. You dreamt of Vishnu not because you are connected to him, but because you are Vishnu. One could say we are both connected through Vishnu.'

'Sorry, what?'

'Consider Vishnu to be a tree . . . We, that is, Anirudh and Krishna, are two branches of that tree. We have different paths, but we are connected to the same tree. So you can dream of Vishnu directly, and you can dream of me because I am a part of Vishnu, same as you.'

'And Bhoomidevi? I also saw her in my dream once, after I had gained some energy-conversion abilities. Am I connected to her as well?'

'Bhoomidevi is connected to everyone and everything, Anirudh,' the all-knowing god answered. 'And only you saw her during your battle against Kalanayaka because she chose to be visible only to you.'

TWENTY-FOUR

'So how do I find the answers to all these questions I have in my mind?' Anirudh asked Krishna as they sat on the wet sand.

Meow was resting on the boy's lap.

Krishna smiled, saying nothing.

'I still don't get why you won't tell me answers directly . . .'

'Well, I don't want to spoon-feed the answers to you, Anirudh, lest I deprive you of any learning that you may come across on your quest.'

Anirudh was silent now, stroking the black furry being on his lap.

'Besides,' Krishna continued, 'I have already revealed the answers. You just need to recall them.'

Anirudh looked at Krishna in awe, the latter's face bore a grin now, dimpling his cheeks.

'When?' the boy asked, almost out of breath with excitement.

'During my time . . .'

The boy's brows furrowed in thought as he gazed at the fiery sea. His mind was now a screen on which images flickered—of Krishna and anything related to the dark-skinned god.

His focus was interrupted by one picture. It had Arjuna sitting dejectedly next to his chariot, while Krishna stood next to him, talking to him, advising him.

The creases on Anirudh's forehead melted and a smile appeared on his lips.

'Your words to Arjuna . . . The Divine Song . . . Does the cryptic song bear the answers I seek?' Anirudh asked the god.

Krishna smiled and nodded.

'Great! All I need now is to get my hands on the book, and I am set,' he said jubilantly.

Krishna raised a brow questioningly. 'Why do you need the book when I am here?'

'Are you going to give me the answers, Krishna?'

'Well, no.'

'Then?'

'You have access to my life. We are connected. So why don't you recall the part of my life that you seek?'

Anirudh stared at the lord of Dwarka, looking for an explanation.

'How do I do that? How do I recall your life?'

Krishna spoke a line in explanation and stood up. Anirudh followed suit, making sure that Meow got up first.

'Where are you going now? Are you leaving?'

'Yes, I have said all that I wanted to. Now it's time for you to resume your journey ahead, Anirudh.'

'Resume?'

'Yeah?'

'Pray tell me, dear lord, how am I to resume my journey, given that I am in the astral realm with no way to get back to the physical realm? Even if I find all the answers, how do I get back to the physical realm to act on them?'

'You will find all the answers. Only you can,' Krishna said, in a reassuring tone.

Krishna then turned and started walking.

'Where are you off to?'

'It's time for me to vanish.'

'Will I see you again?' Anirudh asked, with anticipation.

'No, my journey ends here. But then again, should you want to see me again, look inside yourself.'

Anirudh smiled and nodded.

Krishna waved and the avatar reciprocated. The dark-skinned god smiled and vanished into thin air. He had unmanifested himself.

Anirudh turned towards the sea, his eyes fixed hopefully on the dusky horizon. He thought about Krishna's answer to his question of recalling the predecessor's life.

'Meditate. Think of what you seek, and you shall see it. And you will see even beyond what you ask for . . . if you let go instead of fighting.'

TWENTY-FIVE

Jana's cottage,
The night of Kali's resurrection, 2026 CE

In a lawn illuminated by lanterns, Jana was instructing his students to bring first aid and food to the injured Kalabakshakas resting on the grass outside the cottage. Young men and women, dressed in orange clothes, were administering aid and medicines to the battle-worn sorcerers. After ensuring that the situation was under control, he assigned two members of the senior staff to look after the arrangements.

Having relieved himself of his duty, he quickly made his way deep into the dark forest. Soon, he reached a small clearing lit with torches. The forest was still at this ungodly hour. There were just a handful of people in front of Jana—Kalaguru, Bhairava and four others. There was also a large box made of white marble, on which a man was leaning. Kalaguru was now draping a dark shawl around the man who took a step away from the coffin. The man, who was feeble in his movements, was dressed in dark blue robes.

Jana, Ajith's guru, looked at the other two men, who were standing sturdy, like bodyguards. The advisor to Kalarakshasa had addressed them as Koka and Vikoka. He noticed a golden crown hanging from the belt around Vikoka's waist, while a steel sword with a green pommel hung from Koka's belt. Behind these two protectors, against a tree, sat a wizened old man in white ascetic robes. He was shivering with fright, looking at the man departing from the casket.

Jana wondered about the absence of his lord, Kalarakshasa.

After draping the shawl, Kalaguru took a slight step back and looked around at the people in the clearing, including Jana, who was just stepping in.

The Kalabakshakas had teleported to Jana's place some time back, and they were quickly tended to by Jana and his students.

The tall man pulled the cloth draped over him with his long fingers tighter over his chest. With his bloodshot eyes, he slowly took in his surroundings.

His eyes settled on Kalaguru next to him, and he asked in a raspy voice, 'Where's Ashwatthama?'

Kalaguru narrated the events that had transpired at the stone palace. Kali was disappointed to hear the sad demise of his close comrade. Even Jana was shocked and sad to hear the tragic death of his lord.

Kali, hunching and limping, took a couple of steps towards the twins. He then looked at the shuddering old man by the tree trunk behind them.

He addressed the old sage, in a less raspy voice, 'Shukracharya, revive my follower, Kalarakshasa.'

Hearing the Lord of Evil address the prisoner, the two brothers quickly went to the trembling sage and pulled him up.

Kali raised a finger to the white-robed acharya. 'Now.'

Shukracharya, petrified to the core, shut his eyes tight and started muttering the incantation to revive the red-robed sorcerer.

While Kali's focus was only on the mumbling sage in front of him, the others started looking around for signs of the master sorcerer.

But, even after a few minutes, nothing happened.

Shukracharya finally opened his eyes. He didn't see his red-robed captor anywhere in the clearing. His chest fell in defeat.

Kali looked intently at the sage. 'Did you give it your best, Shukra?'

The white-robed acharya nodded, defeatedly. 'Yes, I did.'

'Then why isn't he here?' the Lord of Evil asked of him, his voice now cold. The raspiness had vanished.

'I don't know, I really don't,' said Shukracharya, scared. His mind was also searching for answers to the failure of the resurrection.

Then, Shukracharya raised his eyes to the evil demon and spoke in doubt, 'Maybe they already cremated him with the proper rites?'

Kali stared at the wrinkled man in front of him. He had reached the same conclusion as well.

He grunted softly and tugged at his shawl with contempt. By now he had regained complete control of his motor skills in Duryodhana's body; his movements were smoother now.

He tried straightening his posture, and with his bones creaking with the effort, he stood erect. He massaged his neck and stretched it in circles. Then, taking a deep breath, he turned to Kalaguru. 'What do you think, would the Chiranjeevi have cremated Ashwatthama?'

Kalaguru pondered a while and answered, 'Yes, it is possible. They saw Shukracharya and witnessed your resurrection. So they know that we possess the powers to

🙏 Abhinav

revive the dead. Given that our lord was one of their most formidable enemies, they would do their best to prevent any future resurrections that could embolden our forces.'

Kali considered the words and nodded slowly.

After a moment, he stretched his hands out to the twins, gesturing to the crown and sword in their possession. The brothers held the items out to the Lord of Evil. Kali took the crown first and wore it, smiling with pleasure as he did so. Then, he took the blade and swung it around. He twirled it around until he found himself comfortable with it.

Then, he stepped closer to Shukracharya and the twins gave some room to their lord.

He asked the resurrector in a cold voice, 'Are you sure you didn't make any mistake in your chant, Shukra?'

Shukracharya nodded feebly and answered with a trembling voice, 'Yes . . . I am . . . very . . . sure.'

Kali nodded, satisfied. A sly smile appeared on his lips. 'Thank you, Shukracharya.'

The acharya looked at the demon, puzzled and terrified. 'What . . .?'

'Thank you, Shukracharya, for helping me learn the art of Mrit Sanjeevani. You tried to resurrect Ashwatthama twice, didn't you?'

'How do you . . . know . . . that?'

Shukracharya's eyes widened in a beautiful mixture of horror and surprise, giving Kali the confirmation he sought.

And then, without a warning, he slashed the edge of the sword across the old man's neck. The acharya dropped dead swiftly, crimson blood escaping his throat.

All of the people in the clearing watched the execution with horror. The Lord of Evil used his shawl to wipe the blood off his sword.

'Bhairava,' he sounded, his voice clear and booming.

The advisor rushed to his commander. 'Yes, my lord?'

'Clear him away,' Kali instructed, pointing his blade at the corpse of Shukracharya.

The advisor gestured to the twins, and they quickly hoisted up the acharya and walked away from the clearing.

Kali now turned to the other man.

'Jana?' the demon grunted and beckoned to him.

Jana, trembling with surprise upon being identified by the Demon Lord himself, nodded and bowed in reverence. He rushed quickly to his side.

'Are all the injured men doing well? I hope no one succumbed to their wounds . . .'

Jana replied respectfully, 'All the injured people are being tended to as we speak. We are confident they will recover soon, my lord.'

The lord nodded appreciatively and sent their host off to make preparations for food.

Once Jana was out of earshot, Bhairava asked his lord, 'My lord, if you don't mind me asking you . . . How do you know the art of Mrit Sanjeevani?'

Kali smiled softly and revealed, 'I can read minds, Bhairava. I learnt the mantra when he was chanting it . . . When I heard him repeat the mantra again, I wondered if he was trying, once more, to resurrect Ashwatthama. I confirmed that with the acharya himself.'

Bhairava's jaw dropped. But Kali only responded with a smile and stepped away. He looked at the open coffin lying in the clearing. He raised his hand to it and transformed it into a throne. He smiled when he looked at his handiwork.

He walked towards it and sat on it, sighing in relief. Then, he closed his eyes in thought, resting his head against the marble headrest. Kalaguru moved to the marble seat silently and stood beside it.

Kali opened his eyes and looked at Bhairava with a wicked grin.

'Bhairava, let's go to the stone palace later. Tell Jana to make preparations to shift all of us away from here.'

The teacher of the Kalabakshakas was stunned. 'Are we going to reclaim the stone palace, my lord?'

Kali laughed and replied, 'No, dear Bhairava. Let them keep the stone palace. But we will relocate to some other place soon.'

The guru looked at his lord, waiting to hear further from him.

'I want to go to the stone palace because I am going to pay the Immortals a visit and announce my arrival in person.'

TWENTY-SIX

The Stone Palace,
The morning after Kali's resurrection, 2026 CE

Kali stood suspended in the air with Kalaguru Bhairava beside him, looking down at the stone palace that floated hundreds of feet above the sea. The light orange of the dawn was creeping its fingers across the sky above them. Kali sensed a protective barrier around the structure, which prevented him from teleporting into it.

'Secured from intrusion,' he voiced to Bhairava. 'I had expected that much.'

He cleared his throat and closed his eyes. He then spoke a name out loud, and his voice boomed within the walls of the mansion below him. He opened his eyes, and patiently waited with an infernal smile on his face.

Inside the mansion, Parashurama was suddenly pulled out of his reverie. He was still in the Kalarakshasa's chamber with the others. He noticed that even Kripa, resting on the chair opposite him, had woken from his sleep. He registered the alarm in the acharya's eyes as well. Both had felt a tremendous surge of energy in their surroundings. They awoke Bali and Hanuman who were sitting on the ground, on either side of the chest of books. They had fallen asleep against the wall with a couple of books in their laps.

When the two Immortals opened their eyes groggily, they noticed the alertness in the eyes of their fellow Immortals. The duo sat up, wide awake and vigilant. Parashurama looked outside the window and saw the dawn breaking the sky open. The stormy weather had subsided.

A loud voice suddenly boomed through the room. 'PARASHUUUURAAAAMAAA.'

Immediately, Parashurama ran to the main hall, and the others followed him.

'Kripa, check if there are any breaks in the protective shield,' the axe-wielding lord told Kripa.

Kripa closed his eyes and looked for chinks in the armour he had created. After a couple of moments, he shook his head to confirm that there were no breaches.

'Someone is out there. And my guess is that it is Kali,' Parashurama told the others. They waited quietly for him to continue, concealing their shock.

Their leader instructed, 'If Kali is out there, I wonder what his purpose is in coming here. Kripa, remain here and keep an eye out for any breaches. It's possible that Kali is a misdirection, while the Kalabakshakas slip in quietly as we are engaged outside against the Lord of Evil himself. Bali and Hanuman, be ready to assist Kripa in any manner possible. As for me, I will meet our uninvited guest and find out why he is here.'

The three Chiranjeevi bowed in affirmation.
Parashurama then vanished from their presence.

❧

Outside the palace, in the pleasant orange of the morning, Parashurama appeared in front of his guests. He saw that the tall frame of Kali was dressed in dark blue robes. A golden crown adorned his head. A sword hung from his waistband.

'Kali,' Parashurama acknowledged with a curt nod.

'Oh sire, I am pleased to see that you recognize me. Didn't hope to see me so soon, did you?' the demon replied cheekily.

'Well, how can I not recognize the Demon of Evil! You were lying dead inside a coffin only a few hours ago. I hoped to see you sometime, since I already knew Shukracharya had resurrected you when he left here with the others.'

'Ah yes, that is true. Well, in other news, Shukracharya has left the earth altogether.'

The news caught the Immortal off guard, but he maintained a stoic expression.

'I killed him, in case you were wondering,' said Kali.

Parashurama stared at him with a blank expression.

'But his death wasn't in vain. I learnt the art of Mrit Sanjeevani from him, so that counts for something. I will keep the art alive.'

Hearing the appalling revelation, Parashurama's eyes grew wide. The demon's face wore a sly smile.

They stared at each other for a couple of moments. Then, pointing to the stone structure below him, Kali spoke, 'I hope the stone palace is living up to your expectations . . .'

Parashurama smiled and replied, 'As long as it is keeping you and your band of minions out, it is certainly living up to my expectations.'

Kali's smile melted at the quip. He gnashed his teeth in anger.

Parashurama cut to the chase and asked, 'Why are you here, Kali? I am sure it is not to inquire about our well-being.'

Kali laughed and shook his head. 'Of course not. I don't give a damn about you people, nor about the stone palace.'

He continued after a pause, 'I came to announce that I am here. And now that I am here, I am going to unleash the reign of evil upon humans.'

Parashurama replied, 'As long as we are alive, we won't let that happen.'

'Well, you can try to stop me. But I have learnt that Kalki has been killed by my trusted man, Ashwatthama. So good luck trying to stop me now.'

'Ashwatthama got what he deserved for killing a god, didn't he?' Parashurama retorted.

Kali gritted his teeth in response.

'Besides,' Parashurama continued, 'so what if Kalki's not there. We will fight you and stop you. We will give our best shot at taking you down, Kali. We'd rather face defeat than accept it without a battle.'

Kali was furious at the comments made by Parashurama. He had expected him to be afraid, but he was staring into the heart of courage.

Suppressing his rage, he spoke in a cold voice, 'So be it, Immortal. You shall face defeat soon.'

Saying this, he vanished along with Bhairava.

TWENTY-SEVEN

They stared at the sky above. White clouds sailed gently across the blue expanse. The garden was quiet, except for the intermittent chirping of birds.

Avyay turned to Anirudh, 'What do you think of the world?'

Anirudh turned away from the sky and looked at her, trying to understand her question. Even though they had only met earlier that day, they were getting quite comfortable with each other. Inexplicably.

Understanding his puzzlement, she explained her question. 'Do you find that there is too much evil? I mean, do you think that the world is evil enough to warrant our presence, our births?'

Anirudh didn't reply immediately, he was silent as he considered her question. After measuring his thoughts, he spoke, 'Yes, I do find the world disturbing . . . There are things out there, the situations . . . people are delusional, distracted.'

'Somewhere along the way, mankind lost its path?'

'Yeah . . . Those words pretty much cover what I intended to say . . .'

Avyay smiled ruefully. 'And Kalki's task is to bring humanity back to the correct path—out and away from the fog of delusion.'

'Not just delusion, it's the manic self-obsession as well,' he told her. 'That's the most bothersome of all.'

'And yes,' he added, 'the task isn't an easy one. I don't even know how we can go about it without disappointing people or drawing criticism from them.'

'Not to mention the hatred?'

'Oh yeah, there's that as well.'

'What do we do? How do we do it?'

Anirudh sighed and looked at her with a smile, expressing that he was at a loss for words.

'Well, we shall start somewhere,' he said at last. 'We have to. We just can't leave things as is . . . However drastic the measures, we have to set things straight. That's why we are here. That's the reason why EOK has been around for centuries. We have the resources for it, and we have to use them.'

Avyay couldn't help but wonder out loud, 'Krishna did make sure that we have the power to get things done! So, thanks to that.'

They shared a laugh, thinking of Krishna's blessing to them. Anirudh cast a cursory glance at her but stopped when his eyes met hers. And his eyes held hers.

'What?' she asked, feeling conscious and curious.

Without controlling his words, he spoke, his voice a bare whisper, 'Damn . . . It's a big, dark world out there, and in your eyes . . . In your eyes, I see the light of strength and will to make everything blissful for everyone out there.'

Avyay's slumber was disturbed by Sadhika shaking her by her shoulders. Mumbling groggily, she sat up. She looked out of the open window and saw the sunlight pouring into her room. Even though a few hours had passed, it seemed like it had only been a few minutes since she fell asleep.

The dream about her and Anirudh in the garden was fresh in her mind. Then, seeing Sadhika in her room, her mind reeled. The previous night's memories flooded her.

Anirudh . . . Tears rained down her cheeks when she realized that he had left her.

Sadhika panicked looking at Avyay, and she too burst into tears. She sat close to her and took Avyay into her arms. She patted her head and consoled her as Avyay rested her head on Sadhika's shoulder. They remained that way for a while.

Then Avyay lifted herself away from her friend's embrace and controlled her tears. Wiping her wet cheeks and composing herself, the avatar asked, 'What happened? Why did you wake me up?'

Sadhika told her softly, 'We have been called to the EOK mansion.'

'What? Why?'

'They attacked the stone palace last night.'

Within the hour, the Immortals and the others were seated around the large table in the dining hall. Parashurama sat at its head, while the rest of the five Immortals sat to the left of him, and Avyay, Dweepa, Acharya Sreedhar and Sadhika sat to his right. Siddharth and Safeed were standing against the wall behind Avyay and Dweepa. Since Sreedhar, Dweepa and Avyay didn't have an objection to Safeed's presence, the Immortals didn't mind it either. He was, after all, a close friend of Anirudh's. Parashurama asked Avyay about Anirudh's cremation and last rites. After they finished discussing it, they turned their attention to everyone at the table. It was time to explain why they were called upon urgently.

On Parashurama's request, Hanuman took the lead and narrated the events that led up to the attack on the stone palace. Then, the axe-wielding avatar took up the thread of narration and explained the chain of events ending in the moment of Kalarakshasa's death and the disappearance of the Kalabakshakas with Shukracharya and Kali.

'I tried to trace them, but they were moving too quickly,' Hanuman added.

Everyone took in the words silently.

'So, is the stone palace still there or have we destroyed it?' Siddharth asked.

'It is still there. Kripa has placed protective enchantments around it, so no one can trespass,' Bali answered.

After a moment, Sadhika, resting her elbows on the table and cupping her face in her palms, spoke, 'So, Kali is gone, and so are Shukracharya and the others. It is just a matter of time before we see Kali in action.'

Kripacharya spoke, 'Well . . . About that . . . There is one more reason why we called for this meeting.'

He went on to narrate their activities after the Kalabakshakas teleported and their discovery of the books and Krishna's aid in telling Ashwatthama about Shukracharya. Then, Parashurama informed them about Kali's visit to the stone palace. He also revealed that the Demon Lord had learnt the art of resurrection from Shukracharya, and then killed him. This revelation brought about an air of tension and horror in the room.

Avyay thought out loud, 'So, Kali is alive and kicking . . .'

No one uttered a word.

Dweepa cleared his throat and turned to Parashurama. 'Lord Parashurama, did Kali mention anything about Kalarakshasa? Are we sure that Kalarakshasa hadn't accompanied Kali and Bhairava?'

Parashurama looked at Kripa and then back at Dweepa, 'Yes, we are sure, Dweepa. There weren't any breaches to the perimeter when Kali was around. Kripa had an eye on it. And he definitely wasn't present with the other two.'

Dweepa nodded and his silent contemplation merged with the wave of quietness that was already in the room.

After a few moments, the silence was broken by an unexpected person.

'Are we sure that Kalarakshasa, sorry, Ashwatthama, is dead?' Safeed asked Parashurama.

Kripa sat up, his eyes curious. While the others were attentive, Parashurama's lips had a slight smile on them. *This is the second time that someone has expressed doubt over Ashwatthama's death. Is there something obvious I am missing here?*

'What makes you say that, Safeed?' Kripacharya asked.

Safeed explained, 'Last night, Siddharth described the battle between Kalarakshasa and Anirudh, with some vivid narration. From that, I learnt that Kalarakshasa was immortal, because of Krishna's *curse*. So wouldn't this curse make him invincible? Didn't he say the same thing when he was fighting Anirudh—that weapons could wound him, but not kill him?'

Hearing his words Kripa's eyes shone with hope and he turned to Parashurama. The avatar looked at him and scratched his beard in thought. But he immediately stopped it when Vyasa, the compiler of the Vedas, spoke.

'He has a point there,' he said. 'See, if he was dead, then Shukracharya would have been able to revive him. If not Shukracharya, then Kali himself would have attempted it. And he would have definitely brought the resurrected Ashwatthama to the stone palace to rub our noses in it. But since Kalarakshasa isn't dead in the first place, he couldn't be resurrected.'

Parashurama added his side of things, saying, 'I checked for signs of life in the sea after Ashwatthama fell into it. But I didn't detect any.'

At this, Safeed involuntarily burst into a laugh. Everyone stared at him, but Parashurama looked amused and turned to him questioningly.

After realizing the inappropriateness of his outburst, he spoke, 'I am sorry about that. I just found it funny when you failed to detect any life signs of Ashwatthama. He is the guy who kept the entire stone palace hidden from all of you. That's the level of his prowess! So if he wanted to cover his own signs of life from you, it is, perhaps, just a child's play for him.'

Parashurama nodded appreciatively. 'That's true.'

Siddharth reasoned further, 'Meaning that he couldn't be resurrected because he was still alive. Which begs the question—if he is not being resurrected, wouldn't Kali be curious as to why? We are hypothesizing that he may be alive and has shielded signs of his life. But what's Kali's take on this? Does he, too, believe that Kalarakshasa is alive? Or is there something else at play here?'

'I am going to hazard a guess here,' Vyasa answered. 'Of course, Shukracharya would know better, since he was a master in the art. I believe that resurrection fails to work after the last rites have been administered on the deceased. So if Kali thinks that we performed the last rites for Ashwatthama, then he wouldn't think beyond that.'

Sadhika added, 'Plus, he was there in person at the stone palace today. So he might have checked for signs of life as well, and found none.'

Vibhishana, who was silent till then, finally spoke, 'I am not really sure that he survived the fall. He had taken the full blow of Asi and Parashu to his chest. Such was the intensity of those two weapons that he was flung out of the chamber, crashing right through the marble wall!'

'Vibhishana, the intensity with which we flung our blades, they would have sliced right through a person, dismembering that being,' Parashurama said. 'But Ashwatthama took the force of the weapons and it was still only embedded in his chest.'

Siddharth spoke, 'Lord Parashurama, my knowledge of your past isn't that great, but tell me this, isn't the Parashu, your axe, a gift from Lord Rudra?'

'Yes, it is.'

Acharya Sreedhar caught the line of thought that Siddharth was following. He, with a glimmer of excitement in his eyes, looked at Siddharth and said, 'And Asi was wielded by Rudra the first time.'

Then everyone caught the meaning behind the question Siddharth had asked.

Safeed posed the question on behalf of everyone, 'So does this mean that the axe and the sword cannot kill Ashwatthama because he is the embodiment of Rudra? And that these weapons can only wound him, correct?'

'That seems to be a possibility, yeah,' Parashurama nodded

Vibhishana leaned in, his brows frowned in doubt. 'Then, by that logic, Asi shouldn't kill Vishnu either. Asi was given to Vishnu by Rudra himself. And Vishnu is the keeper of the sword. So, if that's the case, how come the divine blade killed Anirudh?'

TWENTY-EIGHT

EOK Mansion,
The day before Anirudh's death, 2026 CE

Hearing the word 'death' caught Avyay off guard.
'No, no, no . . .' she replied, with panic in her voice.

Her breathing became heavy and she started hyperventilating. 'Stop talking about such absurd stuff . . .' she hissed angrily.

'Hayati . . .' Anirudh said softly.

The voice caught her. She looked into his eyes, and they were two pools of serenity. Death didn't seem to bother him.

Confirming her thoughts, he told her, his voice a soft caress, 'I have already accepted death, Avi . . .'

He gave her a few moments, to wrap her head around the idea, before he spoke again.

'You promised that you would support me in my plan,' he reminded her.

She recalled her words to him when he was at her home a few months back. Having remembered them, she reluctantly forced herself to listen to his words.

'How can you even think of this . . .' she asked, struck with incredulity.

Anirudh just smiled and answered, 'There's no other way . . .'

'There must be *something*! We can definitely think of something!' she cried.

'There are no other options left, Avi . . . I have been trying every other option and none of them have worked. I tried to understand from the Immortals about the workings of a soul, but they weren't able to help. Another alternative to reach the soul was through becoming a yogi, of the highest prowess, but that will take a lot of time. And I really don't have time on my side . . . So yeah, the only door left with me is death . . . The deep dive.'

Avyay's breathing had calmed down during his talk, and she was now turning over his words in her head.

'Why do you say you don't have time? Because Kali and others could be a barrier? You needn't worry about them, I will keep them engaged and protect you from harm . . .'

Anirudh smiled. 'I appreciate that, Avi . . . But Kali is not a concern of mine. I don't think he has arrived yet. My instinct tells me so . . . Regardless, the true evil in this world is not him. It is something far worse and more sinister than Kali . . .'

Avyay nodded, her lips wearing a soft curve. They had discussed this previously as well. 'Mankind . . .'

He nodded, 'But that's not the focus at the moment . . . There are far more important things at stake.'

'Like?'

'My departure and how to go about things after that . . .'

'I am sure you have something in mind,' she replied curtly.

'Yes, I do . . .'

It did little to calm her distress. She knew he had made up his mind, and he had accepted death. And suddenly, his possible absence dawned on her, and it consumed her whole. The anger, the frustration, the impatience . . . all those melted away.

'Anirudh . . .' she said, her lips quivering. 'I . . . love . . . you,' she whispered shakily as tears drained her strength. Her hands stretched out to embrace him, and she spoke in a defeated tone, 'I cannot . . . live . . . without you.'

Anirudh took her into his arms and rubbed her back softly, trying to console her. She rested her head on his chest, sobbing softly. But he spoke no words in response. Noticing that he was silent, she looked up at his face.

'Don't you love me, Anirudh?' she asked him, partly astounded and partly disappointed at his silence. She had expected him to respond in kind.

With a soft smile, he wiped her wet cheeks dry and answered, 'I love you, Avi. But . . . the threat facing us is too large for me to be selfish.'

'But Anirudh . . .' Avyay started, but she was cut off by him.

'Listen, Avi, I love you. There is no denying that. But we have a responsibility, don't we? We are humans, yes, but there's more to us. If I shy away from my responsibility, and I don't attempt to thwart Kali because I love you, then maybe, one day, we'll both hate the fact that we couldn't rise above ourselves. And it may not stop at hate, it may ascend to regret too, Avi.'

Avyay stared at him, just blinking at him . . . understanding him. Wordlessly, she hugged him and rested her head on his chest. She felt his arms envelope her.

༄

She looked straight at him, her eyes boring into him. 'How long have you been wondering about this "death" thing? Has it been long?'

'Ever since the day I first asked you about death. At your house.'

Avyay's jaw dropped.

'So all the questions about the differences in our dreams . . .'

Anirudh nodded, 'They were to check my hypothesis that one doesn't require a physical body to . . . work around in this world.'

Avyay nodded, recalling the conversation she had had with him. She was trying to understand Anirudh's game with death, and she had also given in to his plan, since he was as stubborn as they come.

After a few moments, she asked him, 'So death is not going to stop you? How will you stop Kali after you are dead? Also, what's the guarantee that you will definitely find the answers after death?'

'I know being alive won't get me any answers, so I'd rather try the alternative. I have a chance of stopping Kali once I understand what a soul is . . . And no, death is not going to stop me.'

He paused and looked at her, a smile spreading on his lips, and continued, 'If I am not wrong, I may be able to return as well . . .'

His words took her breath away, and she gaped at him wide-eyed. 'Return, as in?'

'Return in the flesh . . .'

'How? How can you do that?'

'Well, let me not reveal it now. I don't want to get your hopes up . . . If I do get back, I shall tell it to you then.'

Avyay exhaled, her patience thinning.

'Are you going to let Kalarakshasa kill you just like that?' she asked him.

'Of course not, death has to be earned. It will definitely be an interesting fight, should it come to that. He would be fighting for his life, I would be fighting for my death . . .'

Avyay stared at the figure in front of her; Anirudh was completely laidback about the idea of death.

'So tell me, how do we go about things after your departure?'

Anirudh then set off on the most important conversation they'd had till date.

TWENTY-NINE

'Well, after my death you can go about things however you want to . . . It will be the break we are looking for,' Anirudh said.

'What?' Avyay asked, leaning forward.

'My death will be a distraction for the enemy. It will make them lower their guard. This event will make them lose their focus. Currently, I am being watched, Dweepa is being watched. Every acquaintance of mine is probably being watched. But should I leave the game unexpectedly, they'll think that they have won. And they would stop watching us briefly, if not permanently. And this lack of monitoring is critical for us. This will give you the freedom to do whatever you want to, unobserved by enemy forces.'

Avyay slowly nodded, considering the soundness of his plan.

After a couple of moments, she asked, 'Leave the *game* unexpectedly?'

Anirudh smiled, 'Of course, it is a game! We have been playing this game for a long time now. But the actual game begins after my death. It will be our element of surprise! They will be in the dark and you . . . you will be in the light.'

Hearing about this *death* thing time and again, Avyay frowned. 'Do you really have to go through with this plan of yours?'

'I have to . . . because we have no time to lose. We have to figure out how to defeat Kali,' he replied, trying to pacify her.

Avyay just sighed, fully aware of the fact that it was a battle she had already lost. The person sitting in front of her had already made up his mind, and there was no way to change it.

'Plus, it is not just about defeating Kali. Like I said earlier, it will also take the spotlight off us. It's a "two birds one stone" victory scenario.'

She considered his words and nodded as he continued.

'Defeating Kali is more a game of brains, than of brawns . . . It will be a conflict of wits . . .'

The word 'conflict' made Avyay recall a conversation between Krishna and Dweepa—the first one.

'Anirudh, do you recall the conversation between Krishna and the first Dweepa? The one where Krishna revealed the need for two Kalkis—one would be a destroyer and the other a preserver?'

Anirudh smiled and asked, 'Are you wondering which one of us is playing what role?'

She nodded. 'Who are you? Who am I? What do you want to do—preserve or destroy?'

Anirudh breathed deeply and then told her, 'Avi . . . The two of us needn't worry about it. We need not make that decision.'

'But Krishna said that it is up to us . . .'

'I believe that Krishna is wrong in this matter . . .'

'Krishna, wrong?! How so?'

Anirudh just smiled broadly, enigmatically.

THIRTY

Astral Realm

Anirudh went down on his knees and pulled Meow into his arms.

'Hey, Meow! I will be going now. You take care, okay?' he told the furry creature.

The cat placed a paw gently on Anirudh's thigh, who just laughed as he rubbed the furry being's head and neck affectionately and nudged her to join the other animals.

Meow meowed and bounded away. Alone now, Anirudh looked around the beach. He had thought of a calm place to meditate. Given that he was in a realm outside the bounds of time, he wanted to take advantage of it.

'Travel to any place with the speed of thought,' he muttered to himself as he closed his eyes.

A smile appeared on his lips when the image of Sage Dweepa's modest accommodation appeared in his mind.

When he opened his eyes, he was standing in a small clearing surrounded with trees. There was no beach or sea in front of him. But what caught him by surprise was that

Sage Dweepa's hut wasn't there. Anirudh looked around for Dweepa's house but couldn't find it.

Maybe settlements don't make their way to the astral realm either, he concluded.

He turned around in place, taking in the environment. The orange sun had covered the treetops with a shade of fiery gold. Birds and insects of various hues and trees of different classes caught his eye as he revolved.

He found the place to be soothing and calm. He sat down on the ground and took a deep breath. Sage Dweepa's lessons came to him as he closed his eyes. He shut out his surroundings, though there wasn't anything to shut out. It was quiet all around him.

However, instead of exerting control, he let himself go— his imagination took over. He started conjuring images of Krishna's story, from the ninth avatar's childhood to the god's presence on the field of Kurukshetra . . .

Arjuna sat down at the back of his chariot, overwhelmed with the sadness of the impending war, dejected at the prospect of becoming victorious by killing his kin.

Anirudh turned to the heavy-hearted Pandava. Breaking the silence he had held ever since he set foot on the battlefield, he started, 'O Arjuna . . .'

THIRTY-ONE

*A*nirudh stared at the forsaken island. Krishna had left his physical body and had ascended to the divine realm. The opulent city of Dwarka stood bereft of its inhabitants. The people had left the city some time back, with all the wealth and belongings they could carry, and were escorted by Arjuna to Indraprastha.

Time seemed to stand frozen over the remnants of the territory. Anirudh was standing in a forest overlooking the island city in the distance. Next to him was Sage Dweepa, who was unaware of his astral presence.

Then, with no warning, the ocean rose. With its mighty limbs grasping the island, the waters entered the lavish mansions and flooded the streets and gardens. Anirudh could feel the resistance of the city walls, and the breach of their resistance against the onslaught of the blue ocean. And he could also feel the rush of the turbulent flow coursing through the land.

Barely moments later, the ocean, victorious in its endeavour, breezed along normally. There was no trace left to speak of a grand city like Dwarka that had existed on that very spot. It was all smoothed away.

Anirudh turned to Dweepa and saw that the sage had his hand covering his mouth, aghast. Tears were streaming down his cheeks.

Anirudh smiled melancholically, as he realized why Krishna told Dweepa to witness the doom of the city of Dwarka.

He turned around and started walking deeper into the forest. As he strolled through the lush trees, a butterfly caught his attention as it flew towards a flower. Anirudh followed the fluttering insect to its destination. He stood over the flower and the butterfly, drinking the nectar. Involuntarily, he smacked his lips, tasting the sweetness of the nectar in his mouth. He scrunched his brows in curiosity. How am I able to taste the nectar?

As soon as he thought those words, a strange sensation came over his index finger, as if it were being sucked on. He rubbed the finger with his thumb, trying to shake off the feeling but it didn't help. The fragrance of the flower assaulted his sense of smell. His brows burrowed deeper into his forehead. He was breathless now. Panic was gripping him. The taste of sweetness in his mouth was overwhelming. He tried to spit out the sugary saliva but his mouth wouldn't listen to him. He tried to stop breathing, but he couldn't hold out for long.

He was trying to fight the feeling off, but it was overpowering him.

Then, suddenly, he recalled Krishna's last words. And you will see even beyond what you ask for . . . if you let go, instead of fighting . . .

Anirudh exhaled from his mouth, preparing himself for the unexpected. He released his hands and let them hang freely by his sides. Gulping down the sweet water in his mouth, he inhaled the overbearing fragrance of the flower.

One moment he was looking at the butterfly on the flower, and the next, he was looking at the flower up close in front of his eyes. Using the proboscis extending out from his mouth, he relished the nectar that came out from the flower. The instant after that, he was looking at the butterfly perched on top of him, surrounded by his petals. He felt himself drop down a green tunnel and stretch out into the mud. He had numerous fibrous extensions spreading out into the dark brown earth. He held the roots of the plant firmly in his grasp, giving it nutrition and support. As he passed through the mud, he ensured that he was gripping all the plants securely. He found himself entering thick roots and ascending the bark of a tree. He spread into the branches and then spread himself further. He felt the wind caress his green foliage. Then, he flew off from one of the branches, his black feathers fluttering in the sky. He heard a loud caw that erupted from his own beak. He looked up at the crow flying across his ocean-green expanse. He let himself drown into the depths. With his orange fins propelling him, he swam around the flora of the underwater sea, and started eating them. He let his long, slender body be nibbled at by the orange fish, happily providing it with energy and food. Interrupted by a dolphin passing by, the fish scurried away. He ignored the scurrying fish and exerted his thick fins pushing himself towards the surface, his rostrum guiding him upwards. Shooting out of the water, he found himself flying through the air and soaring higher. He saw the dolphin dive back into the ocean. He was bodiless now, drifting across the ocean.

He reached a city and brushed against a group of people in a marketplace. From behind his shop's counter, he handed some coloured bangles to a woman, and took a couple of coins from her in exchange for the sale. He felt his coloured, circular bodies land inside her cloth bag, nesting himself against the potatoes. The constant swinging of the bag made his brown, tuber body brush against the glass bangles, making them clink. He held the vegetables and bangles firmly inside his cloth body, protecting them from the small fire on the road whose heat he could feel. He saw the cloth bag pass by, with the bangles clinking inside it, while his orange body flickered in the wind. As he stretched his fiery limbs into the air, an apple rolled on to the ground in front of him, which was promptly picked up by a man. He felt himself tossed in the air by the hand of a man trying to negotiate a better price for his red and luscious body. He looked at the blue sky spread above him. He was flying away from the apple, one with the wind again. He soared higher and higher, into the infinite blueness. From afar, he looked down at the inhabitants of the city. They looked like ants, roaming the earth beneath his vast, blue body. He floated away from the blue planet. He sped across the darkness in his glowing, meteoric body. He saw a star zip past his rocky body, which was basking in the severe glow of the golden globe in front of him.

He looked at the numerous planets, asteroids, moons and stars spread out in front of him. He ensured that his limbs stretched as far as they could, touching everyone with his warmth and light, removing the darkness temporarily from their faces.

He saw the yellow sun glowing fiercely, illuminating the visages of all the beings in his dark body, which was spread out in all directions.

His body had no end, no beginning and no middle. He was present in everything, and he was present in nothing as well.

Anirudh opened his eyes and looked at the clearing around him, surrounded by the translucent trees. He was back in the astral realm. He had all the answers he sought, as well as the ones he didn't seek.

THIRTY-TWO

Outside the Stone Palace,
The night of Kali's resurrection, 2026 CE

As soon as the ocean swallowed him with a thirsty gulp, Ashwatthama was jolted awake by the water splashing across his face. He found himself pushed deeper into the watery grave by the two blades sticking out of his chest. His reflexes kicked in—he conserved his breath and paddled in the water, making his descent gentler. He looked down at the two weapons and tried to tug at them. But the pain caused him to grit his teeth and give up on the effort to pull them out. He had allowed Asi to strike him lethally, as Krishna's boon made him immortal. When he thought of the axe in his torso, he recalled Parashurama and his fellow Chiranjeevi.

Ohh no—the Immortals would know that I am alive! he realized.

He knew of their prowess in detecting signs of life, so he conjured a shield around himself that would hide his vital signs from prying eyes.

I am just tired of playing good and bad now . . . Kali has been resurrected, so it is time for me to be on my way . . . Oh how much

I seek solitude! I don't want anyone to find me . . . he muttered inside his head as he brought up the enchantment around him.

A couple of moments after he conjured the barrier around him, he felt the weapons being tugged powerfully from his chest. The pain was excruciating as he felt his torso being ripped apart. With a heave, the divine blades exited his body and his chest fell with a swoop. He saw the two weapons fly to the surface. But he didn't follow them up. The pain in his chest was blinding him now. He closed his eyes and conjured a breathable bubble around him, covering his body. The bubble kept the water out and gave him oxygen to breathe. Taking a deep breath, he gave in to the darkness that filled his senses and passed out due to the pain.

There stood the dark mouth of a cave before him. He looked at the gravel-and-snow ground in front of the cave. He discovered that the cave was a part of a mountain. He saw the ice-covered peaks around him. Snowflakes whirled around him in the cold breeze.

'Come to me, Ashwatthama,' a familiar voice beckoned him. The voice made him feel safe about the place.

With his eyes still heavy with tiredness and his consciousness still not fully awake, he found himself floating in the deep waters. The cave in the snow-capped mountain stood profound in his mind. The familiar voice was inviting him to the mountain. He tried to place the voice but couldn't bring himself to strain his mind. So he let it go. He wanted to escape the watery abyss surrounding him. With a final effort, he thought of the snow-covered mountains and teleported himself to the cave he had dreamt of. And as the energy drained away from him, he slipped into darkness again.

When his eyes opened, there was no water around him. There was no air bubble keeping him breathing. Instead of the cold of the sea, he found his atmosphere warm. He was lying on his back, on firm ground. He looked around and found himself in a dimly lit chamber made of stone. About a foot away from him was the only source of light—a fire. Beyond the fire was a door-like gap in the chamber wall. He saw that it was dark outside and there was a snowy breeze blowing about. When he saw the snowflakes, his eyes opened wide.

I made it . . . I made it to the cave, he lauded himself.

On the wall opposite him, closer to the entrance, he saw Karna's *kavacha* resting against the stone. He had worn this tough hide before his battle with Anirudh and he hadn't removed it since. There were two large bloody gashes on it.

He was about to lift himself up when pain erupted across his chest. He let his torso fall back to the ground. He looked down at his upper body and was surprised to find it bandaged. He ran his fingers over the cloth. It seemed to be covering some green-coloured paste.

As he grazed his fingers across the dressing, he heard a voice speak to him. 'You shouldn't exert yourself, Drauni . . .'

The familiar voice from the dream, Ashwatthama recognized.

The suddenness of the voice had alarmed him, but he was feeling better now. He located the source to be deeper in the cave. The inside of the cave was drowned in darkness. He heard a light ruffle as the speaker got up and walked towards him. The mysterious person finally stepped into the light and sat on their haunches next to him, saying, 'Those are some really bad wounds, son of Drona, and they need plenty of rest and healing.'

The yellow firelight illuminated the speaker's face— swarthy in complexion, wearing a dimpled grin. This man was the last person the sorcerer expected to see. One could easily mistake him for his predecessor, but not Drauni, who was well aware of the distinct facial features of the two people.

Ashwatthama was staring, in disbelief, into the face of the boy he had supposedly killed.

Anirudh . . .

THIRTY-THREE

While Aswathhama was taken aback by Anirudh's presence at the Himalayas, the question about Anirudh's death by Asi had stunned everyone sitting around the dinner table at the EOK mansion. Parashurama looked at everyone's face, expecting an answer. His searching gaze finally settled on Avyay, and he was surprised by what he saw. She had a broad smile on her face.

'What do you know that we don't know, Kalki?' Parashurama asked intently.

This brought everyone's attention to Avyay, and they saw the mysterious smile on her face.

She turned to the wielder of the Parashu and said, 'Asi cannot kill Anirudh. Not without his permission.'

Saying this, she got up and walked to the end of the table. She requested Vibhishana to fetch Asi, and he went to get the celestial blade for her. He returned quickly with the sword. Unsheathing it from its scabbard, he placed Asi on the table in front of her.

Running a finger along the blade, she spoke, 'Asi cannot kill . . .'

But she stopped midway along the blade. It had started glowing softly at her touch. She picked up the sword and it kept glowing. Everyone noticed this mysterious behaviour of Asi. With a face filled with curiosity, she placed the blade back on the table and took her hand away from it. It grew dull and went back to normal immediately. She requested Vibhishana to take the sword in his hand. The Immortal did so and it remained its dull self. She asked him to pass it to Hanuman. Hanuman took the sword and held it. The divine blade lit up softly. She motioned the blade to be passed around, and it changed hands quickly. Soon, it was back on the table, in front of her.

Looking at the people around her, she ticked off names as she spoke, 'Asi didn't glow in the hands of Lord Vibhishana, Maharishi Vyasa, King Bali, Acharya Kripa, Safeed, Sage Dweepa and Acharya Sreedhar. It glowed in the hands of Lord Hanuman, Lord Parashurama, Sadhika, Siddharth and myself.'

'The blade glowed in Lord Parashurama's hand and mine because we are avatars of Vishnu. It glowed in Hanuman's hand because he is a form of Rudra himself.'

Turning to Siddharth and Sadhika, she said, 'What I am unable to account for is the blade glowing in both of your hands—why did that happen?'

'Well, let's keep that mystery for another time, shall we?' responded Parashurama.

She eyed him curiously, so did the others, except Siddharth and Sadhika, who remained expressionless.

Parashurama pointed to the sword in front of her and asked her, 'Weren't you saying that Asi cannot kill Anirudh?'

She nodded, and said, 'Asi cannot kill Vishnu or Rudra.'

Then she picked up the sword, looked at Parashurama and said, 'Try your best to not defend against it.'

Looking around to the others, she said, 'Watch this carefully now.'

She flung the sword towards the Immortal with the intent to kill him. Parashurama remained calm, having been warned, and allowed the glowing blade to approach him unobstructed. When it was roughly a foot away, he felt everything in the room go still. Avyay was frozen in time, and so were the others. The blade trembled violently, growing brighter and brighter, before finally exploding into a bubble of white light. When the radiance ebbed, he saw a swarthy man in place of the sword, his form resplendent like that of the moon. Parashurama recognized him to be Asi. The divine being bowed to the Immortal and requested himself to be deflected and returned to his hand. Parashurama granted the request. Immediately, a ball of white light filled the space around Asi and exploded. This time, when the light faded, he saw the divine blade back in its place. Soon, everything unfroze. The sword shot away from Parashurama and then circled back to him and waited by his side. The Immortal stretched out his hand and the sword shifted itself into his palm.

Everyone stared at the proceedings with wide eyes. Since they hadn't seen Asi in his human form, Parashurama related to everyone his interaction with Asi.

Avyay concluded, 'Since Lord Parashurama agreed to Asi's request to deflect himself and return to his hand, the blade did so. Had he insisted that the blade strike him dead, then Asi would have had to obey. That's what happened in Anirudh's case. He must have told Asi to continue on his trajectory and kill him.'

'But why would he want Asi to kill him?' Hanuman asked.

'Because he wanted to die,' she revealed.

Everyone's mouth fell open at that.

'What? Why?' Dweepa asked, controlling his surprise and anguish.

'Well . . . He had this dream about Krishna and Kali conversing with each other after Duryodhana's defeat in the war. And during this interaction, Kali had asked Krishna how he intended to destroy him, since his soul would always remain alive. If he were to be killed a million times, it still allowed him to return the next time, and the times after that. After this dream, one question bothered Anirudh deeply: how does one destroy a soul? So he started looking for answers but couldn't find any. He then decided to enter his soul form and find the answer for himself. And to enter the soul form quickly, he chose the only option that was immediately available to him—death.'

'Why didn't you tell us any of this, Avyay?' Parashurama asked, deeply concerned.

'Because he forbade me from saying anything.'

'So his questions about the workings of the soul were an attempt to find out if the soul can be destroyed?' the axe-wielding Immortal asked.

Avyay nodded.

'And . . . He set out to find the answers on his own,' Kripacharya spoke out loud.

'Yes,' muttered Avyay.

THIRTY-FOUR

'We should get moving now,' Parashurama addressed the group in front of him at the mansion. 'I will head back to the stone palace with the rest of the Immortals. We'll start training and recruiting people to battle Kali so that we are ready when the time comes.'

He then turned to Avyay and asked, 'Kalki, what do you plan to do?'

'I'll head back to my home,' she replied. 'I will check on Anirudh's parents too. I also have to read his diary, he left it for me. I will come back here should there be any need.'

The Immortal turned to Sadhika and Siddharth now. Sadhika spoke up, 'I will keep Avyay company. I can manage work from her place.'

'And I will take stock of all our offices and see how things are. We need to be on our toes and ensure that we are capable of handling Kali,' said Siddharth.

Safeed spoke up as well, 'I will head back to my pub and keep an eye out for any movements that may indicate Kali's involvement.'

'That will be good,' said Parashurama as he finally turned to Dweepa.

Dweepa gave voice to his thoughts, 'I have one purpose in my life—to be there for the Kalki avatar. So I will be around Avyay should she have any need of me.'

Avyay affirmed that with a nod of her head.

Once the plans had been laid out, Parashurama took leave of Acharya Sreedhar, and alongside the Immortals, vanished into thin air.

From the gallery, Parashurama looked down at the students exercising in the grand training hall of the stone palace. There were instructors roaming between the disciples, correcting their postures and techniques.

After they had arrived at the stone palace earlier in the day, Parashurama dispatched his fellow Immortals to consolidate their ranks so that everyone was at the same place. He felt that it was time for them to train harder since Kali had now returned. It was only a matter of time before they had a showdown with him.

When they first laid eyes on the grand hall, everyone marvelled at the variety of training equipment and facilities. Parashurama's observation of the practice was interrupted by a cup of steaming hot tea served by Dhanvantari. The Immortal accepted the beverage from the medicine expert with a smile of gratitude.

Parashurama had requested Dhanvantari and his team to come to the stone palace and take up residence there so that they could impart their knowledge of medicine to the recruits.

'Do you find this place a welcome change from the cold mountains?' the avatar asked.

Sipping from his cup, Dhanvantari replied, 'I guess so. It is nice and breezy here. I do miss the cold fingers of the Himalayas, but this place serves me well.'

The Immortal nodded. 'I don't know if you know yet, but there's a bunch of great texts in Ashwatthama's chambers. Perhaps you can find something of use in those books.'

'Yes, Kripacharya told me about them. I will take a look in a while.'

'Also, you can start the lessons whenever you want. Just let Kripa or Vyasa know, and they will arrange it for you. In case you need to go to the Himalayas to pick any herbs, ask any of us, we'll take you there and bring you back. We are happy to help you, Dhanvantari.'

Dhanvantari smiled and bowed in gratitude.

In Kalarakshasa's chamber, Parashurama and Vyasa waited for Hanuman to return from the urgent assignment they had sent him on.

A while back, Parashurama had recalled the conversation with Kalanayaka out of the blue, and he remembered that the sorcerer had told him of Jana's cottage, where he was a student. So he had sent Hanuman to check if Kali was there.

'I should have thought of this earlier,' the avatar muttered, disappointed.

'Well, I should have remembered too,' the great sage opined.

'Better late than never. That counts for something, doesn't it?' Vyasa ventured.

Before the axe-wielding Immortal could reply, Hanuman appeared out of thin air.

'There's no one at Jana's place. It looks like they cleared out some time ago,' said the ape-god.

'Are we sure he was there?'

'Yes . . . I found Shukracharya's remains at the cottage. I have surrendered his body to Kripacharya and the others in the hall. They will perform the required rites.'

Parashurama grunted softly, angry at himself for realizing it so late.

'What were you planning to do if we had indeed stumbled into Kali there?' Vyasa asked.

'I would have been able to keep an eye on him of course . . .'

'That's all right then. If you were planning to attack him, then I would be forced to remind you of the conversation Kali had with Krishna, about which Avyay told us . . .'

The axe-wielder nodded at the words.

'So I guess we will have to wait for Kali to make his move now . . .' Hanuman said, resignedly.

THIRTY-FIVE

Once she had checked on Anirudh's parents, Avyay went to her house. She found Sadhika in the living room, typing away on her laptop, while Dweepa sat on the ground, deep in meditation. Nodding to Sadhika, she walked to her room and shut the door behind her.

Avyay clutched the locket under her shirt and held it tight. It was a reminder of Anirudh. She closed her eyes and took a deep breath, letting herself lean against the door gently. She was, for the first time, truly alone. Tears rolled down her cheeks. Though he was primarily her partner, she mourned him for the different roles that he played all his life—a friend, a son, a student, a god, an avatar, a thinker . . . The death was of one person, but the voids it created were innumerable. She had never felt death in this depth, never fully realized the horrendous impact it left on people. Though she knew that Anirudh had chosen his death, she still couldn't make her peace with it. She longed for him. Her head bowed to the pain in her heart and she shook amidst the tears.

Then, after a few moments, Avyay drew a long breath. She stood upright and wiped her tears. *I am the only Kalki now . . . I have to move forward according to the plan.*

She had brought his belongings from the EOK mansion earlier that day. She glanced at Anirudh's diary and folders lying atop the table beside her. Then, she turned and looked at Anirudh's whiteboard. It had all of his scribbled notes intact. She softly ran her finger along his handwritten letters.

Heaving a sigh, Avyay picked up his diary, and settled herself on her bed. She started sifting through the pages, which were filled with paper clippings and scribbles.

She ran her finger over a clip with the headline, **'Speeding Mercedes Mows Down Auto and 2 Cyclists'**.

Below it was Anirudh's handwriting, which read, *'20-year-old, drunk driving. 3 people killed. How to prevent this?'*

Avyay traced his handwriting, feeling him in the ink. She felt every stroke of the nib that he had etched upon the page, she felt every curve of the letters and imagined his voice speaking those words aloud. She let him melt her again. Closing her eyes, she held the page close to her chest as streams of sadness released themselves from the prison within her heart.

It felt like hours had gone by, though only a few minutes had passed, when she finally opened her eyes and let the diary fall on to her lap. Drying her tears, she reminded herself of her mission again, tasked to her by Anirudh.

She flipped through some more leaves of the diary and came across more newspaper snips bearing headlines, and Anirudh's scrawls below each of them.

'College student kills 18-year-old over rejection'. *'Why can't people stomach a "No"?'*

'Two killed in a 'Hit and Run' as Political Leader Opens Fire from Car'. *'Too much power to politicians? And make gun control stringent?'*

'Woman's father arrested for attack on inter-caste couple'. *'So, two things come to my mind here: love and caste.*

Why can't people accept love marriages easily? If you give birth to a child, then you have also given birth to their freedom. The child is entitled to make all decisions and face their consequences as well. It is the parents' duty to accept the child's decision. And if the choice is a wrong one, then the parents should support the child even during the rough times and help them free themselves of the unhappy union. As parents, their priority should always be their children, and then, later, the society. Parents should never make a choice against their child so that the society perceives them pleasantly. Should a choice ever arise between choosing to save their child or the institution of marriage, what should a parent choose, logically and sensibly? It's as simple as that.

'Caste has been a long-standing barrier to people having the freedom to love anyone of their choice, honour killings are testimony to this fact. Why does caste stand as a problem in a marriage? Souls have no caste. Life and death don't happen based on caste. Then, why are humans so worried about caste when it comes to marriage? It is, after all, about the union of two souls. What role does caste play in this?'

Beneath this text, he had written a line and underlined it for emphasis.

'What is the role of caste in our lives, anyway?'

Just then, she heard a knock on the door, and saw Sadhika enter the room.

'Hey, you all right?'

The avatar nodded, making space for Sadhika to sit on the bed beside her.

'Anirudh has collected a lot of newspaper snippets, with his thoughts about them . . .' the Kalki avatar said, handing over the diary to her.

Sadhika took the diary with an intrigued expression and browsed through the pages.

'I agree, some thought-provoking stuff indeed.'

Handing the diary back, she asked, 'What do you plan to do?'

Avyay shrugged her shoulders. 'Think for a while. I might start with the drunken-driving problem.'

'Ahh, I see,' Sadhika said. 'I am personally inclined towards the love and parental-love aspect . . .'

Avyay nodded. 'It's true, isn't it?'

'I feel that some parents feel that they need to control their children. "If I have produced you, you belong to me, you owe your life to me and you will do as I say" is the typical attitude many of them have. They let society dictate what should and should not be instead of letting happiness in. Parents would make their children walk through hell if it were something that society perceived as correct in its eyes. How do we address things like these, Avyay?' Sadhika asked grimly.

'These are mindsets that we are talking about. People are not going to change easily, or soon, I guess,' Avyay responded.

After a pause, she continued, 'Well, I would say that when we are talking about children, and about people in general, we are discussing souls. Their freedom and independence are being taken away from them, right from childhood. So we will have to do whatever it takes to better the situation for them.'

'True, whatever be the price, it is less compared to the freedom of the individual soul. Also,' Sadhika wondered out loud, 'I am guessing that this scenario of parents is present mostly in the older generations of parents. And up to some extent, it is because of different cultures and societies. What do you think?'

'While that may be true, I also feel that the "values" and traditions could pass down generations and places. So we may still see the oppression of freedom at some places.'

'True . . .'

After a deep breath, Avyay spoke, 'My desire is to give every soul its freedom and independence. If someone misuses this, then that person will be punished. Because now that I think of it, it's not just wrong parenting that needs rectification. It's relationships as well—friends, married couples, employer–employee relationships, teacher–student relationships—all of these should be devoid of selfishness.'

'In simpler words, you are suggesting that we rewrite the way humans perceive other humans,' said Sadhika.

'In simpler words, yes. I am.'

Then, after a pause, the avatar added, 'Not just the way humans perceive other humans but also the way humans perceive other living beings . . .'

THIRTY-SIX

The Himalayas,
2026 CE

'How . . . did . . . you . . . I had killed you,' Ashwatthama said to Anirudh, not able to comprehend the presence of the young avatar in front of him.

'Oh, you killed me, all right,' Anirudh confirmed as he sat cross-legged next to the son of Drona. 'But death was not the end of the journey for me, Ashwatthama. It was just another chapter in my life.'

His listener looked at him with furrowed brows.

'Death is the *final* chapter, Anirudh. Not *another* chapter. How does one return from death?'

'How did Kali return from death?' the avatar asked with a smile.

Drauni's eyes widened in surprise. 'How do you know that Kali has returned? You weren't even there . . .'

'Oh, Ashwatthama! I know many things,' the young man said with a mysterious smile.

He continued, 'I even knew that you weren't dead, and that's why I told you to come here. Who else knows that you survived the attack of those two divine weapons?'

The wounded sorcerer stared at him curiously. Then he answered the question that was posed to him earlier, 'I had preserved the body of Kali. So he was able to return to life.'

'Okay. Let's hold that thought there. Do you know of Kacha, Shukracharya's student? What's his story?'

Ashwatthama nodded and narrated the legend he had heard. 'Kacha was the son of Brihaspati, the teacher of the devas. Shukracharya was the teacher of the asuras. The battles between devas and asuras were generally one-sided because the slain asuras were brought back to life by Shukracharya. To remove this disadvantage, the devas sent Kacha as a student to the teacher of asuras so that he could learn the art of Mrit Sanjeevani. Kacha became a student of Shukracharya and he was liked by the teacher immensely. The asuras, knowing that the son of Brihaspati was there to learn the esoteric art of resurrecting the dead, decided to thwart the devas in the best way they knew possible—by killing the beloved student. The first time they killed him, they cut his body to pieces and fed them to the jackals. Now, Devyani, daughter of Shukracharya, had a . . . well, a soft spot for Kacha. She, on finding that Kacha hadn't returned from his daily routine, feared that he had been killed. So she spoke to her father and told him to revive Kacha. Moved by his daughter, he revived him. When asked, Kacha told his guru what had happened to him. The asuras were furious that Kacha had been revived, but they didn't stop their attempts to thwart him. When they killed him the second time, they ground his body to a paste and mixed it with the ocean. However, Shukracharya was able revive his student again. The third time around, the asuras killed Kacha, burnt his body and mixed his ashes in the acharya's wine. Seeing that Kacha was missing again, Devyani rushed to her father. When the guru tried to revive him, he realized that Kacha was inside his stomach. Explaining his presence in his teacher's belly, Kacha informed his guru of his tragic death. After being emotionally driven by his daughter's plea to see Kacha alive, the teacher of the asuras revealed to her that Kacha could come back to life only by ripping apart his stomach, which would kill him. Devyani was aghast and torn at the thought of losing her father in exchange for Kacha. She implored her father to think of some other solution. Then Shukracharya decided to teach the deva about Mrit Sanjeevani. Thus, after having come back to life, Kacha revived his teacher, too, using the art of revivification.'

After Ashwatthama completed his narration, Anirudh asked, 'Do you know why I asked you about Kacha's story?'

Ashwatthama shook his head. 'To estimate my knowledge?'

Anirudh replied, 'That's true. But I also want to draw your attention to the details of Kacha's deaths and his revivification each time. And compare them to Kali's revivification. What's the most obvious difference?'

Drauni mentally ticked off each of Kacha's deaths and compared them to Kali's. And his eyes grew wide in surprise.

'Kacha's deaths resulted in him losing his body, while Kali had his body intact. Which means, Sanjeevani works regardless of the state of the body . . .'

'Yes,' Anirudh responded. 'So coming back to the question I had asked earlier—how did Kali return from death? You told me it was because you had preserved the body. I just proved to you that the body doesn't play a role in it. So what's your answer to it now?'

The son of Drona shrugged his shoulders.

'Come on, Drauni, think, think, think. You are missing something obvious.'

But it failed to turn the wheels of the sorcerer's mind.

Anirudh sighed and told him, 'Well, I will give you a hint—Antyesti.'

Ashwatthama furrowed his brows upon hearing that word. 'Antyesti, the last sacrifice. The ceremonial last rites performed upon the death of a person. What about it?'

'What is the objective of the last rites?'

'To surrender the body to the five basic elements and to release the atman from its physical vessel,' the learned scholar replied.

'Correct. Kali and Shukracharya tried to revive you but failed. Rightfully so, since you are still alive. But that's a secret between us alone. They assumed that the Sanjeevani method failed to revive you since you may have been cremated with all proper last rites by the Immortals. Now, their assumption is wrong, but it holds reason. A person who has been cremated, and for whom Antyesti has been performed, cannot be revived because that person's spirit is free and unbound.

'In Kacha's case, though his remains were burnt and reduced to ashes, no last rites were performed. His spirit was in this realm. So he was brought back to life. In Kali's case, the Antyesti ceremony was performed for Duryodhana, not for Kali. Duryodhana's soul had departed from its vessel. So Kali, being on the same plane, could make his way back to Duryodhana's body, where he was previously resting, since no rites were performed for Kali.'

Anirudh explained further, 'So the core of revivification is union of the soul with the body created using the five elements. The body is perishable, but the atman is immortal. Antyesti deals with surrendering the body to the five basic elements, because the body, and this whole universe, is made up of the five basic elements—air, water, fire, sky and earth.

The soul can never be created, but the body can. That's the secret to the Sanjeevani technique.'

'I see . . .' Ashwatthama said, deep in thought.

'So coming back to my question once again—' said Anirudh.

'Did someone revive you as well?' asked Ashwatthama, cutting him off. 'Since you are here, I am assuming that you hadn't been cremated. That's a bit shocking too. Given that you have people who care for you, and all of them learned people.'

Anirudh smiled. 'I have been cremated with all customs in place.'

Ashwatthama's jaw dropped. 'What? Then how are you here? Is there someone more learned than Shukracharya in the art of Sanjeevani? Skilled enough to create a soul . . .'

'The soul cannot be created, Ashwatthama,' Anirudh reminded the wounded sorcerer.

'Ah yes, I forget that. Well, then tell me, how did you return?' he asked, curious and impatient.

'Well, I created my body using the five elements, and then made it home for my soul.'

'Oh right!' Ashwatthama groaned, feeling stupid. 'You are an avatar of Vishnu. You can very well do anything, I suppose . . . I guess the avatar of Vishnu knows everything in this cosmic universe.'

Anirudh looked at Drauni quizzically. 'Avatar of Vishnu—me?'

'Yeah. You are the last avatar of Vishnu, Kalki. Aren't you?'

He saw that Anirudh's face now wore an undecipherable smile.

THIRTY-SEVEN

'Well then, be an enigma if you want,' said Ashwatthama, looking at the enigmatic smile of Anirudh.

He looked outside the cave, at snowflakes dancing in the breeze.

'Why did you bring me here?' he asked the young boy.

'Well, I saw that you were planning on enjoying your solitude. So I thought I'd rather give you company, and care for your wounds too.'

Ashwatthama quipped, 'Well, perks of being the avatar—access to all the private thoughts and all bits of information. Well, if you actually know everything, tell me what's happening out there . . .'

'Well, the Immortals have taken over the stone palace. Kali had established temporary headquarters at Jana's place, but then moved from there. He also paid a visit to Parashurama at the stone palace, announcing his return and revealing that he killed Shukracharya. And also that he has learnt the art of Mrit Sanjeevani.'

'What the hell!' Drauni blurted out.

'Well, you asked for it,' the boy replied.

'How did Kali learn this?!'

'He told Shukracharya to revive you, and then he simply studied the old man's thoughts.'

'Damn!' Ashwatthama grunted. He couldn't help but wonder about Anirudh. *Does he know the future? Does he have the ability to look into Time?*

'Let me ask you something—did you know all this was going to happen?' he asked the boy.

'No.'

'But you knew Shukracharya was going to get killed, and that Kali was going to learn Mrit Sanjeevani . . .'

Anirudh nodded his confirmation.

'Then why did you not stop these events from happening?'

'Dear Ashwatthama,' said Anirudh. 'Remember, fate will always have its path. Even though I possess the knowledge and power to turn the path of destiny, I seldom interfere with the flow of things.'

Ashwatthama looked aghast at the avatar. These very words were uttered to him in the forest by the lord of Dwarka. 'Krishna,' he gasped. 'So you know all of Krishna's conversation with me?'

'Yes, every moment of it.'

'So you knew I was going to attack you once you had Asi, didn't you?'

The young man shook his head and answered, 'We were counting on you to attack me, since you sent Kalanayaka to attack Sage Dweepa and me outside his house. It was an unplanned trip and we realized that you were after something. So we were expecting an attack. But I didn't know that you were looking for Asi or that Krishna had told you to resurrect Kali after I had retrieved the divine sword.'

'When did you learn of Krishna's conversation with me?'

'After my death.'

Ashwatthama sighed softly. *His afterlife is a bloody mystery . . .*

'Why did you save me?'

Anirudh squinted at him. 'How does one save an Immortal?'

'Well, what's this then?' he asked, pointing to the dressing across his chest.

'Healing and saving are two different things, son of Drona.'

'Besides, you are here also because,' Anirudh continued, 'you too have a role in the coming battle, and beyond that as well.'

'Coming battle?'

'The battle against Kali . . .'

'And what's beyond that?'

'You'll see . . .'

'How do you know all this?' Ashwatthama asked.

The boy remained silent.

He asked him, 'Well, if you are not the avatar of Vishnu, then who are you?'

Anirudh looked at the swirling breeze outside. 'I am Anirudh, and I am the avatar of Vishnu . . . I am every avatar of Vishnu.'

Drauni waited, his brows knit in curiosity.

Anirudh turned to his listener. 'I am also Vishnu. I am Rudra. I am Brahma.'

'I am also that fire beside you,' he said, pointing to the fire. Looking outside, he said, 'I am the snow that's floating outside, I am the breeze that's holding the snow in its arms, I am the mountain inside which you are resting, I am the moon whose light falls on its peak, I am also the sun whose rays will illuminate the mountaintop tomorrow, I am the bird that flies

161

across the sky, I am the worm that searches for food in the earth and I am the fish that lives in the ocean.'

Turning back to Ashwatthama, he said, 'I am also you. I am Hanuman, I am Vyasa, I am Dweepa, and I am Bali. And I am Kali too.'

Ashwatthama found himself speechless when Anirudh concluded, saying, 'I am everything and I am also nothing.'

THIRTY-EIGHT

Avyay's House,
2026 CE

'How do humans perceive other living beings?' Sadhika asked.

'Yeah,' Avyay replied. 'Humans' perception of animals, plants, trees—the nature around them.'

'Are you referring to their lack of concern towards the environment?'

'That, and also their careless attitude towards animals and trees.'

Sadhika raised her brows in question.

Avyay pointed to the folders on the table.

'One of those folders is dedicated only to man's actions against nature. Anirudh collected articles that mention those horrific acts.'

'Like water pollution by industries, deforestation, et cetera?'

'Not just those, I have also come across articles about poaching and violence against animals. He has also collected articles about, say, how the last Cape Buffalo in a Delhi zoo died, possibly due to consuming plastic.'

Sadhika sighed and rested her head on the bed.

'Then there were a few other clippings about humans attacking wild animals who enter their habitation.'

'Well, how else can we expect humans to react when they are under threat?'

'Well . . . why deforest on a massive scale in the first place and take away the animal's home. The land first belonged to the animals, not us.'

Sadhika got off the bed to pick up the folders on the table. Choosing the one on animal cruelty, she emptied the papers on to the bed and leafed through them.

'I see that he has collected articles about zoos and circuses as well,' she said.

Avyay nodded. 'Yeah, he was against cruelty to animals. He has always been of the opinion that we should abolish circuses, aquariums and zoos. He wanted animals to always remain in their natural habitat, their home. He didn't wish to see them caged or trained for the amusement of humans.'

'Can't say I disagree with him . . .'

Avyay came across a couple of pages and handed them to Sadhika.

Her companion studied the papers and frowned. 'The torment against cows for their hide, meat and milk . . .' she murmured gravely.

'Yeah,' the avatar replied. 'Not just cows, he has also collected articles on goats. And pieces about bovines being tortured,' she said, sifting through the sheets.

'You spoke to him about these?'

'I did, yeah. He wanted to end this abuse against animals. He wanted to shut down the industry, or industries. He was very unhappy with the way animals were treated, male children killed after their birth, the children separated from their mothers, the repeated and merciless impregnation of females for milk, and then finally discarding them once they stop yielding milk . . . It pissed him off really badly.'

Sadhika, with eyebrows still knit, asked, 'Well, if he ended the industry, then what about the impact of the closure? Had he considered the far-reaching impact to food habits and culture? The dairy farmers, factory workers and many more people, they would all be out of jobs. What about them?'

Avyay laughed slightly, 'He wasn't giving a damn about what happens to the industry or the people. He said that humans can, and should, take care of other humans. But there's no one looking out for mute and exploited animals. So he wanted to act solely in their interest.'

After a few moments of pondering, Sadhika asked, 'How do you plan to go about this?'

Avyay sighed, tucking rogue strands of hair behind her ears. 'I don't know where to start. There are so many solutions to any problem, but those solutions could have their own impacts as well. We have to analyse each problem and all its potential solutions, then weigh every solution and choose the best one from all of them . . . There's a lot of work involved, Sadhika. And I honestly don't know how we will narrow it all down to a single ideal solution. And even if we did locate optimal, or best, solutions, next comes the roll-out and implementation of the solutions.'

Sadhika smiled and placed an encouraging hand on the avatar's shoulder, giving it a squeeze, she said, 'Listen . . . The Esoteric Organization of Kalki is all yours. We have thousands of people employed just to serve you in whatever way you want. We can even recruit a thousand more. All you need to do is ask, or command, and they will get you whatever you want. So, all the analysing, weighing the pros and cons, et cetera, can be left to the experts. It's not your concern. You just need to make a decision after looking at the detailed solutions they give you.'

'And what will we do after I decide? How do I go about implementing the solution?'

Taking her phone out from her pocket, Sadhika grinned softly. 'There's something you need to know . . .'

She touched a screen a couple of times, and Avyay could hear a number being dialled from the device's speaker.

'Hey, Sadhika . . .' a voice spoke from the other end.

Avyay recognized this to be Siddharth's voice.

'Hey, Sid. I believe it's time for Avyay to know about Clause Zero.'

'What's Clause Zero?' Avyay asked curiously.

'All right, just give me a minute,' Siddharth's voice came through the speaker.

A moment later, their friend spoke through the phone, 'Avi, check your mail. I have mailed you a document.'

THIRTY-NINE

The Himalayas,
2026 CE

Ashwatthama was standing at the mouth of the cave. He had started walking around a bit now. However, his torso still ached when he exerted himself, and every movement was a strain to his body. But it felt good to be mobile. He looked at the sun shining bleakly through the mists, on to the snow outside the cave.

He looked down at the gashed natural mail by his feet. He placed his palm over it and muttered a few words. The thick hide disintegrated into ash and flew out the cave.

He heard the boy's voice ask him, 'Don't you need it anymore?'

Ashwatthama clicked his tongue. 'I never needed it. Immortal, remember? I just wanted to keep it away from Kali. I have no intention of helping Kali . . . And I see that you have mastered death, and thus have no use for this mail. Else, I would have offered it to you. So this skin is no longer of any use.'

He then turned to Anirudh, who was sipping herbal tea. 'Do you possess the ability to look into the future?'

Anirudh looked up at his companion, with a brow raised questioningly.

Drauni explained, 'You told me that you knew Kali would learn revivification, and that he would kill Shukracharya, and also all those events that transpired . . . How did you know these incidents were going to occur beforehand? How do you know the future? You told me that you don't know the future, but you seem to know these events.'

Ashwatthama, clutching the dressing across his torso gently, walked towards Anirudh.

Anirudh looked at the bandage; he had changed it some time back. Pointing to it, he asked Drauni, 'You saw the wounds when I changed the dressing today. How long do you think it will take to heal completely?'

The sorcerer's curiosity was piqued not only by the question but also the direction of the conversation. But he answered, saying, 'Well, the gashes are still there, although smaller now. So I guess around two days more and they should heal completely.'

'Two days?' Anirudh asked. 'How did you come to that figure?'

'By observing the pace at which the wounds are healing . . . It's not tough to come up with an estimate.'

'Your injuries will take thirty-one hours to heal completely, Drauni,' Anirudh spoke with a smile.

With a grimace of strain drawn across his face, Ashwatthama sat on the floor, resting his back against the wall.

'Saw that in the future as well?' Drauni asked, impassive and devoid of any surprise.

Anirudh laughed and shook his head. 'What is "future", Ashwatthama?' he asked.

'I don't get your question.'

'What is the future comprised of? How would you define it?'

'Plainly speaking, things that are going to happen in the course of time ahead—that's future.'

'I am glad you put it that way—things that are going to happen. Now tell me this: how do things happen?'

The former leader of Kalabakshakas just raised a brow in response.

'Okay, I will answer that,' Anirudh obliged. 'See, things that are going to happen—let's call them events instead of things—they don't happen out of nothing. Every single event in the future has its root in the past or the present. Thus, future is a consequence of these incidents of past and present. So, to know what's going to happen, all I need to know is the past and present.

'Let's take your wounds as an example. I know the effect of the medicine in great detail, and I also know how it works when the body rests and when it is active. I am also aware of when you rest and when you're active. Based on that, I am able to gauge the time it will take for the cuts to heal completely.'

'Are you all-knowing then?' Drauni asked.

Anirudh laughed. 'Well, I am all-knowing, yes. But I can't predict that which doesn't exist, can I? I can't predict the unsown. Like I said, events of the future are rooted in the past.'

'Okay,' Ashwatthama said. 'So, basically, there is nothing set in stone as such? The future is not defined. You predict it based on events that occur and their outcomes, right?'

'Yeah, you could say that.'

'So you wouldn't have been able to say for sure that Kali was going to learn the workings of Mrit Sanjeevani?'

'I was sure of it. I brought Shukracharya into the picture and Kali as well. I know Kali really well, so I knew what his next steps would be because I know how he thinks.

'Here, let me walk you through Kali's thought process when he saw Shukracharya. Kali knows that the art of revivification is very valuable. He wants to learn it for himself so that he can benefit from it later on. Also, once he learns the art, Shukracharya would be the only one, apart from Kali himself, who knows how it works. While he doesn't mind the acharya knowing the art, he is wary that someone else may rescue Shukracharya, like the Immortals, and may use the revivification science to their benefit as well. They had already conquered the stone palace and killed you, and thus had proven themselves to be formidable enemies. And Kali realizes that if he was to lose the preceptor of the asuras to his opponents, then this would upset the upper hand he has. Thus, he kills Shukracharya and ensures that he always has the advantage. So there you have it. Once you know Kali well enough, you will be able to predict his actions.'

Ashwatthama struggled to digest his words. And when he spoke, it was with distaste. 'So you led Shukracharya to his own death . . .'

The avatar replied, 'Ashwatthama, don't speak of death with such a tone of revulsion. It is like sleeping after a long day and waking to another day, in another life. And yes, Shukracharya had completed his final purpose with the resurrection of Kali and imparting the knowledge of it to the demon, so it was time for him to leave his body.'

'How can you be so casual about death! Don't you have any value for life?'

'I value life, Ashwatthama. But I value death too. They are two sides of the same coin. Just like sleeping and waking—one cannot exist without the other. Sleep is something that you look forward to, and so it is for waking up too. If you can look forward to both of them with positivity, why not look at life and death the same way?'

'Because life brings someone into this world while death takes them away from this universe. When you sleep and wake, you are still in the same universe. That's why one can look forward to it. There's a vast difference between sleep and death, Anirudh.'

'What happens when someone dies, Drauni?'

Drauni shrugged his shoulders. 'The soul is released from the body . . .'

Anirudh nodded. 'That's correct. The released soul is still in the same universe, like you mentioned for sleep. Everything around you, the visible and invisible, belong to the same—one—universe. What sleeping and waking is to your physical body, living and dying is to the soul—the eternal existence.'

Ashwatthama was silent.

Anirudh continued, 'A soul is eternal, Ashwatthama. It has no birth or death. Using your physical body, you experience life when you are awake, and when you are asleep, you don't live actively. Likewise, when the soul enters the body, it is able to experience the world through the senses of physical existence. When it exits the body, it return to the universe, and remains senseless until it enters another body.

'So to answer your question, I value life and death since they are the soul's experiences,' Anirudh concluded. 'And thus, I don't mind Shukracharya's death. He is heading for the next part of his journey.'

The sorcerer stared at the avatar. 'How can you . . . be so laidback about these things?'

'If you witness the things as they are meant to be, then you will find it all simple. Death is being mourned, while birth is being celebrated.'

'Tell me, should unfortunate and untimely deaths be celebrated as well?'

'Death—unfortunate or untimely—is still death. Whether you sleep less or sleep more, you are still going to wake up and carry on with life. With death, your soul is going back into the universe. Your journey continues. But if you mean unfortunate and untimely in the sense that their deaths have been unjust, then the perpetrators have to be punished. Justice should be delivered. Because no one has the right to grant unjust death to anyone. *No one.*'

'I see . . .' Ashwatthama ruminated on the words.

Then, the son of Drona asked, 'How do you read thoughts?'

FORTY

Kali's Camp,
2026 CE

There was a gusty breeze around the plateau. Standing at the beak of a cliff, Kali studied the lush green land below him. There was a large lake at the centre of this greenery. Surrounding this green vastness was a range of stone hills, and he was standing atop the nearest one overlooking the expanse. To his left, on clear grounds, stood a stone castle that he had produced out of thin air. Inside and around this structure, the Kalabakshakas were setting up their base camp.

Happy with the progress, Kali sat cross-legged on the cold stone surface. The evening sun covered the lands with a hue of amber.

Bhairava stepped closer to the Lord of Evil and asked, 'What's next, my lord?'

'Take over the world . . .' his master replied with a smile.

'Sure, my lord. Shall I introduce you to our men who are working in high places all over the world?'

'Are they in positions of power? Or are they in positions of influence?'

'Sire?'

Turning to his aide, Kali explained his words. 'Can they execute decisions? Or can they present suggestions to decision-makers?'

'We have people in both these places, my lord. But more of the latter . . .'

Kali nodded. 'That's all right. I have the highest influence over all of humankind. So I can get whatever I want done through them whenever I want.'

'How so, my lord?' Bhairava asked, incredulity lacing his voice.

The demon motioned him to sit next to him. 'Let me tell you a story.'

The personification of evil started narrating. 'After the end of the great war and Duryodhana's demise, I left his body and started wandering around, biding my time, waiting for my era to arrive. After Krishna died, my time had finally come. Yudhishthira, the then emperor, renounced his throne. He crowned Parikshit, his grand-nephew, as his successor, and he ruled from Hastinapura. He was the grandson of Arjuna, and son of Abhimanyu. Since it was my time, I set out to enter Parikshit's kingdom. Parikshit was touring the outskirts, on a hunting game, and I met him in a forest on my way to his kingdom. He was warned and educated about me by his preceptors and elders. And the forewarned king understood who I was, and he denied me entry to his region. As a matter of fact, he was ready to kill me. But I requested him to grant me shelter in his kingdom, under his protective sight. And he, being a king, couldn't refuse me. After taking my word that I will behave, he gave me four places to make my abode—gambling dens, brothels, drinking taverns and slaughterhouses. But since these locales were rare in his kingdom, I begged him for more. And the ruler obliged. Parikshit gave me one more place to reside—gold.'

Kali paused and looked at Bhairava, who was listening to him with rapt attention. Kalaguru recollected Shukracharya's words about Kali's attachment to gold.

'Then?' his companion asked of him.

Kali smiled and said, 'Let me put it this way, he was wearing a gold crown. He insulted a sage soon after, and as a consequence, he died a few days later.'

'After Parikshit died, I was no longer bound by my word to him. I was no longer restricted to his kingdom. I spread my influence across the world. Do you know how many abodes I have today, Bhairava?'

The evil lord didn't wait for Bhairava's reply. 'Innumerable,' he said. 'There are so many bars, brothels, slaughterhouses and casinos, jewellery shops . . .'

After a pause, the lord asked, 'Do you know the best part about being *me* in today's world?'

Bhairava shook his head.

'Gold!' Kali spoke animatedly, 'So much gold in the world . . . Almost every house has a fragment of it . . .'

Kali allowed a wicked grin to appear on his lips before he continued, 'And to top it all—even the gods have so much gold with them . . . Golden thrones, golden chariots, golden idols, gold plates . . . Temples have gold in some form or the other. I feel that the temples are made for me, and not for the gods.'

He turned to Bhairava. 'Despite having so many places of worship, there is a scarcity of goodness. On the other hand, even though I am not worshipped in any form or at any place, evil is present everywhere. It's as if the gods don't exist at all.'

'Well, that's great, isn't it, my lord?'

'I don't know, yet. Humans . . . They are greedier. If I offer them a finger, they would want a hand.

'And there are some . . . You offer a finger, they would not accept it. You offer a hand, they would still not accept it.

'Be wary of such people, Bhairava. These people of strong resolve make me believe that there is goodness in this universe, and this power of goodness is really strong and formidable.'

'Do you really believe that there are no gods, my lord?'

Kali laughed out loud. 'Regardless of my belief, I can say for sure that they have no interest in the affairs of humans. Else, there wouldn't have been any inequality in the world. There wouldn't be so much injustice.'

'That's right, my lord. Kalki would not have succumbed to his death so soon . . . He has now proven without doubt that he was after all just a young mortal.'

'That's actually good news, Kalaguru. Kalki is dead; I didn't know that this would happen. I was waiting to fight him.'

Bhairava said, with a tone of caution, 'Well, the Immortals are still around, Lord Kali.'

'Yeah, they are. But Kalki! He was supposed to be my nemesis. I was waiting to vanquish him. And make him watch the world suffer.'

'But do you think it would have mattered to him? Like you said, he wouldn't have cared about humankind anyway.'

'Maybe . . . maybe not,' Kali said, in a dissatisfied manner.

Bhairava nodded.

After pondering a while, the evil lord said gravely, 'Humankind is more evil than me, I believe, Bhairava . . .'

'And is that a problem, my lord?'

'Well, Bhairava, let me ask you this. You are my adviser. And you are also the primary guru of the Kalabakshakas. Now, what if I make a new student the teacher of your students instead of you?'

Kalaguru had a measured response, and said gently, 'And why would you do that, my lord? A student's duty is to learn, not teach. He can serve that purpose when he is qualified to do so.'

'Ah, Bhairava. You have mentioned the very word I sought—purpose. What is the purpose of humankind?'

'Ummm . . . To grow and prosper? Become the best?'

'Yes. A human's purpose is to become their best version. Become *god*. But do you see humankind heading in that direction?'

Kalaguru shook his head.

'I am Evil because I am that. I have made it my purpose to spread corruption and evil. I want to rule the world.'

Bhairava nodded, and asked, 'So I am guessing that humankind being more evil than you is a problem. Isn't it, my lord?'

'Yes, Kalaguru. You are correct. Humans are greedier and hungrier than I am. They are capable of twisting my arm and dominating me, if a chance should appear. So I confess that I am a bit wary of these people of yours who possess position and influence in high places . . .'

'But, my lord, they are trustworthy. There is no doubt about their loyalty.'

'Bhairava, don't teach me about loyalty. Everything has its price. Even the loyalty of your people. And for some, the price may just be my downfall. Like we discussed, give them a finger and they'll go for your hand. Greed. One of the terrible sins that consume this world . . .'

FORTY-ONE

Avyay's House,
2026 CE

Avyay sat back from her laptop, still in disbelief over the document she had just read. Clause Zero was still displayed on her screen.

'Is this a real thing?' she whispered, her mind blank.

Sadhika, seated next to her, nodded.

'And every president has signed this?'

'Yup,' Siddharth's voice sounded from the phone.

Avyay took a deep breath. 'How come I never knew of this? Did Anirudh know?'

Her companion shook her head. 'Anirudh didn't know of this. We wanted some time to understand him before we revealed it to him. And not all of them know of this. Just a handful of us—Lord Parashurama, Acharya Sreedhar, Siddharth and me.'

'Not even Sage Dweepa?' the avatar asked, surprised.

'Nope. He will know of it if he were to take up Acharya Sreedhar's position,' Siddharth informed.

Avyay nodded. 'So this Clause Zero document will allow me to present my proposals to the president, I take it? And they would have to accept and implement it?'

Sadhika answered, 'Well, you can submit your proposals, yes. But they would not be accepted and implemented right away. These proposals would be studied and vetted first, obviously, and would go through the normal flow of perusal through committees and approvals. The implementation will be done after all the approvals are in place.'

'Hmmm, that's good. But how does Clause Zero help me exactly?'

Through the phone, Siddharth's voice answered, 'To put it plainly, it would help you present things to the highest level, directly, removing all levels of bureaucracy in between.'

'And all this is possible just because I am Kalki?'

Sadhika smiled. 'No, of course not. Tell me, are you considering making things better because you are Kalki?'

'No! I really want to make things better. You know it too. I'd feel this way even if I wasn't Kalki.'

'Correct, I know it. So this document, whilst offering you a VIP pass to the highest echelons of power, is not just a privilege . . .'

'It is a matter of responsibility,' Avyay concluded.

'Exactly!' Siddharth responded.

'I see now. I was wondering if this document allowed me to break the laws and do things directly. I am glad it doesn't. It would be too much power for a person to wield.'

'And that is by design, Avyay,' Sadhika commented. 'The idea of this document, when conceptualized, was to give you enough power to cut through the standard, tedious procedures, but not give you powers to override all protocols put in place.'

Avyay sat in thought for a few moments.

Then she said, 'It is a matter of huge responsibility. While EOK would do the heavy work of researching and presenting me with information and proposals, I have to study them thoroughly and understand the impact well. I have to question every move myself, since we are talking about billions of people here . . .'

After a pause, she continued, 'It is expected of me. I am to bring my best game every time, aren't I?'

Sadhika nodded with an encouraging smile.

Avyay hopped off her bed and went to the easel next to her wardrobe. She turned it, making the whiteboard point towards her bed. She sat on the bed and glanced at the board.

Picking up Anirudh's files, she announced, 'Let's start then, shall we?'

FORTY-TWO

The Himalayas,
2026 CE

'How do you read thoughts?' Anirudh considered the question put forth to him by his companion.

He rested his back on the cold, rocky wall of the Himalayan cave before answering.

'Well, thoughts are made of energy. Anything that a living being does requires energy. Even when you think, you are spending energy performing that action. And energy is readable, if you know how to read it. So that's how I can read your mind. I can even read minds that are miles away from me.'

'How do you do that?' Ashwatthama asked, his mouth wide open.

'It's simple. Energy connects everything in the world. So I can read anything, anywhere. You know how telepathy works—sending thoughts over distances. That requires energy as well.'

Ashwatthama closed his mouth and started pondering the words he had heard. 'Come to think of it, you can only read someone's thoughts in the present. You can't read a person's thoughts in the future or in the past.'

'No, I cannot read future thoughts. The energy doesn't exist in the present moment. How can I read something that doesn't exist? But past thoughts, yes, I can read them since that energy will always remain.'

'Would I be right in saying that you can get knowledge of the entire past and all the current events, and based on it, you reliably predict what could happen in the next moment?'

'Reliably, perhaps. If there are no changes introduced by humankind or nature, I can predict what's going to happen the next minute, and over the course of time.'

Ashwatthama raised a hand to scratch his chin, thinking. 'So that means you wouldn't have any way of knowing if I would ever attempt to take Asi or not . . . By you, I mean Krishna, of course. I could have chosen to abandon the pursuit at any time.'

Anirudh nodded. 'But . . . you wouldn't have been able to do it. See, I knew you well enough. I was sure that you wouldn't deviate from the task assigned to you. I had given you purpose in your otherwise aimless life. So I proceeded once I knew that the odds were in my favour.'

'But still, it is possible that I could have deviated from the mission if I thought so?'

'Yes, that was possible.'

'So even the best laid plans can go awry if someone thinks something even slightly different than you expect of them . . .'

'Yes . . .'

'Don't you feel scared of losing control and your plans not coming to fruition because of someone who does differently than what you'd planned?'

'No. I am not scared at all, Ashwatthama. The future, like you deduced earlier, is not set in stone. While I can predict what could happen based on my knowledge of the happenings in the universe, the variable of human factor always remains. And that is by design. Mankind has the freedom to make choices—good or bad, that's up to their discretion. Everything happens as per the decisions, the choices. My predictions are based on their characters, like I was able to predict Kali's actions.'

'So you just use people for your grand design . . . Don't you?'

Anirudh laughed and shook his head. 'No, of course not. I don't have any grand designs. I have created the universe as well as humankind. I have imbued them with a sense of decision-making. Whether they do justice by it, or injustice, that's their choice. It's their decision. But there is no design governing the events.'

'If there is no design, then why did you need to make plans for Kalki from your time as Krishna? Your whole Kalki avatar *conspiracy* was designed to keep me off your scent and to ensure Kalki got all the help he needed. The purpose of the Kalki avatar is to restore the balance of the universe . . . Isn't that the grand plan?'

'The plans Krishna had, those were for Kalki, not for the universe. It's like looking after one's own in the vast, wide universe. To help Kalki obtain the tools needed to aid him in his stand against his enemies and to accomplish his purpose.'

'I don't get it . . . See, Kalki's role in the universe's balance is not of your design, so you say. But all the preparations were for Kalki, thus in consequence, in aid to restore the balance. Which is the grand plan, I take it?'

'This is the second time you mentioned this "grand" plan of restoring the balance. Let me be clear, there is no plan on how the balance is going to be restored. All I know is that I want it to be restored. Coming to Kalki's role, I didn't define his life at all. His life's journey was a series of *his* decisions, including his death, which he *chose*.'

Ashwatthama's jaw fell open. 'What do you mean by that—he *chose* his death?'

'You weren't the only person Asi asked if he could deflect rather than strike. Kalki was asked that as well, and he chose to be struck. He chose his death.'

'And why would he do that!' Drauni gasped.

'Well, he had his reasons. I will tell you later.'

'He . . .?' Ashwatthama spoke, his eyes narrowed in scrutiny as he realized what had been happening.

Anirudh's eyes met that of the sorcerer, and he knew the forthcoming question.

'You are Kalki . . . Why are you referring to yourself in the third person?'

'Kalki died, didn't he?' Anirudh asked.

Ashwatthama gave a nod in acknowledgement, but countered, 'But you are Kalki. And Krishna too . . . You told me this yourself . . .'

'Kalki, Krishna, the avatars, and everything in this world—all of you are a part of me. I am everyone and no one at the same time. So I end up using the third person when talking about fragments of me.'

'I see . . . And there is no point in asking you who you are, since you would rather answer it later,' the injured sorcerer complained.

The young man just smiled.

After a pause, the son of Drona asked, 'Now that the Kalki avatar is no more, what about restoring the balance? Do you have contingencies for it? The Immortals?'

'Well, they are there, and there's Dweepa and many more. Mainly, there's Avyay—'

Ashwatthama cut in, 'Ahhh yes, Avyay. Your partner . . . Don't you feel like meeting her? She would be happy to see you alive.'

Anirudh smiled plainly and replied, 'She would be happy to see *Anirudh* alive, not *me*. And I don't want to meet her, or anyone, yet. There's still time.'

'And why is that? They would be happy to have your support. It would be a morale boost, right?'

'Well, I have some news for you, Ashwatthama. And I am revealing this since you are no longer with the Kalabakshakas. Avyay is also Kalki. There were two Kalkis all along, and you only took one out.'

Ignoring his companion's dropped jaw, Anirudh proceeded to explain Krishna's plan and rationale for having two Kalkis.

'I see . . .' Ashwatthama said, considering the revelation. 'So things happened after Bhairava ran away from the hut. Well, so Kalki isn't really dead like Kali thinks. There is another Kalki in the picture.'

'And that's why she doesn't need my support. She can very well walk the path to accomplishing the purpose, with the support of the Immortals and others behind her. She can lead the battle against Kali . . .'

'A battle, you say, which I will be a part of?' Ashwatthama asked, reminded of Anirudh's words about his role in the future.

'Yes, definitely. I will be there too . . .'

Ashwatthama's eyebrows shot up with surprise. 'If you are going to be there, does it mean you know how to defeat Kali?' he asked, curiously.

Anirudh simply smiled.

After seeing that no response was forthcoming, Drauni heaved a sigh and spoke, 'Well . . . You hold on to that mystery. Secrets and you, *inseparable*. But I know this . . . Evil will be removed from this world and humans will be rescued by you, the God.'

Anirudh rested his head against the wall, and asked, 'Ashwatthama, do you really believe that humans need to be rescued by the *God*?'

'Meaning?'

'Well, I am of the opinion that humans don't need rescuing as such.'

Ashwatthama scratched his dressing, and mumbled, 'Well, I am of the opinion that there are many humans who can benefit from your help, Anirudh. Plus, the world's a much better place without Kali.'

Anirudh chuckled softly. 'Oh Drauni . . . You are so learned! Yet you fail to understand a simple truth. Sadly, Kali knows this truth, and not the humans.'

'And which truth is that?'

With a deep sigh, Anirudh answered, 'That humans are at the mercy of their fellow humans. Not at the mercy of gods . . . or even Kali for that matter.'

FORTY-THREE

2026 CE

Avyay was standing at the head of a conference room table in an EOK-owned office building. The existence of EOK was not known to the public. After Sadhika introduced Kalki as a client of the firm to the attendees in the room, Avyay smiled and nodded at the people. She took in her audience— EOK's think tank. She was surrounded by the lead specialists and subject-matter experts of various fields across the globe. They were seated around a large, rectangular, wooden meeting table, with their electronic tablets before them.

'I am thankful to all of you, for meeting me on such short notice. We are exploring certain options to solve some core problems the country is facing. These issues are going to be highlighted to you. You have to perform impact analyses on them. As in, if we are to implement it, then we need to first find out if it will work, how much good it will do and to whom. And more importantly, the negative impact on people.'

She then looked at Sadhika, who, in response, pressed the screen on her phone. A few seconds later, the tablets in front of the attendees chimed. All of them opened the document they'd just received and started reading it. The first page listed the subjects of analysis:

1. Shelter
2. Medicine
3. Education
4. Food
5. Clothing
6. Justice
7. Flora and fauna

Then, the page flipped and each consequent page bore a problem statement and a brief description. Avyay described each subject as she went through the list.

Shelter

'Living conditions are extremely poor, and no human should have to live like this, where even the basic needs aren't met properly. We need plans and statistics to figure out how to go about shifting people into new households that have better, hygienic accommodation and how to maintain it over the years.'

Medicine

'The pandemic that occurred a few years back was a sure eye-opener. The lack of medical infrastructure is frightening. While we did eventually leave the pandemic behind, the cost was too high. We need to build more hospitals, medical colleges and dispensaries in the country, right down to the villages. We have to be prepared for all kinds of disasters, and that's another objective here. We should also check the feasibility of providing medicines at a cheaper cost or for free.'

Education

'There is a serious need to revisit the education we impart to children today. There is no focus on moral knowledge and personal growth. There should be a focus on education that helps people grow to be good individuals with strong values and principles, rather than mature them into people who just go into any line of work mindlessly. So there is a need to figure out how to include this in the curriculum and way of schooling. Further, free schooling for underprivileged children needs to be looked into, as well as how it is being carried out.'

Food

'The target here is to introduce daily meals—like soup kitchens. Three times a day would be ideal for those living in poverty; they, too, have a right to nutrient-rich food. This set-up is going to be large and intensive since we have to reach out to people in the most remote of neighbourhoods. So primary points to consider here while designing the solution is the effort to get things up and running—like getting a place to cook the meals; the resources required for the process, such as groceries, packaging, etc.; quality checks; optimizing food production; dealing with leftover food; distribution of the food; and other logistics. We have to keep in mind disaster situations and scenarios.

For example, how do we handle this operation in the event of a tsunami or a pandemic that involves a lockdown. The idea is to avoid the failure of the system, since once we have this up and running, many would depend on this. Many points need to be thought about and you will find more when you work on this.'

Clothing

'The goal here is that everyone should have decent and sustainable clothing to cover their bodies in every season. So, to accomplish this objective, we will produce and supply clothes free of cost for the people who need them. We will supply formal clothes, casual clothes, uniforms and footwear. We also want to provide them with seasonal wear, like sweaters, raincoats and the like—again, free of cost.

'These points cover our agenda on food, clothing, shelter, education and health. We task ourselves to get these fundamental needs across to everyone in the nation who doesn't have access to it.' The page flipped.

Justice

'Murders, violence against women and children, robbery, assaults, corruption—all these are happening in sickeningly significant numbers. Does this mean that people have lost their touch with humanity, or is it the case that the legal consequences aren't enough of a deterrent? While we do have good laws in place, it doesn't seem to be enough to deter people from committing a crime. How does one ensure that the very thought of a crime and its legal penalties are enough to prevent people from committing it? We would need to go back to the textbooks to study the current laws and the human psychology to figure out how we can address this issue. Do we need stringent laws? At the same time, we need to see if laws are fair to people too.'

Avyay smiled softly when the next point came up on the screen. This reminded her of Anirudh.

Flora and Fauna

'In the previous points, we have been considering the human aspects of society. But now we talk about plants, trees and animals—which should be considered equally, if not more, important. They are *nature*. We share this earth with them. And we cannot neglect them. So the idea is to preserve nature. Hence, we need to look at stopping deforestation, over-fishing and pollution of the environment. Further, laws and actions against illegal trade of animals and exotic species needs to be stopped, and we need to look at poaching of wildlife. Same goes for all forms of entertainment involving animals. We need to look for ways to rehabilitate these gifts of nature back into their natural habitats Every single bird, animal, plant, flower, insect and tree deserves the freedom that we humans yearn. We are going to give them the rights that belong to them.

'That concludes our agenda for the day,' said Avyay. 'Thank you for listening. We will need to study many more problem areas and find solutions, and this is just the beginning. We need to do everything to find ways to change our world for the best.'

❦

EOK Mansion,
Later that day

'I'd say this list is good,' said Siddharth, looking up at Avyay and Sadhika from the sheet of paper that he was perusing. It contained the points and summaries they presented to the think tank.

'It's not all, though. There's still more work to be done,' Avyay confessed.

He nodded. 'These points, when resolved effectively, would help humanity reach a better place, won't they?'

Sadhika replied, 'Not all of humanity, I suppose. You see, the think tank will study these issues at a national level first. We will have to see how it goes, right from the research to the implementation, and then we can scale it to a global level.'

'I see. That makes sense,' he nodded and turned to Avyay. 'So when you said there's more work to be done, did you mean scaling these to a universal level?'

Avyay shook her head. 'The points mentioned in this list address the basic needs of a human life, and nature to some extent. There's more to do, and that's a separate list that I have barely started working on.'

'And what's on that list?'

Avyay opened her phone, tapped it a couple of times and slid it across to him. On the screen was a bulleted list.

- Climate change
- Preservation of nature—oceans, wildlife, forestry, greenery
- Poverty
- Unemployment

- Health
- Good food and clean water

He studied the list silently. After he reached the end, he returned the phone, saying, 'That's off to a good start. Let me know when you want to talk to a larger or even an international think tank. I can get you in touch with them.'

'I definitely will. I still need to gather my thoughts on what I need to ask the experts. Something along the lines of what I did for the points pertaining to human life.'

'When do you want to start working on this list?' Sadhika asked.

'Well, right now! Things are still happening out there without any break in pace. So we might as well start now . . .'

FORTY-FOUR

The Himalayas,
2026 CE

'Humans are at the mercy of other humans, and not at the mercy of gods. Why do you say that?' Ashwatthama asked.

'Because gods are a fantastic concept, Ashwatthama. Humans, by their deeds, become gods or goddesses. And every human can become a god. For example, why do you call me a god?'

'Because you are all-knowing.'

'Like I said earlier, I don't know the future.'

'But the rest, you do—all that is happening and all that has happened. So aren't you all-knowing?'

'But not the future. I can't predict what every individual is going to do tomorrow. So, no, I am not all-knowing in the sense you mean, Drauni. And the art of learning of past and present events—that's not restricted only to me. You can learn them as well. Anyone can learn it. I am just a guy with the power of vision among the blind. That doesn't make me a king or a god.'

Ashwatthama considered the words for a while, and then spoke, 'But what about gods like Rudra, Brahma, Vishnu, and goddesses like Lakshmi, Saraswati, Durga?'

'All of them are human representations to look at, and to request strength and energy from. They are representations of attributes like knowledge, wealth, preservation, justice, creation, destruction . . . People cannot fathom nothingness, and thus cannot bring themselves to ask anything of a shapeless, invisible entity. That's why we have faces and figures—a form to look up to—so that humans know whom they are conversing with. So that they know whom they are asking something of. How do you gain the force of Rudra upon will? It's upon request, isn't it?'

Ashwatthama nodded but he said agitatedly, 'But . . . This thought . . . that there are no gods. That is blasphemy.'

Anirudh chuckled, and replied, 'Gods and blasphemy, both are creations of man. Picture this. The citizens are at the mercy of a government, the poor are at the mercy of the rich, the illiterate are at the mercy of the literate, the weak are at the mercy of the strong . . . Humans are at the mercy of other humans, in some way or the other. Tell me, Drauni, if there exists an almighty God, then would this disparity occur? Wouldn't God, or gods, look at it all and serve justice?'

Ashwatthama was silent a moment. Then, he spoke, 'So, are you at the mercy of other humans?'

'No, because I exist inside every human. I am every human.'

After a think, Ashwatthama asked, 'If there are no gods per se, then how will the balance be maintained? Or how will things become ideal?'

'Humans will have to achieve this on their own. They are blessed with the sense of right and wrong, and the power to make decisions. They aren't walking pieces of furniture.

They can act in the interest of the greater good or for their own good.'

After a pause, the former Kalabakshaka asked, 'In that case, humans can achieve equality in the truest sense, can't they?'

'Yes. And even godhood.'

'Will they . . .? Achieve equality and godhood, I mean . . .' Ashwatthama asked, curious and anxious.

The boy just smiled and said, 'I hope they do.'

FORTY-FIVE

Bhoomidevi was in a grove, surrounded by tall trees, covered in dense greenish-brown leafy foliage. She was limping slowly, dragging her other foot with each step. A thick bamboo cane acted as a walking stick for her.

Suddenly, she staggered towards the nearest tree for support. Pain exploded in her abdomen as trees were felled in large numbers to make way for new malls and transport stations. Clutching her belly, she rested her back on the wood, drawing in deep breaths. She was so fragile that even the plucking of flowers hurt her.

It hadn't always been the case that the picking of flowers or axing of trees hurt her so mortally. Aeons ago, when she was healthy and young, the picking of flowers felt like soft pinches. However, as time passed by, with the assault of humankind on her body, she became very fragile. Blood trickled slowly from her abdomen, dripping down her fingers. Every small act against her, inflicted upon her by humans, took a heavy toll on her. It pained her and wounded her badly.

Suddenly, her arm started throbbing with pain. It felt like someone had singed her skin. Losing her balance because of the pain, she let go of the cane and crumbled to the base of the tree. She clutched her forearm with her bloody fingers, trying to calm the pain. She realized a vast forest was ablaze in the Amazon. She groaned in pain, her body twisting in agony. Her eyes, once as deeply blue as the ocean, were now grey, with coloured flecks polluting the greyness.

Lying against the tree, she tried to take in a deep breath, but her lungs were barely functional. Even the attempt to breathe in resulted in her coughing up blood. She looked down at her hand in distaste. She tried to ignore the skin of her forearm turning black and melting away, but she was unable to. The agony brought tears to her eyes, and her eyes dripped more dirt down her face.

She felt a calf being pulled away from her mother, depriving the child of her first milk. Her sad, shivering lips expressed her disappointment at being unable to nourish her children.

She closed her eyes, resignedly. She longed for peace. She longed for her health. She hoped that humankind would mend their ways soon and nurse her back to better health.

Seeking respite, her thoughts wandered to Anirudh. Her longing intensified. She longed for his soothing touch on her skin, his soft lips to brush her cheeks, his melodious voice to tell her that everything would be fine.

She wanted to call out to him, but she held herself back. He was on a mission. He would come to her eventually, she knew that. She could feel him in the Himalayas, and she heaved a sigh of relief, knowing he was alive and well. She conjured a shield around herself, to prevent him from realizing her disintegrating state of health.

'It's just a matter of time . . .' she consoled herself, tearfully.

With painstaking effort, she got up with the support of the tree and the bamboo stick. With tortoise steps, she exited the grove and a breezy ocean greeted her. Tired, she sat down on the shore. Her tears didn't stop as she felt a thousand knives were gutting her forearm. The skin on her forearms started melting away. The wounds wore an air of finality.

Yet, against all odds, she still hoped that humankind would reward her forbearance by tending to her wounds and restoring her to best health.

FORTY-SIX

Kali's Camp,
2026 CE

Kali sat down with a huff on a heap of grass. Kalaguru stood beside him respectfully. The two of them had just finished a rigorous exercise of sorcery. On the vast ground in front of them, the black-robed warriors were training hard for combat. For around a month, Kali learnt the Kalabakshakas' ways of battle. He also imparted his martial knowledge to them. The training was severe and thorough.

Kali motioned the teacher of Kalabakshakas to sit beside him. With his eyes on the sorcerers' training, the lord asked his commander, 'Have we received confirmation about the location of the weapons?'

'Yes, my lord.'

'Can your sources be trusted, Bhairava?'

'Yes, my lord. They are Kalabakshakas themselves, and they trained under me long ago. Now, they are in senior positions of interest and they give us classified information whenever we need it.'

'Good,' the lord responded with a nod.

'Should we initiate talks with the world leaders?'

Kali took his eyes off the soldiers and looked curiously at Kalaguru. 'What do you want to talk about?'

'Well, we can hold them to ransom and extort whatever we want, can't we, my lord? Given the destructive powers of our weapons, they will agree to our terms and conditions immediately.'

Kali laughed and patted Kalaguru's back. 'Oh, Bhairava! I am not here for the talking, am I? I am here to spread destruction. And I want to defeat those immortal followers of Kalki.'

With a sudden movement, Kali clutched the throat of his adviser. Bhairava's eyes widened in horror. His hands were struggling against the vice-like grip of his lord, but the hold was too strong. He could feel his air supply being choked.

The man started pleading for forgiveness, but ignoring his pleas, Kali whispered in a cold voice, 'Don't you ever think, or suggest, that I ask for what I want, Bhairava. If there is something I want, I will take it.'

Letting go of Bhairava's neck, Kali said in a menacing tone, 'After the destruction is done, I will dominate the whole world. The people will be at my mercy. I will have all the pleasures and treasures at my service.'

Bhairava, still trying to catch his breath, mumbled, 'Yes, my lord. True, indeed.'

Kali smiled and patted his adviser on the back softly. 'You will see it all, Bhairava.'

'Yes . . . yes . . . my lord.'

After catching his breath, he asked the Lord of Evil, 'What is the next step, my lord?'

Kali looked at the soldiers training on the ground in front of them. 'Are we ready for battle?'

Bhairava answered immediately, 'Yes, my lord. The Kalabakshakas have undergone rigorous training and are now ready for battle.'

'Well, that's great news. For as soon as we launch the attack, the Immortals and Kalki's allies will come at us non-stop. So we should be prepared for it. Are we prepared for it, Bhairava?'

'Yes, my lord,' he confirmed. Then, after a pause, he asked, 'How will they attack us, my lord? Aren't we hidden from their eyes?'

Kali smiled broadly, his face radiating evil glee. 'I will let them know of our location, Bhairava. After what I am about to do, they will most definitely seek me out. And I want to be done with them at the earliest, so that no one stands between me and world domination.'

Bhairava nodded.

After a moment's consideration, he asked, 'When do you intend to execute your attack, Lord Kali?'

'At the earliest possible moment.'

Kali got up and summoned the twins with a loud command. They had been supervising the combat training. Bhairava, too, got up and stood next to his lord as Koka and Vikoka quickly made their way to Kali and bowed to him.

'Tomorrow, we start preparing for the attack,' Kali addressed the three of them. 'Bhairava confirmed the locations of the weapons, so we will commence the attacks once our preparations are done.'

After a pause, he commanded, 'Koka and Vikoka, you will coordinate the attacks with me. After the attack, all three of you start the preparations for the battle. We can expect the allies of Kalki to visit us in a day or two after we strike. And we should be ready for it.'

Saying this, Kali dismissed them with a wave of his hand.

FORTY-SEVEN

The Stone Palace,
2026 CE

Avyay and Dweepa entered the dining hall, which now acted as the war room in the stone palace. She had teleported alongside her guardian only a minute ago, after an urgent call from Sadhika.

The Immortals were already present in the room and were facing the large monitors on display. Safeed, having been brought in by Hanuman, was taking care of the set-up; he had divided the monitors to display news feeds on one half and the people at EOK mansion—Sadhika, Acharya Sreedhar and Siddharth—on the other. He also connected the audio output to a couple of speakers.

'What's going on?' Avyay asked.

'There have been nuclear-bomb explosions all across the world,' Safeed said.

'What?!' her jaw dropped. She could feel her heart pound against her chest. 'Where?'

'Several locations across the globe—Asia, Africa, America . . .'

Dweepa, calm even in chaos, quickly grabbed a spare laptop and powered it up whilst also dialling someone on the phone.

'Casualties?' he asked, concerned, looking at the news feeds.

'The rescue operations have just begun, but as of this moment, the total, considering all the impacted areas, is reaching a thousand,' Vibhishana said, not looking away from the large monitors.

'That's too little, isn't it, given that you mentioned these are nuclear explosions? We have seen bombs with lesser power wipe away cities.'

Parashurama answered, 'The casualties are few indeed. Even we are wondering how that's possible. We also noticed that a few explosions were at remote locations—uninhabited villages. A few of them are at totally isolated locations like forests or large lakes.'

'Those are strange areas to target . . . And how do we know these are nuclear explosions?' Dweepa asked.

This time, Kripacharya answered, saying, 'The seismographic readings alerted the authorities to the explosions. The heat signatures of these places shot up exponentially and suddenly, without any warning. The intelligence agencies of the impacted nations sent out surveillance drones, and for all the areas covered until now, they reported back highlighting the presence of radioactive substances in the soil and air of these areas. The drones are still analysing the other areas of explosion. We have satellites scouring the earth for more such incidents. We should have more information in some time.'

Safeed typed away on his laptop for a few seconds, and then, directing everyone's attention to one of the screens, he announced, 'The list of areas is tabulated, along with casualties. As and when more information is available, I will update this.'

Everyone's eyes were fixed on the luminous screens. On display, they saw a table containing three columns—Place, Continent and Casualties. Most of the places on the list had zero casualties, and the rest had casualties ranging in the hundreds.

'Almost all the continents are covered, I see. This is an assault on a really large scale.' Avyay gasped. Everyone took in the information with disbelief.

'This is something unimaginable. I never thought I'd see this day . . .' Parashurama whispered softly.

Avyay nodded and pursed her lips. She turned to the monitor connected to the EOK mansion. 'What are we hearing from our sources? Who is behind this?'

'No idea yet, Avi. No one has come forward,' Sadhika replied.

'They are still getting a hold of the situation, assessing the next steps and getting rescue teams out,' Acharya Sreedhar said.

'How's the president?' she asked Siddharth.

'In the nuclear bunker. All world leaders are in their nuclear shelters,' he answered.

'We need to keep our eye on every piece of news . . . fresh blasts, attacks, anything irregular.'

'Yes. Our people are reaching out to every available outlet and seeking information,' Safeed replied.

Avyay turned to Sadhika. 'Get the list of the timings of the blasts. We need to figure out if they're coordinated attacks.'

Sadhika nodded and exited the screen.

'Siddharth,' she continued, 'check again with our government source and let's analyse all the intel they've received.'

Siddharth gave her a thumbs up and disappeared from the screen.

'Acharya and Sage Dweepa,' she spoke addressing the two of them, 'can you please get all the EOK people on standby across the world?'

They nodded and set out to work, but Acharya remained on the screen.

Vyasa, impressed with Avyay's quick thinking, asked her, 'What's the plan, Kalki?'

'No plan yet, Maharishi. Just trying to get everything in place in case we come up with a plan.'

She looked around and found the person she was looking for. Hanuman was seated in a chair. His face was supported by his palms, and his elbows were resting on his knees. His eyes were sad as he stared at the news footage.

'Hanumanji, can you please bring Dhanvantari here immediately?'

Leaping up from his seat, Hanuman nodded. He disappeared into thin air to get Dhanvantari, who had gone to the Himalayas a couple of days ago to collect valuable plants and meet his students and friends.

Avyay now turned to Safeed. 'Did you hear any word or gossip related to these attacks? Any whispers in your pub?'

Safeed immediately shook his head. 'If there was even a slight mention of something of this scale, I would have known.'

Avyay sighed and sat on a chair. She complained out loud, 'This doesn't make sense! How come there was just no intel? How can such a huge attack be pulled off without a single leak?'

'You're right. Let me check the dark web and see if there is something there,' said Safeed.

Just then, Sadhika appeared on the screen via her laptop. She spoke, 'Based on the reports, all the explosions happened roughly at the same time.'

'Also, no intel whatsoever at the moment from anyone,' said Siddharth, who had also joined back.

Suddenly, Avyay got up and rushed to the screens. Addressing the two of them, she spoke, 'Do we know how these bombs were deployed? Were these airdropped? If we find even one clue, that can help us.'

Just then Dweepa spoke, 'All EOK members around the world are on standby.'

And just as he finished, Hanuman appeared with Dhanvantari.

'That took quite some time in the era of teleportation,' Kripacharya said, stepping forward to help the medicine expert with his bag.

Dhanvantari bowed briefly to Kripacharya. 'Yes, I learnt what had happened. I was getting my notes on radioactive substances and their effects on nature and the human body, thus the delay,' he said.

'So what can we do now?' Parashurama asked.

'All we can do is make life less painful for the survivors,' said Dhanvantari. 'The science and intention behind any and every weapon is destruction—to bring about an irreversible change in the environment. I will need some time to consult my notes. By the way, do we know the number of people affected and the method of deployment?'

Parashurama nodded. 'As of this moment, the casualties are low. Totalling thousands. However, we are not yet aware of the method of deployment.'

'I see . . . Let me know when you hear something.' Saying this, the medicine expert walked to the back of the room.

'Okay . . . I have something,' Sadhika suddenly announced. 'The intel is that it all seems to be ground deployments.'

'At least we are getting some information now,' Acharya spoke. 'I'm going to receive satellite images of the blast sites in some minutes. I will send it to you all.'

'Thank you, Acharya,' Avyay responded.

'This is weird,' Siddharth suddenly muttered softly, his words coming through the speaker.

'What's weird?' Sadhika asked.

'According to the initial analysis reports I have, the area of impact seems to be quite small. Like a few hundred metres, I guess. The fireball radius is roughly 15 metres or so.'

'Fireball radius?' Avyay asked.

The weapons expert, Kripacharya, answered, 'When a nuclear bomb explodes, it creates four impact circles—and the circles are concentric. The centre one is called the fireball, which is the core of the explosion. Nothing survives inside this circle. After the initial explosion, there is a shock wave— this is the second circle. Generally, everything in the radius of the shock wave's influence is destroyed as well. The third is the radiation exposure. The fourth is the fallout, which happens when the radioactive particles in the air, due to the explosion, fall to the ground. The fallout area is determined by conditions like wind direction. Now, the size of the rings depends on the power of the bomb. The more powerful the bomb, the larger the circles' radii.'

Having explained this, Kripacharya turned to Siddharth and told him, 'If you are sure that the impact area is around 15 metres, then the bomb is a small one.'

Turning to Avyay, he added, 'And that should explain why the number of casualties is low. If the bomb is indeed that small, then the numbers won't increase exponentially. The impact area is less.'

Siddharth responded, 'I will check if the impact area is small with all the other explosions.'

Parashurama wondered out loud, 'If the intention was destruction, then the bombs would have been larger . . .'

'Maybe the perpetrators were facing some constraints in transporting large bombs, and they went for smaller explosives?' Bali interjected.

Sadhika replied, 'I will check transport around the sites.'

After a couple of minutes, Siddharth's voice came through, 'Confirmed, all the explosions are small-scale.'

Dweepa's update followed. 'Our sources in various governments are saying the same: casualty rate is low and the injured are being found and treated. Most of the blasts have occurred in remote, isolated locations.'

Safeed finally looked up from his laptop and announced, 'There's no word on the dark web either.'

'Something strange is happening,' Vibhishana said, scratching his chin.

A sudden silence filled the room. The former ruler of Lanka wasn't the only one who thought that way. The strangeness of the attacks worried everyone.

Acharya Sreedhar spoke up, breaking the quiet, 'Safeed, I have sent across the satellite images of the blast sites.'

Safeed gave him a thumbs up and clicked away on his console. After a couple of moments, the satellite images appeared on the screens.

Kripacharya moved closer to the screen, so did Dhanvantari and the others.

'I think so, we should move now,' said Dhanvantari to Avyay and Parashurama. 'Given that the areas are small, there's a good chance to contain the radiation.'

The two avatars exchanged a glance, chiming in with a 'Yes'.

Dhanvantari then turned to the large screen. 'Sage Dweepa and Acharya, can EOK spare some resources?'

'Of course,' Acharya responded. 'How many do you need?'

'As much as you can afford. And I am hoping we can avail resources on a global scale?'

Acharya nodded. Dweepa spoke, 'I will coordinate with you regarding the resources. It will help if I accompany you.'

'That will help,' confirmed Dhanvantari.

'I will help with teleportation,' said Hanuman. Looking at the medicine expert and the sage, he asked curiously, 'Where are we off to?'

'Well,' Dhanvantari said as he packed his belongings, 'First, we are off to a mountain to collect some herbs and shrubs. Then back to the Himalayas to set our remedy plans in motion.'

After the bag was packed, they disappeared into thin air.

'Now, here is something really out of place,' Kripacharya said.

Everyone's attention turned to the warrior-teacher. His eyes were focused on the map.

'What happened, Kripa?' Bali asked, stepping closer to him.

'Who, in their right mind, would blow a nuke in the middle of a barren desert?'

FORTY-EIGHT

'What?' Vyasa asked in disbelief.

Kripa pointed to a spot on the map. 'Right there. The Sahara. It's barren all around. It could be a testing site as well, but it doesn't seem to be a test.'

'It fits the pattern of the other remote explosions,' Safeed chipped in.

Avyay asked Sadhika and Siddharth, 'Can we confirm this isn't a test? And the blast size too?'

Siddharth came back in a moment and confirmed the occurrence of the blast. 'The blast is small-scale. Just like the others.'

Avyay held her head, frustrated. Closing her eyes, she took a deep breath before coming back to the present. 'It's a strange occurrence, so let's focus on the Sahara.'

Sadhika nodded. 'I can see this was also ground deployment. Let me access satellite footage of the moments before the blast.'

Suddenly, Safeed spoke up, 'So the bombs are small, so we are under the impression that the terrorists are under resource constraints, but if that were the case, they definitely wouldn't be blowing bombs in the middle of the desert, would they?'

Avyay thought for a second and asked Safeed, 'Was there any talk of deals—buying and selling of nuclear materials on the dark web?'

'Already checked. There's nothing.'

Avyay pursed her lips in thought. 'So they were either really secretive in terms of procuring the materials, or . . .'

She stopped abruptly, 'Acharya and Siddharth . . . Any chatter from our people in the governments about missing nuclear devices or materials from national inventories?'

They nodded and set to work.

Meanwhile, Safeed started clicking away on his keyboard, working on the satellite images that Acharya had sent earlier.

After a couple of moments, he splashed new images of maps on the screen. Pointing to the maps, he explained, 'I have highlighted the blast sites that have no possible casualties, like the desert site we saw, in blue. The others are marked in red. There are twenty sites in total, 17 are blue and 3 are in red.'

All of them looked at the map and saw that there were quite a number of blue dots on the screen, to everyone's surprise.

'Is this an attack gone wrong?' Parashurama thought out loud.

'The sites are spread across the globe, and the blasts are almost simultaneous, if not actually synchronized. These two facts indicate that this attack is something that was tightly coordinated. The odds of this going wrong . . .' Kripa left the words hanging in the air.

'There are also a couple of blue dots in the Indian Ocean and the Pacific Ocean,' Bali said, peering at the map.

'That's interesting. Let me see if there is any pattern in these random blue dots,' Safeed said, readying himself to work the keyboard again.

'I am sending across the blasts' radii to you now,' Siddharth told him.

'Ummm,' Acharya's voice came through the speaker. 'Well, we spoke with the sources, and at least a couple of them can confirm that there are one or two nukes missing from their armouries.'

'And the military didn't know? How . . . How many bombs have been taken, and what was the size of these weapons?' Kripa asked, shocked.

'Sending you the briefs now,' said Siddharth.

'Well, it is possible that these nukes were divided into smaller nukes. It may account for half of these devices used in these explosions,' said Kripa.

'We should await confirmation from the other sources as well,' Siddharth responded.

'Yes. Also,' Acharya spoke, 'it seems that there's no hard evidence of the theft. They are checking the surveillance footage, but as of this moment, they haven't found any records of anyone accessing their secured armoury vaults. It is impossible to take the bombs out without any personnel noticing it. As of yesterday's routine checks, the weapons were all accounted for.'

'That's strange,' Vyasa replied.

'Well, I found something even stranger,' Sadhika said as she accessed the monitor remotely, bringing up a video on the screen.

All eyes were on the video that played on the screen. It showed the barren land of the Sahara from the sky. Suddenly, a flash of bright light appeared in the vast emptiness and a mushroom cloud appeared. They could see the shock wave spreading across the sandy expanse.

'That's strange. Where's the bomb?' Kripa asked.

'Now, look at this,' Sadhika said as she rewound the footage. 'I've just slowed down the same video and have zoomed in the video frame.'

The sandy expanse was the same as before. However, this time they saw a small black dot appear on the sand out of the blue. The scene remained for a couple of moments before the dot exploded into a flash.

'What? How did that happen? Did it appear from underground?' Vibhishana asked.

'No. Not underground . . .' Parashurama answered. Turning to Sadhika on the monitor, he asked, 'Did it appear out of thin air?'

She nodded. 'Seems to be the case.'

'That would explain things then. It connects the dots . . . the pattern in the blue dots I was looking into,' Safeed said, now back on his screen. He pointed to the map he had put up on the monitor. 'So, I was looking to see if something connects these locations. I found nothing. But then, I found something else. Can you see the green dots?'

Siddharth read out the names of the places that the green dots indicated, 'Lhotse, Kangchenjunga, Ismoil Somoni Peak, Annapurna.'

'All of these are mountain peaks,' Bali said.

'Who sets off nuclear bombs on mountain peaks?' Vyasa asked, curious.

'The same person who sets them off in deserts and oceans,' quipped Sadhika.

Suddenly Parashurama spoke, 'What are those four green spots on the screen? Are there other mountain explosions?'

Safeed shook his head.

But just then, Sadhika interrupted, 'A couple of other locations show the same black dot appearing before the detonation. So safe to say, the bomb deployment is a mystery.'

'Well, not a mystery as such, I guess,' Safeed answered.

Everyone looked at Safeed with curious eyes.

'The bombs from the inventories vanished without a trace, and these explosives, perhaps smaller ones made from those missing bombs, made their appearance without a trace,' he said as he walked to the monitors.

'And I have found one thing that could probably connect all of these. But before that, I have just one question that needs answering—What's the intention behind these attacks? We have already agreed a while ago that it isn't destruction because heavily populated areas, government buildings or officials weren't targeted. Further, it seems that the bombs were taken apart and dismantled to make new, smaller bombs to target obscure and empty terrains. But why? Wouldn't it have been effective to topple governments or destroy cities? Maybe the bombs were deliberately made small in size to keep the casualties to a minimum. Having said that, we have seen explosions in remote, sparsely populated places too. What I am trying to say is that the message is clear: the attackers can attack at any place and any time. What remains to be found is the intention.'

'Seems like warning shots,' Vibhishana said.

'We have to get the whole list of bombs that were stolen, so we can tally how many nukes were used from that list,' Acharya mused.

Vyasa asked, 'The thing now is: What's the warning for? And more so, what do we need to do to stop future explosions?'

Safeed quietly said, 'Find the attacker and end him.'

Parashurama turned to Safeed suddenly, a movement so quick that it alarmed everyone.

'You know who it is, don't you? It's connected to the green dots—the mountain sites—isn't it?' the axe-wielder said.

Safeed walked back to his workstation and tapped a couple of keys. On one of the monitors, the table that showed the list of impacted places had a column added to it. *Blast Radius*.

'I think so, I can only propose my hypothesis. I think that these mountains were chosen on purpose. They are among the tallest, so they are easily noticeable. Unlike the deserts and the ocean, there is something that stands out in these mountains. What makes these mountains special is not their heights, but their blast radii. These mountains have the largest fireball radii compared to other sites.'

Tapping a key, he said, 'I have rearranged the list based on radii.'

On the table, the four mountains took their places on top, their impact radius ranging between fifty to thirty metres.

'Kangchenjunga, Annapurna, Lhotse, Ismoil Somoni,' Avyay said, reading the names listed in the table. 'What's special about them?'

'Well, look at their first letters—K, A, L, I.'

'*Kali*,' Parashurama whispered. 'He is calling out to us. He's calling us to fight him.'

A collective gasp escaped around the room.

Sadhika ventured, 'But . . . If we do that, we can be sure that we are walking into a trap.'

'While that may be the case, we know what's going to happen if we *don't* comply. More destruction, perhaps more powerful than this time,' Kripa opined.

A silence fell over the room. Avyay was deep in thought and Parashurama noticed this.

'What's on your mind?'

'There are two fronts here—one is the blasts themselves, which has resulted in the loss of innocent lives, and therefore requires medical attention. And then there's Kali, who is eager to meet us in battle. And so, we have to handle both these situations. Ummm,' she paused for a moment, 'I guess we'd need Hanuman in case we are heading into battle with Kali.'

'I'd suggest that you take Dweepa and Hanuman with you. I will work with Dhanvantari to aid the people. There are EOK people as well. So it's not like we are alone. Stopping Kali is a priority now,' Acharya Sreedhar responded.

'I'll stay back too. I will help Acharya with the coordination,' said Sadhika.

'Me too, I'll need to coordinate from here with the governments,' Siddharth piped up.

Avyay was a bit disappointed. 'But you are both warriors. Shouldn't you be out on the battlefield? You are among the people who can harness the power of Asi . . . just as we saw today.'

Siddharth smiled softly and said, 'If you are talking about people who can unlock Asi, then I should tell you that you have Hanuman and Lord Parashurama, in addition to yourself. Also, it's safe to assume that you will be wielding Asi the entire time. And about us being warriors, well, you have seasoned, immortal warriors with you. We are no match against them. They have seen battles, so they can guide you and fight better than us.'

Sadhika added, 'True. We will be of more help here with reports and stats. Plus, we know the workings of EOK and were trained in this for ages. Siddharth has to deal with all the governments and he has our president to liaise with.'

Lord Parashurama added, 'Good points. Strategically speaking, it makes sense.'

Vyasa, too, voiced his thoughts, saying, 'Like you said, Avyay, there are two fronts. We, the Immortals, can go up against Kali with all our might. But we need people on the other side too and Acharya Sreedhar, Sadhika, Siddharth and Dhanvantari will be better placed here.'

'Yes, I agree now. All valid points. Let's get to work now,' said Avyay, nodding.

With this out of the way, Kripacharya and Acharya Sreedhar set off to fetch Hanuman, Dhanvantari and Dweepa, who were in the mountains collecting herbs. Sadhika and Siddharth wished the warriors the best and set off on their tasks. Safeed readied his console to help the duo remotely with whatever support they might need.

A couple of minutes later, Dweepa and Hanuman appeared in front of them, along with Kripacharya. Parashurama brought them up to speed on the developments.

'I will get the EOK warriors ready,' said Dweepa without waiting further, teleporting with Kripacharya to assemble all the warriors at the stone palace.

After they went, Kalki asked the de-facto leader of the Immortals, 'Lord Parashurama, how do we go about searching for Kali?'

'Leave that to me,' the axe-wielder lord said.

He retired to a corner of the room, sat down and closed his eyes. The people left in the room looked at the Immortal close his eyes, and were about to turn away, leaving the avatar to his work, but Parashurama opened his eyes at that very moment. Everyone exchanged glances as the Immortal got up urgently.

'Did you find his hiding place so quickly, Lord Parashurama?' Vyasa asked, echoing everyone's thoughts.

'He is making no effort to hide himself, Maharishi Vyasa.'

FORTY-NINE

Avyay stood with the Immortals, taking in the vast land before them. They were standing at the edge of a large ground that was patched with grass and dry lands all over. They were hidden by a small forest beneath a hill. The place was surrounded by hills all around, and a strong wind made its presence felt across the flatland.

In the afternoon sun's white glow falling across the stretch of land, Avyay surveyed the flurry of activity about a hundred feet away from her. Kali's forces were taking positions, readying themselves for the battle. There were people hurrying in and out of a mammoth stone castle. Her hand instinctively went to Asi's hilt, the blade hanging from her waist. Vibhishana had returned it to her before they left for Kali's camp. She turned around and saw Dweepa and the others organizing the warriors under the cover of the trees. She noticed the sword forged by Krishna hanging from his waist. Sadhika had given the blade to him when they were staying at her place. She looked at Lord Parashurama on her left, who was also carefully studying the forces that were arraying themselves before them. To her right were Kripacharya and Maharishi Vyasa, with their hands stretched out before them. They were trying to break the invisible barrier that prevented them from proceeding to the ground. Kali had set up a formidable defence. But, thankfully, Kripacharya had found a spell in one of the ancient texts in his nephew's possession. So, he was able to work through the defences and bring down the barrier.

After a few restless minutes, Kripacharya and Vyasa gave an affirmative nod to the tenth avatar. As soon as they stepped back, they heard cries of war boom towards them from the enemy lines. A moment later, they all saw shapes of fire, water and earth missiles heading towards them. Avyay turned to Dweepa, who nodded back at her, letting her know that the warriors were ready.

The Immortals formed a line alongside her and started defending against the missiles approaching them.

Avyay raised Asi, which was ablaze with white luminescence now, and flung it at the enemy ranks. As soon as the blade left her fingers, Dweepa commanded the warriors to charge. Immediately, waves of Kalki's followers sped past the avatar and the Immortals, striking the enemy while defending the onslaughts. Asi slashed through enemy ranks, bathing itself in the blood of its victims. This sight brought a surge of courage in the allies of the avatar. As the two armies clashed, numbering in the thousands on each side, there were sounds of swords clanging and thuds and splashes and hisses. Avyay summoned the blade back to her outstretched palm. Dweepa reached her as she caught the sword.

Parashurama, who was studying the enemy lines, spoke with grave concern, 'I don't see Kali or any of his important warriors yet.'

Vyasa had noticed their absence too. He closed his eyes and opened it after a couple of moments, 'They are near the castle.'

'Is there any way to take him out?' Avyay asked. 'If we do so, then we will break his army for good.'

'Not at the moment, he has a protective barrier around him.'

'Ummmm . . .' Hanuman interrupted. 'We may have a problem.'

His eyes were transfixed on the battle in front of them. The Immortals, Kalki and Dweepa looked at the ape-god and followed his gaze. Dweepa's and Avyay's jaws fell open, while the brows of the Immortals shrunk in worry.

'I shouldn't be surprised, but I am,' Bali said. Vibhishana nodded, confirming that he thought the same.

On the battlefield, the enemies who had fallen to the attacks were now rising from the dead.

'Kali!' Avyay hissed. 'He is using the Mrit Sanjeevani mantra, isn't he?'

Vyasa grunted in affirmation.

After a couple of moments, the axe-wielder avatar spoke, 'We knew he possessed the power, so the only option we have left is to fight his soldiers until we get to him.'

He turned to Kripacharya, and instructed, 'Kripa, look for a way to bring Kali's barrier down. Also, let us know if the barrier moves with them.'

Kripa's eyes narrowed in doubt.

The sixth avatar rephrased his question, 'If we make him step out of the barrier, like provoke him to enter the battle, on to the ground, will he still be protected by the barrier?'

'Yes, the barrier will be around him always.'

The avatar grunted and turned to face the battlefield in front of him.

Taking his axe off the hook on his back, he told the fellow Immortal, 'Then find a way to break the barrier, Kripa. Sage Vyasa, you stay back with him and help him.'

Kripa and Vyasa nodded.

Parashurama armed himself with his blade and announced, 'Others, let's enter the fight and keep the energy of our warriors alive. We can help check the count of the enemies until we are able to bring down Kali.'

Everyone nodded and armed themselves. Avyay, Dweepa and Vibhishana took out their swords. Hanuman and Bali conjured *gadas* out of thin air. They swung the large maces gently, getting their wrists accustomed to the weight. After everyone exchanged a nod, they teleported into the heart of the fray.

Once they left, Kripa and Vyasa quickly rushed back to a particular tree a few feet behind them. Their eyes were set on a cloth bag resting on the ground. Vyasa settled down next to the tree while Kripa sat beside him, sifting through the contents of the satchel. He took out two stringed bundles of pages, and handed one bundle to Vyasa, while he kept the other one for himself.

'What are we looking for, Kripa?'

'Maharishi, we are looking for a way to destroy a barrier made of Kali's blood.'

The great sage's eyes widened with shock. 'What do you mean "made of his blood"?'

'Well, the barrier is made of powers I haven't seen before. They are dark. And I could sense that they are connected to his blood.'

'So, does this mean that as long as there is blood in his body, the protective shield will remain?'

Kripa nodded gravely, adding, 'Even a drop of it should keep it alive.'

Vyasa shook his head, his face contorted with worry. 'That's truly dark.'

After considering the situation for a moment, Kripa spoke, 'So we should look for ways to remove the blood from his body.'

'I don't think we can even prick him as long as the barrier exists, but yes, we can look at that option.'

'What else can we do?'

'Find a way to destroy the enchantment without depending on Kali or his blood,' Vyasa said, and he received a nod from Kripa in acknowledgement.

Vyasa, using telepathy, informed Parashurama about the barrier's power.

Soon after that, the two Immortals started flipping through the texts, trying to figure out how to remove the protective shield around the Lord of Evil.

FIFTY

When Kalki and her allies made their way into the fray, they were greeted by a furious war around them. The air was hot and smelled of iron. The ground was red and wet. There were cries of assault and wounds all around them.

Amidst the clangs of the swords, Avyay let Asi cut swiftly through the bodies of their enemies. Hanuman was swinging his mace around, sending enemies flying. Dweepa and Vibhishana also moved with dexterity, taking down enemies with their swords. Bali hammered his gada on the black-robed sorcerers. Parashurama deftly cut down enemy ranks with his axe. The avatar and her warriors had a single objective—kill everyone as many times as you can.

Parashurama, after receiving the information about the mystery of Kali's barrier, relayed the same to the others. And everyone's minds echoed the same thoughts: 'Why is Kali using a blood barrier? And how did he manage to conjure it? And how do we break it?'

After telling Kripa and Vyasa to keep searching for a solution, he brought his focus back to the fray.

Kali saw the movements of the two armies from the distance. Jana, Bhairava, Koka and Vikoka stood next to him. He saw that his people were falling. The ground in front of him was awash with red. Jana was about to join the fray when his lord stopped him by raising a hand. Jana stopped in his tracks and looked at his dying soldiers. After a couple of moments, the Lord of Evil waved his hand towards them. The warriors got up as if from a deep slumber. Jana watched in amazement as they all rejoined the battle as if nothing had happened to them. He bowed in gratitude to the lord and stepped back.

Even though the opposition was strong and thriving, the warriors of Kalki had killed the enemy's soldiers seven times over, and the exertion was catching up to her fellow warriors. Avyay noticed this. She signalled to all the EOK warriors to fall back while she coordinated with the Immortals on holding down the fort. The Chiranjeevi quickly formed a wall as the other soldiers stepped back to grab their breath. Avyay flung her divine blade at the evil warriors and she too caught her breath alongside Dweepa. Asi flew through the hordes of enemies, decimating them. The black-robed sorcerers fell around them, giving them a brief respite. Avyay clasped Asi on its return to her and looked at Kali and his aides standing at a distance.

After regaining their composure, the EOK warriors readied themselves for battle again. Avyay wielded Asi, but then stopped in her tracks. The Kalabakshakas weren't rising from the ground. She looked around at the Immortals, and their faces were contorted in confusion as well. But their stances were ready and alert. Then, everyone's eyes turned to the Lord of Evil, to check if he was around. To their surprise, their eyes found him walking in their direction, with his aides acting as his bodyguards.

As he neared them, he noticed the shining blade in Avyay's hand. 'I see that Asi has a new wielder, now that Kalki is dead.'

Parashurama, with his guard still up, smirked and replied, 'That's Kalki, Kali.'

Kali's head turned suddenly to Parashurama, his eyes narrowing, failing to conceal his surprise. The heads of his aides followed suit as well, their eyes settling on the axe-wielding avatar. His curved blade glinted in the bright sunlight, but the relish of having taken them by surprise was even more bright on the avatar's face.

Kali spoke in a cold rasp, 'I thought Kalki was dead. Didn't Ashwatthama kill him?'

'There are two Kalkis,' Dweepa said.

Kali's breath froze at learning of this deception. So did that of his aides.

Parashurama added further. 'Anirudh passed away, yes. But she . . .' he said, pointing towards Avyay, 'She was kept hidden and safe.'

The Lord of Evil looked at the tenth avatar, and she stared back at him.

Then, Kali broke the gaze, laughing. 'I am so glad to see you alive, Kalki. I am really happy.'

Creases of curiosity appeared on Avyay's face.

'Well, now you will get to see me destroy you, and this world of yours,' he said laughing. 'I was disappointed that Ashwatthama had killed Kalki as I was hoping to kill your world in front of you. But now that you are here, let me show you my powers . . .'

Saying this, Kali stepped back and closed his eyes and joined his hands in prayer. Everyone looked at the evil lord anxiously, including his own aides.

After a few moments, they heard a rumbling sound and the ground started shaking slightly. A dusty wind swept through the land. And the rumble grew louder. Then, at a distance, near the stone castle, a few whirlpools of winds started appearing, small and at a distance from each other.

Soon, from these dust swirls, three tall men emerged, decked in battle armour.

Vyasa, who was viewing these developments from afar, looked at the people through his mind's eye. And he relayed the identities of these men to his allies, saying, 'Narakasura, Hiranyakashipu and Hiranyaksha!'

On the bloody ground, the Immortals, Dweepa and Kalki exchanged worried glances. Then they all turned to the dust swirls behind the three warriors. The winds spread out and became a tempest, which soon withered down and revealed what it shielded in its core: scores of men dressed in battle gear stood as the last wisps of wind vanished around their feet.

'They are soldiers of these three demons,' Vyasa revealed, his fearful eyes meeting those of Kripa.

Parashurama looked around at his allies, and their worries were more pronounced. He glanced at the EOK warriors and saw despair in their eyes. Their faces already wore defeat. He looked back at the scores of resurrected warriors who now stood near the castle.

Avyay's gaze, having moved from the resuscitated demon lords and warriors, settled on the evil lord's face. His face wore a smile of victory and relish. He was enjoying the effect of his surprise on her allies' faces. She cursed Kali softly under her breath. But Parashurama heard her and this drew his attention to Kali and Kalki. He looked at the evil lord and saw that Kali hadn't yet resurrected the sorcerers lying dead on the ground. He then looked at the glowering blade in Avyay's hand. He called out to her, and she looked at him. Parashurama pointed his axe at Kali and told Kalki one word, urgently, 'Asi . . .'

Avyay didn't lose time thinking. She flung the divine blade towards the evil lord. *Asi can break through any evil barriers*, the axe-wielder and Avyay realized.

As soon as the sword left Kalki's hand, Kali instructed his aides, 'Arms.' His four aides quickly conjured four spears and armed themselves.

Asi flew through the air, and everyone's eyes followed the blade closely. The blade, its velocity lightning-fast, rushed to Kali and then stopped a foot away from him. A red translucent wall appeared in front of the sword, and it was stopping the sword from breaking in.

Parashurama wondered out loud, echoing the others' thoughts as well, 'How is the barrier able to stop Asi?'

Back at the tree, Kripa asked, 'How come Asi isn't able to penetrate the barrier? Kali is the supreme evil . . . Asi is designed to eliminate evil. What's preventing Asi from entering the barrier?'

'I don't know, Kripa,' Vyasa sighed, scratching his forehead. His eyes roamed helplessly over the spread of books in front of him and Kripa.

'I didn't know it was this hard to figure it out . . .' a voice spoke from the trees behind them. They heard the footsteps walking over the dry leaves, approaching them. Vyasa was about to get up to defend them, but Kripa kept his hand on his wrist. He looked down at the acharya's tight grasp and stopped, and then looked at his face. Kripa's face wore a look of horror.

'I know that voice . . . I have heard it before . . .' he gasped.

The next line uttered by the martial-arts trainer froze the sage's breath. 'And he had died that day . . .'

Kali, seeing the shocked expression on his enemies' faces, yelled to his armed aides, 'Now. Her.'

Kali's sorcerers flung their spears at Kalki, which travelled fast towards her.

Kali cast a glance at the divine sword a foot away from him. He was feeling proud of his sorcery, which had prevented Asi from killing him. He was appreciating the blazing, bejewelled blade when it zipped back and away from the barrier. His wide, surprised eyes followed the blade, as it headed towards the Kalki avatar. He saw a dark hand wrap around the hilt of the divine sword. Kali's eyes moved up to the wielder of Asi, expecting to see the face of the avatar. But upon recognizing the face of the wielder, he was shocked. The Immortals, Dweepa and Kalki's allies were struck by surprise as well, seeing the protective figure in front of Avyay, with the glowering Asi in his hand. They had all thought him to be dead.

A tall, dark, young man emerged from the trees and stood in front of Kripa and Vyasa. The newcomer's face wore a broad smile.

Kali turned to his followers, and even their eyes wore surprise. Bhairava looked at the figure in front of him, aghast. This man had died in front of his eyes. But there was no mistaking that he was alive now. And in the flesh. There was no mistaking the object his own eyes were looking at intently—the blue gem, afire, on the forehead of the Asi-wielder's face.

Vyasa and Kripa were in complete disbelief. The last time they had seen him, he was lying dead on the beach, having been struck by Asi.

'Anirudh,' the great rishi whispered.

'Is blood evil or good?' the young boy asked, flashing his dimpled smile.

FIFTY-ONE

With a smirk, Ashwatthama cut down the heads of the spears that were headed towards Avyay. The fragments of the lances fell down on the wet ground. Everyone in the vicinity stared at him with shock and disbelief.

'Kalki . . .' Kripacharya gasped, looking at the form of Anirudh standing in front of him.

The eyes of the two Immortals were wide with bewilderment. Not even in their wildest dreams had they imagined seeing the avatar in the flesh.

'You guys are looking as if you have seen a ghost,' Anirudh and Ashwatthama told the people around them.

'You were dead . . . How did you . . .' Vyasa's voice trailed away, as incomprehension took over.

Anirudh drew their attention, saying, 'How, why, what . . . All that for later. We have Kali to deal with at the moment.'

Bhairava took a step towards Ashwatthama. 'We saw you fall to your death . . . How are you alive? We thought they had cremated you,' he said, looking at Parashurama and his fellow Immortals.

Parashurama looked quizzically at Bhairava, and then turned to the son of Drona. 'I checked for life signs, but never found any. So, we thought you had died. Plus, my Parashu and Asi had been inflicted on you . . . How . . . are you . . . here?'

The words brought Kripa and Vyasa back to the moment. And they recalled Anirudh's question.

Kripa spoke, 'You asked if blood was evil or good. It is neither. Blood is life.'

Anirudh smiled hearing the answer, 'True. So can Asi actually destroy the blood barrier created by Kali?'

Vyasa and Kripa allowed the meaning of blood barrier to sink in, and shook their heads in response.

'So there's no way to defeat Kali?'

'There is. But it's not mentioned in any of these books,' Anirudh said, pointing to the books in front of him.

'And,' he added, 'we should get to the other Immortals soon. They need your help.'

As the two Immortals readied themselves, Anirudh informed them, 'There's one more surprise for you both.'

Ashwatthama laughed, and said to Parashurama, 'I never died. I hid my life signs.'

He turned to Bhairava and added, 'You saw me fall, but not to my death. After hitting the water and drowning, I teleported myself to another place.'

'Where to?' Parashurama and Bhairava asked in unison.

They both glared at each other and were about to turn to Ashwatthama when Kali screamed in despair.

'Enough of this!' he said and closed his eyes. He was seething in anger at the betrayal of his once-upon-a-time ally.

And a couple of moments later, the fallen soldiers around them started stirring to life.

Drauni sighed and told the evil lord, 'You shouldn't have. Now they have to die once more.'

Kali laughed coldly, 'They can die a hundred times and I will revive them. You needn't feel sorry about their deaths. As long as I am alive, they don't have any death.'

The black-robed sorcerers woke up and went and stood behind the evil lord in a disciplined manner. Drauni studied the soldiers and looked at Kali. He smiled and said, 'That's just it, isn't it? They will die again, and that's permanent death for them. Since you won't be alive to bring them back.'

Kali looked at Drauni intently and let a smile appear on his lips. 'Your divine Asi failed to reach me and you will all fail to reach me. Tell me, how do you suppose I will die?'

'All of us here may fail to reach you, but there's one person who can.'

'Who?' Kali asked, curious.

Turning to the Immortals and the allies of Kalki, Ashwatthama said, 'There's a surprise for you all.'

As soon as he finished speaking, three people appeared out of thin air next to Ashwatthama.

As soon as Vyasa and Kripa appeared on the ground, their eyes settled on the tall figure of the latter's nephew. Their eyes were wide with surprise. Ashwatthama bowed briefly to his uncle. In the meantime, everyone else was looking in disbelief at the third person who had materialized in front of them. The boy they previously knew as the Kalki avatar stood before them, taking in the battlefield around him—his eyes focused on Kali, his aides and his soldiers. Dweepa and Avyay were too shocked to move or utter a word. Parashurama and the Immortals couldn't believe their eyes.

How could someone return from death? their thoughts agonized alike.

Kali was stunned to see a person in Krishna's likeness stand in front of him. He had an inkling of who this person could be. And Bali's gasp of 'Kalki' confirmed his suspicion. The demon lord's blood raged.

'I thought he was dead!' he screamed at Kalaguru.

'He . . . he . . . he had died,' Bhairava stammered. 'Kalarakshasa had himself killed him. I saw it with my own eyes.'

Kali yelled. 'And it's this same Kalarakshasa, who you told me had died, now standing before us, isn't he?' His lethal tone sent shivers down the spines of his aides.

'My lord . . .' Kalaguru whimpered.

'Shut up, Bhairava!' Kali lashed out. 'Two people who were supposed to be dead are standing in front of me—very much alive. So either I have never met someone as mistaken as you and your people before, or these two people are much more powerful than I thought.'

Ashwatthama turned away from his uncle and moved towards Anirudh. Swinging Asi, he asked, 'Well, how do you want to go about it?'

'I am fighting Kali. You guys decide about the rest,' he said and started heading towards Kali.

'It is a blood barrier! Even Asi wasn't able to pierce it . . .' Parashurama warned him.

'How will you get through that wall when Asi couldn't, Kalki?' Avyay whispered, shocked at the events around her.

Anirudh stopped and turned to them. He studied the faces of the Immortals, Dweepa and Avyay. With a smile, he revealed, 'I can get through anything and everything.'

'Also, I am not Kalki, you are,' he said, looking at Avyay.

Without waiting for any questions or answers, he turned to face Kali. The devil's confident demeanour which he had worn with arrogance a couple of minutes ago, was now totally shattered. He took a step back, in fear, when he saw the young man walking towards him. He commanded Koka and Vikoka to attack him, and the twins hailed a storm of fiery projectiles at the boy.

In response, Anirudh only spared a casual glance at the torrent of missiles, and they disintegrated into dust particles. Everyone was taken aback and shocked by the disappearance of the flaming arrows. Anirudh walked casually towards Kali and stood in front of the blood barrier.

Kali was sweating now, his lips chanting fervently, trying to keep the enchantment strong. With a smile, the young man stepped through the barrier and stood in front of the Lord of Evil. Anirudh's passing through the blood barrier stunned everyone on the field, friends and foes alike. If that weren't enough, his next act made all of them anxious. The boy placed his hand on Kali's head and they both disappeared.

FIFTY-TWO

Ashwatthama was perturbed by the sudden disappearance of Anirudh and Kali, but he quickly composed himself and looked at the sorcerers in front of him. While others were still processing the events that had just transpired, Jana regained himself and rushed, enraged, towards Ashwatthama with his sword drawn. Ashwatthama smirked as Jana came in closer. The smile infuriated Jana further and he swung his blade at his opponent. Drauni sidestepped the attack and drove the glowing Asi through Jana, vanquishing his opponent. The cry of death erupted from Jana's mouth and brought everyone's attention back to the battleground. As Jana fell to the ground, Ashwatthama blocked a fireball headed towards his face. He saw that it was Bhairava who had launched the attack at him.

'I am taking Bhairava,' he told the Immortals. 'You decide the strategy of the rest of the battle.'

He returned Asi to Avyay and conjured a sword out of thin air for himself. Then, looking at the still body of Jana on the ground beside his feet, he announced to the allies of Kalki, 'He is dead.'

'Of course, he would be! You killed him,' Vibhishana commented.

'He is *still* dead. Kali isn't here, so neither are his powers of resurrection,' Drauni whispered.

Parashurama nodded and quickly surveyed the ground, taking in his enemies and friends alike. 'Everyone, now listen,' he stated, 'Avyay and I will go after the remaining two aides of Kali, and Ashwatthama will fight Bhairava. Kripa, you fight Narakasura. Bali, you will fight Hiranyakashipu, Hanuman, engage Hiranyaksha. Now, Dweepa, Vibhishana and Vyasa, the three of you can lead our soldiers and attack theirs.'

The allies of Kalki bowed and quickly proceeded to dispense their duties. Parashurama and Avyay stood on either side of Ashwatthama, their weapons at the ready.

Ashwatthama revealed, 'The two aides you are both taking on, they are Koka and Vikoka. Twin brothers. Excellent fighting prowess and incredible resistance to pain.'

'Will they stand against Asi as well?' Avyay asked with a smirk.

'They will stand really well against Asi,' the former leader of Kalabakshakas answered, which evoked a shadow of horror in Avyay.

'Let me guess,' Parashurama spoke, 'You trained them to withstand Asi, didn't you?'

Ashwatthama allowed a smile of pride come on his face, as he divulged another piece of information, 'And your battleaxe too.'

On the other side, Narakasura, Hiranyakashpu and Hiranyaksha, and their band of soldiers, had moved forward to join the ranks of the black-robed sorcerers. The disappearance of Kali had brought the soldiers to the brink of chaos, but Bhairava had stepped up to take the leadership mantle. He now commanded the evil army.

The Immortals and Dweepa assembled themselves in front of their soldiers. Kripacharya, the expert on weapons, quickly analysed the swarm of soldiers headed their way. He delivered the instructions urgently, 'Hanuman, Bali and I will tackle the three demons. The foot soldiers are of two types here—sorcerers and the resurrected soldiers of the three demon kings. These ancient fighters don't seem to know sorcery, so they should be easier to defeat. Dweepa and Vibhishana, you take on the sorcerers. Vyasa Maharishi, you take on the soldiers. Our warriors can take on whoever is conveniently closer.'

Saying this, Kripa created a bow and a quiver from thin air and handed them to Vyasa, who accepted the weapons with a respectful nod.

'Take a vantage point?' Kripa suggested.

'Of course,' Vyasa agreed with a smile. He loaded an arrow in the bow and closed his eyes. Suddenly, he elevated himself into the air, standing on an invisible platform. Vyasa's lips moved as he chanted a spell. He opened his eyes, and from his position, he shot an arrow towards the approaching enemy line. The attack had commenced.

Dweepa and Vibhishana rallied the EOK soldiers behind them and instructed them to direct their attacks on the foot soldiers. As soon as Vyasa's arrow left the bow, Hanuman, Bali and Kripa rushed to meet their foes—the demons.

One of the enemy soldiers saw that Vyasa's arrow was headed towards him. He was about to raise his shield to protect himself, but he froze when something else happened. The projectile replicated itself into a dozen more arrows and rained down on his fellows. Before he could react, the sage's arrow caught him in his throat and he collapsed.

As the arrows fell from the sky, Kripa engaged Narakasura in a battle, their swords clanging against each other. Bali was heaving his mace against Hiranyakashyapu's arm, while Hanuman was in a fist fight with Hiranyaksha. The three demons were formidable fighters, and they were giving their best efforts to vanquish the Immortals.

As he delivered a cut to the demon's torso, Kripa communicated telepathically with his fellow Immortals, 'I hope when we end them, they remain so for good.'

Vyasa responded, 'They will. As long as Kali is away from here, they will remain dead.'

Hanuman asked, throwing Hiranyaksha down, 'What will happen when he returns?'

Bali swung his mace at Hiranyakashipu and took a moment's breather, replying, 'I don't even want to think about that.'

A Kalabakshaka, seeing Vyasa rain arrows from his elevated position, launched a fiery serpent at the great sage. But as soon as he launched it, it turned into water and lashed back on him. The sorcerer looked stunned by the sudden turn of events, and then saw the reason for it.

Dweepa looked at the attacker. As he impaled the sorcerer with a spear made of stone, Dweepa replied to Bali, 'Same here, King Bali. I hope Kalki is successful in ending Kali's menace.'

Vibhishana pulled his sword out of the body of one of the soldiers and shot an icy blade at a sorcerer who had gained the upper hand on an EOK warrior. He spoke, 'Well, Kalki, or *whoever he is*, will be successful. If he got past the blood barrier, then I am reasonably confident that he will deal with Kali too.'

'*Whoever he is*, indeed,' Vyasa responded to the group.

'Who is he, if not Kalki?' Hanuman asked.

There was a pause in their conversation as they dealt a series of attacks on their opponents, and then Vyasa answered, 'I don't know, to be honest.'

Dweepa, allowing himself to be emotional about Anirudh's reappearance, asked, 'Would he come back after vanquishing Kali? Or would he depart from there, having realized the purpose of his avatar?'

'I don't know, Dweepa,' Vyasa answered. 'But I hope he does come back.'

'Until then, let's do our duty and keep our focus on our enemies,' Kripa spoke.

Everyone agreed, resuming their attacks with a renewed fervour.

FIFTY-THREE

*W*hy the hell did you have to train them so well? Avyay groaned telepathically, after having been thrown to the ground by Vikoka. Her flesh bore numerous scars inflicted by the Kalabakshaka's sword.

I swear, and these twins don't seem to tire at all, Parashurama sighed, exhausted, as he blocked Koka's sword from cracking his skull.

Kalki got up, ready to duel her enemy again. Ashwatthama, who was engaged in a fight to the death, managed to respond amid grunts of victory and pain, *What you are experiencing is a result of training them every day for eighteen hours.*

Non-stop, he added.

When she heard the afterthought, she involuntarily cursed. She thrust Asi against her enemy's torso, and having found a gap, she slashed.

Taking a momentary break while her enemy recovered, she screamed telepathically, *Eighteen hours? Are you out of your mind?*

Ashwatthama smirked as he dodged a slash from Bhairava and delivered a quick swish in return. *You would do the same if you knew that your enemies are the powerful Chiranjeevi. That's why I had to train them well. Besides, they wouldn't settle for less, and I didn't have any qualms in training them then. Also, if the Chiranjeevi were to disrupt the plans laid by Krishna by obstructing me in some manner, I had to be sure that I was able to overcome them and see to the completion of those goals.*

Parashurama slashed his axe against Koka's forearm, while he took a lick of his opponent's blade on his stomach.

Avyay, still chagrined by the strength of the brothers, spoke up, *I don't know if I will be able to combat them for eighteen hours.*

Well, we have to give it our best, Kalki, Parashurama encouraged her.

Avyay grunted and started fighting fiercely against her opponent. Asi glowered, reflecting her ferocity.

When will this carnage end? With Kali's death? she asked, as she delivered a cut across Vikoka's cheek.

Parashurama ducked a swing from Koka's sword, and he slashed his curved blade across the thighs of the sorcerer. *I am not sure. Well, with Kali's death, they will stop being resurrected. So if we kill them all, the carnage will end with Kali's death.*

Ashwatthama cut his sword across Bhairava's belly, and replied, *Let's hope Anirudh gets it done.*

As the sky turned a shade of amber indicating the onset of evening, the warriors of Kali were still putting up a strong battle. On the other side, Kalki and the two Chiranjeevi warriors mounted an equally formidable opposition. Both the sides were severely hurt, but they kept the fight alive through pure grit and determination. The ground around these fighters was scorched and wet and upturned. The three aides of Kali were severely injured, but they had wounded Kalki and the two Immortals equally.

I agree, I have trained them really well, Ashwatthama sighed, having dodged a rope of fire that Bhairava had furiously set his way. *I am proud of them*, he added.

Parashurama and Avyay were busy defending themselves from the determined onslaught of the twins, so all they could manage in response was a grunt.

In another part of the ground, the forces of the Immortals and EOK warriors were engaged in a fierce battle with the demons and Kali's soldiers. Their battle was a lethal mixture of weaponry and sorcery. But eliminating a warrior was a tough job since they kept adapting to the attacks heaped upon them. The field was littered with arrows, spears, swords, blood and gore, fires, puddles and rocks. The corpses of fallen warriors lay unattended amid the chaos of the war.

Where is Anirudh? Avyay asked as she blocked Vikoka's sword jab to her abdomen.

Parashurama, inflicting a fiery whip on the forearm of Koka and singeing him, replied, *I don't know. But wherever he is, he is doing a good job of keeping Kali at bay.*

I agree, Ashwatthama affirmed.

As he clashed blades with Kalaguru, Drauni asked him, 'Bhairava, your lord Kali has been missing for a while now. In all probability, he is dead. What are you all even fighting for?'

Bhairava, as he carefully delivered cuts to the former leader of Kalabakshakas, replied, with a smirk, 'Come to think of it, even Kalki has been missing for a while. In all probability, he is dead. What are *you* all fighting for?'

This conversation was audible to Vikoka, Koka Parashurama and Avyay.

'Anirudh is missing,' Parashurama replied. 'Kalki is right here. And our aim has been to stop and eliminate Kali, which is what we intend to do until the end.'

'And we are fighting to remove Kalki and all the allies of Kalki, which is Lord Kali's command,' Koka replied, delivering a pointed thrust to Parashurama's waist.

Vikoka took a pause, one that was followed by his fellow sorcerers as well. He spoke, 'And as long as Kalki is alive, we haven't fulfilled our lord's command.'

The aides of the Lord of Evil exchanged glances. Then, without any warning, they unleashed a frenzy of attacks upon Avyay, Parashurama and Ashwatthama. The trio were putting up a tough resistance, but they were on the verge of breaking under the fervent assault of the sorcerers. The Kalabakshakas were fighting like spirits possessed.

'For Kali!' Bhairava yelled.

'For Kali!' the twins echoed back.

With that, the three Kalabakshakas launched a powerful assault of sorcery and physical combat on their opponents. Kalki and her allies were staggering back, beaten. Ashwatthama had never seen such martial skills before, and he recognized it to be Kali's teaching. He and the two avatars of Vishnu tried to maintain their resistance, but they broke soon.

They were now beaten and on their knees. Their bodies were reeling from the fatigue of the long battle, the strenuous exertion from the sudden powerful assault from the three Kalabakshakas, and their wounds.

Before they could defend themselves, the three black-robed sorcerers heaved their swords and swung at them.

FIFTY-FOUR

Kali looked at the white space around him. It was a large square-shaped room, aglow with white light. He was seated on a peacock-blue couch. The young boy stood at a distance, facing him.

'Where are we?' the Lord of Evil asked.

'Somewhere we are guaranteed to be left alone.'

'And why do you want to be left alone?'

'Because I want to talk.'

Kali squinted his eyes and asked the boy, 'Talk?'

His companion nodded.

'There's no talking, Kalki. I am going to finish you.'

'I have already mentioned that I am not Kalki. And why do you want to kill me?'

'How are you not Kalki? Your resemblance to Krishna is just too coincidental for you to not be Kalki . . .'

'I agree, I do look like Krishna, and I *was* Kalki. And I continued to use my former physical appearance.'

'Right, you have returned from death, miraculously.'

'So have you.'

Kali glared at him and replied, 'I have returned to the same body. But from the looks of it, though you are in your original body, but you have also restored it to health. Unless you have hidden the gaping hole that Asi gave you.'

'Well, I created this body.'

'And that's the difference! I need a body to host me, whereas you can create one.'

Anirudh remained quiet, smiling at the evil lord.

Kali looked at the avatar, and asked, 'How did you come back from the dead? I mean, where did you get the knowledge to create bodies?'

'I am the creator.'

'Of course you are,' Kali said, grimly.

Anirudh brought the conversation back to his question. 'Why do you want to kill me?'

'I want to kill you and the Immortals, and all your allies, because you all stand between me and my dream of dominating this world.'

Anirudh paced around with slow steps.

'And what would you do if you dominated the world?'

'What do you mean by that? If I dominated the world, then I would have everything at my disposal. I would have power—everyone would serve me. I would have command over the whole world and enforce my rules over the people. I would have all the money and gold. And,' he looked up, 'I would destroy the concept of God. I would become God, and all of humanity my slave.'

'Okay. So be it,' Anirudh said.

Kali squinted. 'What do you mean by "so be it"?'

'I have given you the world to dominate, Kali. Look around.'

When Kali looked around, he was taken aback. The white room was gone. He was in a large palatial palace, with people attending to him. He was seated on a large, plush throne made of gold, with the cushions made of the softest velvet. His clothes were made of the finest silks. Struck with awe, he stood up and started walking around the room. All the furniture and utensils were made of gold and expensive metals, studded with expensive jewels. He saw stacks of gold bricks lined along the walls. He took a couple of them in his hand to appreciate their beauty. As he did so, he heard a man telling him the accounts. He was stunned to hear it run into thousands of trillions. He kept the gold bars back on the stack. Another man gently informed him that it was time for a meeting of his, with heads of various nations who served him now.

Kali's feeling of surprise now transformed into doubt. He looked around, searching for Kalki, and his eyes rested on the swarthy figure standing by the window behind him.

He quickly walked to the window.

'This can't be true,' he told Anirudh.

Anirudh smiled at the statement.

'Why not? Touch your clothes. Don't they feel real?'

Kali ran his fingers over the fabric on his forearm. 'Well, it does feel real,' he said, unconvinced.

'Everything in this room, you touched them, right? They are all real, Kali.'

Kali looked around the room, wondering about the veracity of Anirudh's words.

He looked at the windowpane and touched it. The glass felt real. He found that they were on the top floor, and his window overlooked a beach. The sun glimmered over the white, frothy waves of the sea.

Kali, still not convinced, voiced his thoughts, 'All this is an illusion. You have created all this, to fool me. This is not reality.'

But Anirudh just turned to the assistant and told him to initiate the meeting.

'Are you sure you don't want to take this meeting?'

Before Kali could respond, a dozen holographic figures appeared in the room.

'My lord,' the attendant announced, while bowing to Kali, 'the heads of all the countries.'

The rulers bowed to Kali and greeted him. Kali blinked, unable to comprehend the situation. He beckoned to the organizer. As the young man stepped up close to him, Kali asked him, 'Why are they meeting me?'

Before the organizer could answer, Anirudh answered, 'Why, because you dominate the world.'

The attendant nodded. 'You have to direct them on trade rules between nations, loan disbursements, allocation of natural resources—these are on the agenda for now. The rest can be scheduled for later today, or tomorrow.'

'What? Do I have these meetings daily?'

'Yes, my lord.'

'Why am I deciding all this . . . taxation rules and allocation of resources?'

Now Kalki replied, 'Because you are their boss. You are the supreme ruler. And humanity is your slave, just like you wanted.'

The Lord of Evil turned and looked at the avatar with incredulity written on his face.

'But these are decisions to be taken by humans! Not me—this work is beneath me!'

'The entire human civilization is beneath you, Kali. So they look up to you. They want you to make the decisions, since you are their *lord* now.'

Kali grit his teeth as frustration rumbled through his veins.

He turned to the organizer and asked him, 'What about the loans? Is it because I am the richest?'

'Yes, my lord.'

'What? Don't they have any financial system in place? Can't their banks give them loans?'

'They cannot, my lord. Their monies are currently allocated in various public schemes.'

'If they have monies, what are they asking me for?'

'Well, my lord . . .' the attendant hesitated.

Anirudh came to the aide's rescue, 'They need funds to rebuild their places of worship . . . with you as their deity.'

'What?!' Kali shrieked in awe.

'Yeah. You abolished all gods and established yourself as the sole supreme power of the world. And they need money to make you their god, since their current financial commitments won't allow them to distribute funds to all the cities in their respective nations to renovate their places of worship. If they divert their funds to the cause of rebuilding structures, then they would be depriving their people of some much-needed financial help. And doing so would make the masses unhappy, and they might resent you. And the leaders don't want that to happen, since they want to keep you happy. You are the most powerful and richest person in the world, you are *the* god. They fear that the resentment of the people would infuriate you and you would destroy nations in one swift strike.'

Kali turned to the attendant, exasperated, and asked him, 'Can't they postpone the renovations?'

'No,' Anirudh answered, 'These places of worship are all empty now, and they need a deity. People need a figure to express their faith to, an image to place their hopes on.'

'So,' Kali asked, irritated, 'I should sponsor my own temples?'

Anirudh shrugged. Kali looked at the attendant and the roomful of leaders in front of him. Then, he turned to the dark-skinned young man and stepped close to him. 'All this is fake, isn't it?'

'You saw and felt everything for yourself—how is anything here fake? I gave you what you desired, aren't you happy?'

Kali looked around the vast, rich room. It was real, everything in the room was real. But it didn't sink in, it all felt surreal.

Turning to Anirudh, he said, 'It's all just an illusion.'

Anirudh smiled and asked, 'Well, isn't everything an illusion, Kali?'

FIFTY-FIVE

'So you admit it! It *is* an illusion,' Kali announced triumphantly.

'Well, yes and no.'

Kali looked around and saw that he was seated on the peacock-blue couch. They were back in the white room.

'Of course, it was an illusion,' Kali said accusingly. 'I was not in a meeting with any leaders, and the gold was all fake as well. And you staged the whole thing. You told me yourself that everything is an illusion.'

'Kali, I agree I said that. And it is true, everything is an illusion. The gold, the silks, the people, the power—all that you saw was real, but an illusion as well.'

'What do you mean?'

'Well, tell me this, you felt the gold, the silks, everything. They were real, so you felt it. But think carefully and tell me if you felt happy even for a single moment? I had given you everything, but did you feel complete? Did you feel fulfilled?'

'If all that was real, then you never even gave me a chance to enjoy them fully.'

Anirudh smiled and said, 'Okay. So be it. I am granting you your desires again. And when you feel like you are fulfilled, just utter my name, and you will be back here.'

Kali looked at the avatar and nodded hesitantly. And he disappeared from the white room. Anirudh conjured another couch, black this time, and sat on it, waiting patiently.

After a few minutes, he heard his name uttered. Following that, Kali was back in the white-walled chamber, sitting on the blue-hued couch in front of the boy.

Kali stared wide-eyed at the room, almost in disbelief that he had really returned.

'I am back here?' he wondered out loud, looking around in disbelief.

'So, how was your life? You finally lived the life that you wanted. For fifty years, right? You had everything you wanted. I hope you enjoyed life to the fullest.'

'Well, I did enjoy life. But then, it got boring. There was nothing left to enjoy as such.'

Anirudh smiled and asked, 'For fifty years you lived your life—the life that you desired. And you got bored?'

Kali scowled and told him, 'Well, even fifty years is a miracle!'

'Why did it get boring, Kali? You had everything you wanted,' Anirudh asked with a serious expression on his face.

Kali was hesitant to answer. Partly because he didn't know the answer himself, and partly because he wasn't sure he wanted to answer the avatar. Then he looked at the earnestness on the boy's face.

Kali spoke to himself, wondering, 'He is genuinely interested in understanding me. Kalki kept his word of giving me the life I wanted to live. I have nothing to lose by sharing my thoughts with him, so I might as well tell him. Let's see what his take on things are . . .'

He replied to the waiting avatar, 'Well, I don't know! There was just no joy left in ruling the world. Everything

I did, and kept doing—gambling, drinking, entertaining myself—I just had enough of it. I wanted something more.'

'What more do you want? Do you know?'

'No.'

'So you had all that you wanted, yet you found no fulfilment . . .'

'Well . . . They were gratifying, sure. But they didn't fulfil me.'

'Hmmm . . . why do you think that happened?'

Kali simply shrugged his shoulders.

Anirudh conjured a bar of gold and tossed it towards Kali. 'Does it fulfil you?'

Kali, catching the brick, looked at it distastefully. 'No.'

As he looked at the brick, its yellow gleam grew larger, filling his vision.

He no longer felt the brick in his hand. He felt himself falling into the growing luminescence. He closed his eyes. After a moment, he felt his mouth stretch forward into a distance and suck on something. Sweet liquid gushed into his mouth and he drank it. He opened his eyes and saw that there was a flower in front of him, and his mouth was a long stick-like thing. He retracted his proboscis and stepped back from the centre of the yellow flower. Then, he launched his bee-body off the flower and flew to another. He saw the bee taking off from his body, and he felt a breeze kiss his petals. He flew among the flowers in the forest, gracing all of them with his lively touch, before he dissolved himself in a passing brook. Encouraged by the force of the water on his back, he gushed forth on to the flowers and made his way into the porous soil, to feed the plants in the soil. He felt his earthy body get drenched as he soaked the water to nourish the plants and seeds in his womb, and he took in the sunlight to feed himself. Burning bright as the sun, he spread himself like a warm fire in the sky, showing the world to a crow flying in his light. He flapped his wings effortfully, trying to keep himself flying. His throat was parched. He had scoured and crossed a whole city but found no water. He was thirsty and longed for water. He came across the forest as he flew. He tilted his head and looked down at the flowing brook. With a caw, he swooped down and sat on a rock by the brook. He hopped gently over to the stream and lowered his beak into the flowing water. And he drank his fill of water and quenched his thirst.

When Kali opened his eyes, the gold brick was gone. He felt his cheeks wet and tears still dripped down his eyes. He could feel the fresh water of the brook inside his mouth. Anirudh was seated in front of him, looking at him.

'I was there . . . in everything in the world,' he whispered, overwhelmed with joy.

'You *are* there in everything in this world, Kali.'

Kali slowly nodded, bringing his hands together.

'Are you fulfilled now?'

'I am. Very much so,' Kali said, shivering with joy.

He bowed to the young man. 'How did you make me do that? How was I there in everything?'

'Because I helped you realize that fact.'

'What do you mean?'

'Everything, and everyone, in the world is connected with divine energy, Kali. *Everything*, *everyone*. But they are not aware of it. I made you aware of it now.'

'But why?'

'Because I wanted to break the illusions you held dear in your heart.'

Kali stared at him, his eyes now dry, but his cheeks were still stained.

Anirudh continued, 'You had these grand illusions that money will fulfil you, that gold will give you all that you want, that a life of power will gratify you and fulfil you. But did it?

'And that's the illusion I wanted to break. All these material things you sought—those are illusions that keep you occupied, that hide the truth from you. You, or any other person for that matter, will never find fulfilment in these material pleasures. You may find joy, but you will always want more. The true essence of life—it lies in understanding that everything in nature is connected at a level that is not tangible or experienced by the five senses. Mankind is living in a world that is distorted by these material pleasures, and they have thus pushed themselves away from the core truth, that all are one. You sought all material possessions, but they never fulfilled you. Not even after fifty years! They never brought tears of joy in your eyes. But when I showed you the truth, you found the happiness and the fulfilment you sought. That's because I took you past the veil of maya, the illusion, and showed you the truth—the truth that you are one with the world. And it takes sages years to discover this truth.'

Kali was smiling with joy as he asked, 'Why did you show me this truth? If sages take years of penance to learn, why did you show it to me so easily?'

'You have lived millennia in lust for power and wealth and the pleasures of life. Even when you were sentenced by Parikshit, you were confined to places of material happiness, and you still wanted more of it. So I thought to take you to the pinnacle of your desires and let you feel the incompleteness first. And then, I showed you the truth, which fulfilled you. So, in a way, you have lived a life of penance yourself.'

Kali considered the words he'd just heard.

Anirudh added, 'Also, it was time for you to learn the truth.'

Kali smiled and asked, 'And I guess it was also time to stop me?'

The young boy smiled and said, 'Have you stopped? I thought you had said that you can never be stopped—for a soul never dies.'

'Of course I have stopped. I don't want to go back to the material world. I want nothing of the maya you created.'

'Then what do you want to do?'

'I don't know. I would have asked for death. But death is of the body, not of the soul. How will I attain moksha—my release?'

'What is moksha?'

'The release from the cycle of birth and death, right?'

'Well, yes and no. Moksha means freedom from the material pleasures of the world. Understanding that you are a part of the world, connected to everything—that's freedom. Then life or death doesn't matter. Take Vishnu as an example. He took birth as Parashurama, Rama, Krishna and Kalki. These many births—does that mean he is not a liberated soul?'

Kali replied, 'Of course he is a liberated soul.'

Anirudh smiled and said, 'That's moksha. Knowing that you are a part of the world and serving the greater good in whatever way you can, whether it means taking birth once or ten times.'

'So even death won't grant me moksha?'

'No. But you have already gained moksha, Kali.'

'You mean the truth that I saw—I am one with the universe?'

'Yes. With that knowledge, you have freed yourself from the material world. You don't long to go back there.'

'Then what do I do?'

'Whatever you want to do.'

'Then, what does it mean to be one with the universe?'

Anirudh conjured a white table in front of Kali, and made a few brown wiry objects suspend above it.

'What are these?' the young boy asked.

'They look like roots of some plant or tree.'

'Correct,' Anirudh said. Then, he conjured a miniature tree above the distended roots.

'Do the roots belong to this tree?'

Kali compared the roots of the tree with the ones hanging freely.

'Yes, they are the same. But where are you headed with this conversation?'

Anirudh raised his hand to signal patience. 'Now, you think these roots are separate, right?'

Kali looked at the roots freely hanging and nodded his head.

'But they aren't.' Saying this, Anirudh waved his hand once, and an invisible veil fell away. The separate threads revealed themselves to be connected to the tree.

The young man explained, 'Those separate roots— that's what you think you are, that's what the human race thinks it is. But we are all connected to that tree. Tell me, would it be possible for those separate roots to even exist if it wasn't for the tree? That tree is the universe. Humans are always connected to that tree. All are one with the universe, at all times. You exist because of the universe. But that's not the end of things. Just like the roots nourish the tree, humans help nourish the world, to make it a better place to live in.'

Kali nodded. 'What if the roots stop nourishing the tree?'

'Well, the roots will die in that case. And the tree will produce new roots to nourish itself. Remember, a root is a part of the tree, it is one with the tree, but it is not the tree itself. Being a root, it's a selfless life. You absorb the nutrition and food for the tree and pass it to the tree. The tree will consume it and pass the life to its entirety. A root, in this way, lives in service of the tree, and helps all the other roots, leaves, fruits with its nutrition. The same is true for humanity. Humans should selflessly serve the earth, and then every living being would be taken care of.'

Kali smiled and said, '*Karmany evadhikaras te ma phalesu kadacana.*'

'You have the right to do your duty, but you are not entitled to the fruits of your action,' Anirudh smiled and looked at Kali. 'I am glad you understand it and have realized its meaning appropriately in this context of the tree.'

Kali thought for a bit and asked, 'So death has no role to play in moksha?'

Anirudh shook his head. 'Moksha means you are liberated from maya. You are liberated from your individual identity, from the self. Letting go of your individual identity, that's a death in itself. Moksha is when you realize that you are not an individual root, but a part of the tree. You, being a root, are one with the tree. For humans, moksha is when they realize that they are one with the universe.'

Anirudh, after giving Kali a pause to digest the words, continued, 'So death, by design, cannot play a role in moksha, because liberation is something that happens on a level of consciousness. You have to realize that you are a part of the tree, and you have accept it. And that's possible only when you are alive. Death is but a chapter in your journey. For if you realize that you are a contributor to the harmony of the whole universe, that you nourish it, and that's your sole function, then even your death is a contribution, just like your birth is. Death doesn't serve as a block, but it serves as the next step.'

'So what can I do to contribute?'

'Whatever you want to do. It's your choice.'

'But aren't you going to kill me? I am the Lord of Evil. Isn't it your purpose to vanquish me? Didn't you return from death to end me?'

'Are you the Lord of Evil?'

'I was, wasn't I? So you will end me now, won't you?'

'If you were the Lord of Evil, then I wouldn't have shown you that you are connected to the universe, that the universe and you are one. The purpose of my avatar was to restore the balance of humanity, and of course, to end evil. But you aren't evil anymore, so I am not ending you.'

'Didn't you consider me evil at all?'

'When I was Kalki, yes, I did consider you evil. But now that I am reborn, I have realized the truth. I don't see you as evil. You were an ambitious person, just like most humans on this earth.'

'But I am the personification of evil. This whole era is attributed to me, and I am the root of all evil.'

'You were the personification of evil. Like I said earlier, that person, the evil identity you had held on to, you have let go of it. Kali, the Lord of Evil, is now dead. You have reformed now, haven't you?'

Kali nodded his head.

'And about you being the root of all evil, that's not the case. You have reformed, but out there, I still know humans who are, well, ambitious and unapologetic about their wicked ways to achieve their goals. So this malice will continue existing even after you have reformed, Kali.'

Kali, after spending a moment in thought, asked the boy, 'I am curious. Why did you create evil?'

'The concept of good and evil is a human concept, Kali. If a person earns a crore rupees through illegal means, but donates the money to the needy, he is considered good. But if a person earns a crore rupees through illegal means and uses it for his own self, he is considered evil.'

Anirudh added, 'In your case, you were aiming to rule the world and make everyone in the world your slave, so I had to stop you.'

'And you are going to stop the others too? The selfish humans?'

'I will give them a chance to reform, if they do, then good. If they don't, well, let's see.'

Kali acknowledged with a nod. Then he asked, 'What do I do now?'

'You can meditate and understand more about the universe, or you can start helping people. Whenever you want to die, you can die. If you choose to live and want to leave this chamber and go to some place of your choice, then think of that location. You shall be taken to that place. You have complete freedom to do what you want to do, Kali. Until then you can stay here.'

Anirudh got up, and his couch vanished.

Kali appreciated the words and thanked Anirudh.

After a pause, he asked, 'If you are not Kalki, then who are you? How do you know so much about the universe?'

Anirudh smiled and said:

'Na me viduh sura-ganah prabhavam na maharsayah
aham adir hi devanam maharsinam ca sarvasah'

After saying this, he waved to Kali and vanished.

Kali translated the quote out loud as goosebumps covered his skin.

'Neither the host of gods nor the great sages know of my origin. Because, in every way, I am the original cause of the gods and the great sages.'

Then, focusing his mind on a mountain cave in the Vindhyas, he closed his eyes. He wanted to understand more about the universe and himself first, and then he would help the people to the best of his abilities.

FIFTY-SIX

Parashurama, Avyay and Ashwatthama, with their eyes tightly shut, waited for the huge blades to strike them. But the steel weapons of the Kalabakshakas never reached them. When they opened their eyes, they saw the three sorcerers disintegrating into fragments of light and entering a tall silhouette walking towards them. When the dark figure stepped into the light of the purple sun, Anirudh gave them a smile, as the wisps of glowing light vanished into him.

'In the nick of time,' he said.

The trio, visibly relieved, nodded gratefully and got up to their feet.

The boy looked around the battleground. 'Damn, the battle's still going on!'

Then, all the enemy soldiers and demons, the ones fighting and the ones fallen, decomposed into light particles and swam into Anirudh, vanishing inside him.

The Immortals and Dweepa, who were engaged in battle at a distance, watched the abrupt disapparition of their opponents. Their eyes found Anirudh, and they heaved a sigh of joy.

'Where did they all go?' Hanuman asked as they reached Anirudh and the trio.

'Back into the universe . . . Their work is done for now, they have served their purpose,' Anirudh said.

He waved his hand at the EOK warriors and they disappeared as well. Anirudh added, 'The EOK warriors are back at the mansion, where they will be taken care of by their colleagues.'

Hanuman nodded. Kripa looked at the bruised states of Ashwatthama, Avyay and Parashurama.

'Someone took a good beating, I see,' he said simply.

'Where's Kali?' Parashurama asked, looking around for a sign of the evil lord.

The boy replied, 'He's gone too. You needn't be worried about him anymore.'

Saying this, he stepped aside and surveyed the untidy battlefield. And suddenly, the remnants of the skirmish disappeared, and the field was back to its original texture of patches of dryness and greenery. The huge stone palace melted into oblivion. All traces of combat and inhabitation were removed from the site.

Anirudh turned to the Immortals, Kalki and Dweepa. Their scars healed and their fatigue melted away. Their skin was perfect and they felt rejuvenated. They looked at him in amazement, speechless.

Finally, Vyasa asked, 'Who are you?'

Anirudh smiled but didn't answer. He told them, 'It is time for us to leave as well.'

Avyay, suddenly cautious of becoming luminous dust flakes, asked, 'Where to?'

With a slight grin, he said, 'EOK mansion.'

~

Placing the sherbets in front of everyone seated at the large table, the EOK mansion caretakers left the kitchen. Anirudh stood next to the wall. Siddharth, Safeed and Sadhika had joined them as well.

Acharya Sreedhar asked, 'So neither Kali nor his minions are ever set to return?'

Anirudh shook his head and replied, 'No. They are gone for good.'

Everyone exchanged glances and looked at the boy, whose resurrection and identity was a complete mystery to them.

'How did you return from death?' Avyay asked. She didn't find her old Anirudh under his skin. She realized that this was a different person in Anirudh's body.

Anirudh repeated all that he had told Ashwatthama in the Himalayan cave.

'How did you achieve mastery over the five elements? And well enough to create a body from them?' Bali asked.

Anirudh smiled and said, 'I know them because I am the one who created them.'

There was a silence around the table, everyone considering the words, wondering what they meant.

'Who are you?' Parashurama asked, finally finding his voice.

'I will tell you when the time comes.'

Dweepa, after seeing that Anirudh's true identity was going to remain a mystery for a while, asked, 'So Kali and his evil soldiers are gone. Where does that leave us? Do we shut down EOK, since we have been able to keep Kali away from power? What do we do next?'

Anirudh spoke, 'Only the Lord of Evil and his minions have been stopped.'

Looking at Avyay, he continued, 'But the presence of evil continues in the world.'

She nodded back, understanding what he was hinting at. She said a single word so that others got the hint as well, 'Humankind.'

Turning his attention to others, he spoke, 'So work still remains to be done. About what needs to be done next, and about EOK, I will leave it to you all.'

As an afterthought, Anirudh added, 'There's still the nuclear mess to clear up. So, yeah, that could be a priority.'

Acharya Sreedhar replied, 'Well, that situation's under control. Dhanvantari is out there with his people, healing people and containing the situation.'

Everyone took in the news.

'Anirudh,' Avyay asked slowly. 'What's your plan now? Are you going to be with us?'

He looked at her and shook his head. 'My role, for now, is done.'

'Where are you going?' Hanuman asked gently.

The young man replied cryptically, 'I am going to some place. I have no role to play here since there are more than enough knowledgeable people in this room, and all of you, together, can set everything right.'

'And if we want to meet you?' Vyasa asked, curious.

'You will find your way to me when it is time.'

Vyasa nodded. Ashwatthama asked, 'What about me? Do I come with you?'

Anirudh smiled, 'You are finally home, with the Immortals. The rest of your journey is with them, son of Drona.'

Drauni gave a brief bow, accepting the words of the boy.

Anirudh looked at everyone once, and then announced, 'I'll take my leave then. I leave the world to your care and guidance.'

He paused, and added, 'In my opinion, EOK can't just shut shop immediately. After the nuclear situation is attended to, you can look forward to the research work from the think tank regarding your proposals of making the world a better place. You can use the Clause Zero to take the outcome of the research to the government for review and implementation.'

Avyay and Sadhika's eyes widened in surprise. But, before Avyay, or anyone else for that matter, could ask him how he came about that information, or react to him, he vanished.

Avyay was heartbroken. Her sadness poured out, 'Why didn't he stay? How could he be so heartless and not wait to hear me out? Doesn't he love me any more? I have been waiting for him for so long—he comes back from the dead and doesn't even meet me once. And after he appeared in front of me, he hasn't even spoken to me as such . . . What is wrong with him?'

Dweepa smiled sadly and put his hand on her shoulder and squeezed it softly. Parashurama said in a melancholic voice, already hurt by the words he was going to speak, 'He is no longer *your* Anirudh, Avyay. He is someone else in Anirudh's body.'

'I understood that, Dada. But who is he, if not Anirudh?'

Pointing to Parashurama, Ashwatthama said, 'He is correct. He is no longer the Anirudh we know, or rather, knew. I tried to extract his identity from him, but he didn't reveal it at all. But he did say this . . . He told me that he is Anirudh, he is Kali, he is Kalki, he is Parashurama, he is Krishna, he is me, he is every one of you. He is everything and he is nothing.'

Everyone just looked at each other.

'And once, he told me these words,' Drauni continued, '*Aham atma . . . Sarva-bhutasaya-sthitah . . . Aham adis ca madhyam ca . . . Bhutanam anta eva ca . . .* I have heard these words only once before in my life. I heard them when Krishna said this to Arjuna.'

Parashurama, in an awestruck whisper, translated the words, 'I am the atman established in the heart of all beings. It is I who am the origin, the middle, and also the end of all beings.'

FIFTY-SEVEN

Over a period of twenty-four years

Anirudh wandered the streets under the cover of the dark night sky. He weaved in and out of lanes, localities and cities, observing the life around him.

It was roughly 2 a.m. and winter's icy blanket had settled over the night. His slow, casual trot stopped suddenly when he heard a large *thwack* sound, which was followed by an agonizing yelp of a stray dog. From one of the building gates on the street before him, a dog rushed out and sped off. A man also appeared at the entrance, a bamboo stick swinging in his hand. Anirudh shook his head, feeling pity for the stray creatures who sought shelter in the building's warm corners to keep the cold at bay. And this person whacks the mute beings he considers to be a nuisance. He derived a sadistic pleasure from hearing the animals' hurt shriek. The man glared at the dog until it vanished down the road and lit a beedi, blowing the smoke into the air. As Anirudh walked by, the smoke drifted through his invisible, astral form.

The stifled whimpers of a woman, crying on one of the upper floors of a building that he was passing by reached his ears. Her husband had hit her some time ago, for she had voiced her opinion against him. Her in-laws weren't supportive of her either. She was curled in the corner of the bedroom, her wounds still fresh from the stings and her tears still hot. Her husband was busy watching TV, undisturbed and unapologetic.

In the wee hours of the morning, Anirudh passed by a popular brand's milk factory. The workers were working frantically—mixing water in the milk machines. This milk was then dispersed in plastic pouches, bottles and tetrapacks to the market. So much for 100 per cent pure milk!

Under the pale moonlight, an elderly man sat weeping in the centre of his barren field. The treacherous rains didn't allow him to have any harvest this year. He thrashed his palms wildly on the land, but his frustration didn't subside. In addition to the already existing debts, he had taken one more loan earlier that year so that he could sow and plough for the season's harvest. But he couldn't produce anything. The seeds lay buried under the earth, dead. He looked around at his land hopelessly. There was no more help he could ask for, from anyone. No one could rescue him from the mountain of debts and problems he was trapped under. His life, his hopes, his dreams—they all died with the dry monsoon. He slowly got up and started walking towards his home. *It's all over now*, he told himself. He turned around and looked at his land and the dark sky one last time.

As he strode past a row house, he could hear the voice of a girl crying out in anguish. Her words were met by an angry, loud voice of a man. A daughter was fighting her father to let her marry the man she was in love with, while her father was adamant that she should marry someone of their caste rather than an outsider. Anirudh shook his head and walked on.

He walked by a parking lot, which was empty save for two cars parked next to each other. It was a secret rendezvous between a businessman and an assassin he had hired. The businessman wanted to eliminate a rival, and he had invited the hitman discreetly to take care of the arrangement and execution of it.

He was making his way through the crowds in a city circle. The golden luminescence of the street lights and the car headlights made the surroundings shine like a bejewelled gold ornament. 'Truly, the city never sleeps,' Anirudh noted. The people were roaming around with masks on their faces. It wasn't because of any pandemic. It was because of the pollution. The unchecked levels of polluted air messed with the respiratory systems of most of the population of the nation. The toxic levels were something that the lungs couldn't adapt to. But the younger generation had it even worse, their lungs were affected since birth. How can one help infant lungs adapt to toxic gases? To preserve the public health, the government mandated the use of industry-grade respiratory masks, which would protect the people from the poisonous air.

As he walked past a skyscraper, the tearful gasps of a woman filled his ears. The blade she held over her wrist shivered violently with her shuddering breaths. She wanted to divorce her obsessive, psychotic husband—but he and her in-laws weren't agreeing to it. They weren't letting her leave the house either. She had no support from her own family—they didn't want the taint of divorce on their daughter. She hoped that her family would understand and agree to the idea of a divorced daughter rather than a dead daughter, but her hopes were squashed. And thus, inside the locked bathroom, she held the blade in her hand. Her eyes were shut tight as she tried to bring herself to give up.

Anirudh walked by a hospital. He heard a family lamenting over the sudden death of their son. He was struck with fever and weakness, so the doctor had advised that he be admitted to the hospital. The boy's condition had deteriorated, and the fever had grown worse, and soon the boy had succumbed to his fever. At the very least, the family could get some peace by donating his organs. Inside his cabin, the doctor confirmed the availability of the organs to a recipient. He was posed to earn crores of rupees from this transaction. After all, he had arranged for the organs by inducing death in his patient to harvest his body parts. The life-giver played the opposite role today. His victim was the son of the family weeping in the lobby outside his cabin as they completed the organ donation formalities.

Anirudh passed by a children's garden, which was empty since night had fallen. But there were two men on the grassy ground, and one of them handed a bottle of acid to the other. The recipient kept the container carefully inside his bag, and then gave cash to the seller. The young man walked away with the weapon in his bag—a weapon with which he intended to harm the woman who had rejected his affections for her.

He strolled past a law-and-order station. Inside the station, the enforcement chief was coercing an old couple to sign a statement saying that their daughter had committed suicide, and there was no need for any murder investigation. The parents, under the pressure and fear of torture if they didn't obey, signed the document. The enforcement agency had already tortured them enough and destroyed their peace. As the defeated couple finished signing, the officer nodded to a man standing a few feet behind them. The man nodded back and left the station. The old couple started crying uncontrollably, as they watched their daughter's murderer, an influential politician's son, walk away with no remorse.

In an empty junkyard, Anirudh witnessed a group of men kill two men, whose pleas for mercy fell on deaf ears. After the deed was done, the leader of the gang took out his phone and made a call. A car entered the junkyard and an elderly man stepped out. He walked to the two corpses and peered at them to confirm their deaths. One of the deceased was dressed in a blue shirt, and the other in yellow. The visitor spat, with intense repugnance, on the one wearing the blue shirt, his own son. Then, he turned to the leader and handed him a wad of cash. In a couple of minutes, they had all left the junkyard. Anirudh stepped closer to the victims and looked at them. The two lovers lay spreadeagled on the ground, having paid the price for falling in love with each other. The fact that his son could fall in love with a man—the man couldn't quite digest it, and it disgusted him. And so he took the extreme measure of removing the cause of his revulsion from the face of the earth, and of course, his son's partner too.

Anirudh, intrigued by their conversation, stopped next to two people.

One of them asked, pointing to a tall skyscraper, 'Why can't we stay there? That tall building looks so beautiful! The night makes those yellow lights look so pretty.'

The companion looked at the excited eyes of the speaker. With a sad smile, their words came, 'Iru, you know that those places are not for us. We are outcastes, and our home is this place.' The hand stretched to point across the street.

Anirudh's eyes followed the hand, resting on the intentional community for *kinnars*.

'But why, Charu?'

'That's just the way things are.'

Just then, a couple of bikes appeared on the street. Slowing down to a crawl, the riders heckled the two, and sped off, laughing loudly.

Charu turned and found Iru in tears. Stifling their own tears, Charu found themself saying, 'That's just the way things are.'

Iru, sobbing softly, replied, 'If that's the way things are, then I don't want to live this cursed life. We have no job, no protection, no care, nothing . . .'

Anirudh watched as Charu pulled Iru along and crossed the street, trying to console the latter, telling them to eat dinner and sleep. He watched them vanish into their community. His eyes went up to the skyscraper, and a melancholic smile escaped his lips.

In the forest, amidst the trees, a father and mother watched with evil delight as their two sons hacked a couple to death—their daughter and her husband, their son-in-law. Anirudh observed the whole scene, standing a few feet away from them. After the two men finished the gruesome act, they turned to their parents, giving them the nod. The satisfaction of vengeance gleamed in their eyes. The father and mother patted the shoulders of their two sons with pride.

'You have saved the honour of our family, my sons,' the father said.

'Indeed,' the mother spoke. Looking with disgust at her daughter and son-in-law, she added, 'Your sister nearly destroyed our honour by marrying this filthy, low-caste man.'

The sons set the two bodies on fire and Anirudh watched them leave the clearing.

❧

As the yellow sun started creeping into the black sky, Anirudh's steps slowly came to a halt when he heard the agonized cries of a calf. He paused in front of a cowshed. Inside the shelter, the owner was pulling the newborn child away from its mother. He tied it far from the cow, so that the calf wouldn't drink the cow's milk. He wanted to keep the supply of milk intact for his business. He set to milk the cow, heartlessly ignoring the calf crying out for its mother's warm milk, and also ruthlessly overlooking the tears flowing down the mother's eyes.

'Anirudh . . .' a voice came gently to his ears. It was the voice of Parashurama.

Anirudh smiled softly.

'The Immortals are waiting for me,' he spoke to himself.

He heard his name uttered by Vyasa now. The young man closed his eyes, for he had to now open his eyes.

FIFTY-EIGHT

Parashurama exchanged a glace with Vyasa as they waited for him to open his eyes. Mahabali, Hanuman, Vibhishana, Kripa and Ashwatthama stood behind the two Immortals, exchanging glances amongst themselves.

'Anirudh . . .' Vyasa called out again, to the figure seated in the lotus position.

The Immortals had been trying to trace Anirudh through supernatural means for years, but they never found him. A few minutes ago, they all sensed a sudden energy surge and learnt that it was Anirudh. So, without waiting, they teleported to the source of the energy.

Though they had taken in their surroundings earlier, the Immortals found themselves drawn to the ambience around them again and again. Anirudh was seated inside a hole in the hill face in front of them. The sun was shining with splendour, but it was not harsh. A cool and pleasant breeze kept them company. To their left was a forest that spread out infinitely. And to their right was a sandy beach, which shored the blue ocean. Under their feet was the cold, dewy green grass. The place was filled with tranquility.

Anirudh opened his eyes slowly and adjusted to the bright sun falling into his gaze. He then saw the seven Immortals standing in front of him.

'Well, all of you are here,' he said as he unfolded his legs and stood up.

'You did call for us, didn't you?' Hanuman asked. 'If you didn't want to meet us, then you wouldn't have revealed yourself.'

Anirudh smiled softly.

'What happened?' Parashurama asked. 'If you called for us, then there is something of import on your mind.'

'How are things out there?' Anirudh asked them as he motioned them to sit on the cool grass.

Bali smiled and reverted, 'I am sure that you know the state of things out there. Why are you asking us about it?'

Everyone sat on the grass, forming a large circle, and waited for his response.

'It is true, I know how things are, Mahabali. But I want to hear from you all, I seek your opinion about the situation.'

Vibhishana cleared his throat and answered, 'Well, we are giving it our best. Things are slightly better than before, and we are hoping that they become even better soon. We have been able to achieve some of our objectives—like free meals and free clothing. Clause Zero helped us expedite things and implement them swiftly. We are working on the other things.'

Anirudh nodded. Then, as his eyes moved across each of the Immortals, he spoke, 'I know that you will succeed in changing the environment around humans—I mean, you will get them good food, good housing, good clothes. But what about making human beings *human*?'

The Immortals looked at the young boy, apprehensive of what he was about to say. They were also curious about what he wanted to say, and to see if he was going to make their worries come true.

Anirudh, to explain his words, narrated all that he'd seen during his nocturnal wanderings over the past years. After he finished describing his experiences, he said, 'Humans are not being human. They have lost their touch with humanity—they are still stuck in the old ideas, unreasonable logic. There is no compassion in people towards their fellow humans. At least, not all of them feel compassion. And then, there are some humans who show no compassion towards other living beings either.'

'We will get them there, Anirudh . . .' Ashwatthama said softly.

Anirudh's eyes met those of the Immortal. Everyone's eyes studied the boy's eyes, and then it dawned on them. They realized what was on Anirudh's mind, and they understood why they were here. And Anirudh's next words confirmed their fears.

The boy, in the quietest tone they'd ever heard, a tone of deathly quiet, said, 'No, Drauni, you will not get them there. They are never getting there.'

The Chiranjeevi exchanged glances with each other, their eyes filled with worry and uncertainty.

Parashurama, breaking the silence, asked, 'What's on your mind, Anirudh? Why are we here?'

Anirudh took a deep breath. 'Humans have lost their path—they have no respect for their blessings, they have no empathy for their fellow beings, they don't care about nature and other living beings, they are self-absorbed, they have lost the notion of right and wrong. Though they are progressing in science and technology, they are far from their spiritual growth. They have lost touch with their spiritual self and are running amok, causing havoc and destruction on anything and everything around them. And even educating them doesn't help to a great extent, since their education is merely a tool to qualify them for better salaries and jobs.'

With a tone of finality and coldness, Anirudh spoke, 'Humans, most of them, are no longer human. And this section of non-human beings is going to spell doom for this universe.'

Kripacharya, worried by Anirudh's glum words, asked him, 'What do you want us to do, Anirudh?'

'Nothing, Kripacharya. There is nothing left to do. That's why I called for you all. You need not spend any more energy trying to make humans better. I have planned something, and it is time I informed you.'

The Immortals waited for Anirudh's decision with breathless patience. They remained frozen, speechless, awaiting the words from the boy.

Anirudh spoke in a measured tone, 'I am of the opinion that we must end everything.'

The Immortals gasped. Though they had anticipated it, the truth of the words and reality of the situation gripped them.

Parashurama asked softly, 'Are you sure you want to do this? There is still hope for mankind.'

'Are you sure about that?' Anirudh shot back.

The axe-wielder was unsure how to answer. Anirudh looked at the distraught faces of the Immortals and found no answer from anyone.

'I know my words seem rash. But it is just an opinion. I am not entertaining this prospect on the basis of my patience or anything personal. The final decision rests on someone else. I am considering only one person when I say this, and that person is the most important to me.'

The seven people who sat around him looked curiously at Anirudh.

'That person is Bhoomidevi,' the young man revealed.

The mention of the goddess softened their faces and remorse took over them. Vyasa nodded softly.

'I understand, Anirudh,' the compiler of the Vedas said. 'Even so, I want you to consider things once again. This end . . . it's no little deed. The gravity of what you are suggesting . . .'

The young man smiled softly. 'Vyasa Maharishi, I have considered things for twenty-four years, is that time enough for you? I do understand the seriousness of what I am saying.

'The thing is,' Anirudh continued, 'if humans understood the gravity of their actions, if they had realized that they were misusing nature and the gifts that nature bestows on them, and had they corrected their actions accordingly, then I wouldn't be here having this discussion with you. If they had mended their ways, then I wouldn't even have thought of such a move.'

'But you can set things right, can't you, Anirudh?' Ashwatthama asked.

'Of course, I can. I can make things better with a snap of my fingers. With a single thought, I can *influence* humans to become better. My powers have no limits.'

These words brought forth a question to everyone's minds—*Then why aren't you doing so?*

Anirudh laughed softly and asked a question in return, 'Well, have any of you planted a seed?'

Bali responded, 'We are Immortals, Anirudh. And time—we have had that in abundance. So, naturally, we have dabbled in many, many things. And we have planted seeds as well.'

'Thought so. So when you plant a seed or a stem, do you tell the seed to sprout only one flower and four leaves?'

'No, of course not. We let the plant take its own course . . .' said Bali, and went silent. The words and their meaning dawned on everyone around him.

With a soft smile on his lips, Anirudh spoke, 'In the same way, I have always let mankind walk and grow on their own. It's their journey, and I can't do it for them. I have given them all the knowledge required to make decisions, including a mind capable of formulating solutions to problems. Yet, they choose to ignore the problems, focus on greed and blindly race towards what they perceive to be progress. They don't hesitate to destroy whatever stands in their way to success, be it nature or fellow humans. And the cost of their mistakes is being paid by nature and all of her gifts. So since human beings don't care about nature, I don't care about human beings. I am choosing to care about Bhoomidevi, since I believe I am the only one doing so.'

'But that would destroy life as a whole—human beings and other living beings as well—like plants, trees and animals?' Vibhishana asked.

'They would get destroyed soon anyway at the hands of humans, so why not now? Besides, I don't know if they will be destroyed. That's something that Bhoomidevi and I will decide.'

'So, if Bhoomidevi decides to destroy it all, then you will go along with it?' Vyasa asked.

Anirudh nodded.

'What's your role in this decision? How do you have the power to end everything, Anirudh?' Bali asked.

Scratching his chin, Anirudh replied, 'About my role . . . Let me put it this way. If Bhoomidevi is the mother of creation, then I am the father. So that gives me not only a say but also the power to end everything.'

'Who are you, really, Anirudh?' Parashurama asked.

'I am the One. The one who is present in all and in everything. The one in whom every being is present. I am the one whom no one sees but is present everywhere. I am the one who is without form, and who is eternal. Everything originates from me, and everything ends in me. I am timeless, I am endless and I am beyond all realms and dimensions.'

All the Immortals, awestruck, bowed to Anirudh. Anirudh bowed back.

With a tone of concern in his voice, Vyasa asked, 'Are you sure about not giving humans another chance? Can't you forgive them once?'

'Vyasa Rishi . . .' Anirudh said, taking a deep breath, 'If I am here, in the flesh, then I am not here to forgive. I am here to conclude. If I forgive humankind, then I would be doing injustice to Bhoomidevi, the Mother Nature, Prakriti. Man fails to understand the simple truth—that they are a part of nature. They are not special. I treat plants and animals and humankind the same. But despite their intelligence, they keep choosing to do wrong to the nature around them, to Mother Nature, and I am not going to be silent about it any longer. And that's why I am here. I am not here to warn humankind. I will never interfere, for they are responsible for their actions. I am here *because* they didn't heed Mother Nature's warnings, her reactions. They didn't correct themselves, so I am here. I am here *for* Bhoomidevi.'

The Immortals were silent. There was no more discussion. They knew that it was not in their hands to influence this decision.

'So . . . What about us now?'

Taking a deep breath, he said, 'You can wait and see what's coming, or you can realize your atman and rise above your body and nature. You can become one with the Supreme Soul.'

'And the Supreme Soul is you, right?' Hanuman asked in a just-want-to-confirm tone.

The Brahman just smiled.

'So you are ending everyone and everything . . .' Vibhishana spoke.

Anirudh said, 'I am not ending anything yet. I have to first talk to Bhoomidevi. And if the decision comes to that, then it is the time of pralaya, so everything will end—all that you see, and all that you don't. But despite total annihilation, Prakriti, the cosmic force of nature and matter, will always remain, just like me.'

'Just like *you*, Purusha?' Vyasa asked softly.

The Brahman smiled once more. Everyone bowed to Purusha, who just raised his palm in assurance.

He said, 'If "Anirudh" is more comfortable to utter, then feel free to call me by that name.'

After a moment's silence, Bali asked, 'After the pralaya, will the world start anew?'

The Brahman took a deep breath, and replied, 'It will start again, yes, but I have not yet determined *when* it will. That, again, is Prakriti's decision.'

FIFTY-NINE

'Do you recall that during my last breaths when Asi struck me, I had told you both something?' Anirudh asked of Sadhika and Siddharth.

They were seated under the wide shade of the banyan tree on the beach at Anirudh's 'hideout'.

'I had told you that there's more than meets the eye to you, Sadhika. And that you, Siddharth, are special,' he said.

The two companions nodded and exchanged a glance.

'Well . . . Obviously, I wasn't able to put my finger on the exact reason of your transcendental vibe then. But now that I am beyond Kalki, I can see everything clearly. I am sure that you both know of this, but you have Rudra's blessings on you. Well, he blesses everyone, true. But he has blessed you both with an ounce of his divinity.'

Siddharth and Sadhika smiled, their brief nods acknowledging Purusha's words.

'And this ounce of divinity is why Asi glowed when you held it. Parashurama and the others have known this for long, but Avyay didn't know it then. Neither did I. Why didn't you tell me then?'

'Don't you know the answer already?' Siddharth teased.

Anirudh grinned and scratched the dimple on his cheek. 'Of course I do. You were going to tell me later, after you were sure of me. Just like you withheld the Clause Zero information until you were sure that I was capable of handling it.'

Siddharth's and Sadhika's eyes widened when they heard the bit about Clause Zero. But, reminding themselves of Purusha's prowess, they came to accept the surprise quickly.

'So we are looking at the end of everything, aren't we?' Sadhika asked, looking around the beach.

'Potentially, yes.'

Sadhika and Siddharth sighed, visibly sad.

'How can you consider ending the world without even feeling a bit of remorse, Anirudh?' she asked, almost angry about his detachment.

'Isn't it obvious?'

'Well, you are detached from the universe, I guess? You don't care about what happens to humans, plants, trees, birds, animals . . . Correct?'

'Hmmm . . . You are partially correct.'

The duo exchanged a glance and stared at Anirudh.

He explained, 'I am detached from the world, but I am not detached from Bhoomidevi. And I do care about what happens to plants, trees, animals, birds, oceans, forests, man, woman, about everyone and everything in Prakriti. However, I also treat them all equally. I have no favourites. I have provided everyone with all that they need for their survival. But of all these creations of Prakriti, humans have the most potential to elevate their consciousness to new realms, and to work together and elevate nature to new heights. Humankind has the power to provide to all the beings in nature, to nourish the nourisher. So it is insulting that they are enraptured by the illusions of their imagination, and subservient to their base instincts. If that's not enough, they are snatching the blessings and provisions given to other beings. They are plundering and exploiting nature and the beings in it. And, like I said before, I am more attached to Bhoomidevi than to anything else. So if she is having a tough time, then I am not going to be sitting quietly. And that's why I am here.'

'Whenever Mother Earth is under duress, Lord Vishnu arrives to save her, correct?'

Anirudh simply smiled.

Sadhika asked Anirudh curiously, 'You told us that you are Vishnu, Shiva, Brahma, everything. You are the Supreme Soul, the Para Brahman, Purusha, everything.'

The Brahman nodded.

'So, does that mean Vishnu, Shiva, Shakti—these gods and goddesses don't exist? Are they all lies, a work of fiction?'

Anirudh smiled and cleared his throat. 'Sadhika, tell me this: what's my actual form?'

The two listeners furrowed their brows in doubt.

Sadhika asked back, '*Your* actual form, meaning Purusha's actual form?'

Purusha nodded.

'You are formless, aren't you?'

'Yes. And where am I located?'

'Everywhere?' Siddharth ventured.

Anirudh smiled and dissolved into thin air.

'Anirudh? Anirudh!' Sadhika called, shocked.

'I am here,' Anirudh's voice sounded from above, amongst the branches of the banyan tree. But their eyes found no one.

'Where are you? We can't see you,' Siddharth said.

'I am formless, Siddharth,' Anirudh's voice said from behind them.

They turned around sharply, and the vast, empty expanse of the beach stared back at them.

'Why are you jumping, Anirudh? Just be in one place!' Sadhika scolded.

'I am not jumping around, Sadhika. *I am everywhere*,' Purusha's voice spoke from the sand on the ground in front of them.

'Well, what are you trying to do?' Siddharth asked, slightly annoyed at the playfulness.

The Formless One responded, this time from the sky above them, 'We will continue talking like this now. Honestly, I hope you are comfortable with it. But if at any time you feel like you are fed up with my formlessness, then let me know.'

The duo glared at each other, unable to find a form of Anirudh to direct their frustration.

'So coming to your question about the existence of gods and goddesses,' Anirudh's voice echoed from the sea behind them. 'Discard their forms and focus on their deeds, their attributes, the idea they represent. Brahma, the creator; Vishnu, the preserver; and Shiva, the destroyer. Saraswati, the provider of knowledge; Lakshmi, the provider of wealth; and Shakti, the provider of energy.'

'If you consider these ideas,' Anirudh's voice came from the tree's bark in front of them, 'then all of them act as guiding stars. Humans can create their own worlds, be it a family, a garden, a process. Humans have the power to create, like Brahma. Having created, it is their duty to protect these as well. Even if it isn't their creation, they still have a duty to preserve the world, like Vishnu. To be better humans, they have to destroy their ego. If their world goes corrupt, they have to destroy it as well. Just like Shiva.'

He spoke from the sky above, saying, 'Humans should always act as a beacon of light, spreading knowledge to anyone and everyone, like Saraswati. They should generate wealth and help progress and better the living conditions of other beings and the nature around them, like Lakshmi. They should always use their energy wisely and for the good of people and to help the other living beings, like Shakti.'

When Anirudh spoke his next words, his voice came from right in front of them, and they shuffled back in fear. 'So if you look at the ideas behind gods and goddesses, you will realize that it doesn't matter if they exist or not.'

Sadhika shrieked, 'Can you take form and sit in front of us, Anirudh?'

They heard a soft chuckle and saw Anirudh materialize before them, seated under the banyan tree in front of them.

'What happened, Sadhika?' he asked, feigning innocence.

'Well, you were frustrating us with your invisibility and unexpected presence all around us,' Siddharth complained.

'I wasn't comfortable talking to the formless you. You told me to let you know if I wasn't feeling great about the idea of talking to the invisible you,' Sadhika expressed.

'Yes, I did tell you to inform me, and thank you for expressing yourself freely, Siddharth and Sadhika.'

'To be honest, I tried to be okay with it, but I don't know . . . I just couldn't bring myself to it,' Sadhika said. Siddharth seconded her words.

'I understand that, and that was the intention behind going to my formless self. However, before I delve deep into that, I want to ask you this: if you were uncomfortable when I was formless, did you absorb my words?'

'Ummmm . . . Not entirely,' Siddharth said apologetically.

'No problem, I will repeat my words.' And Anirudh repeated himself.

After he finished, he asked, 'Now, what do you think of my current form? This human form? Is it easy on your eyes, simpler to comprehend?'

Siddharth and Sadhika nodded.

Anirudh smiled broadly, his dimple deepening in his cheek. 'But is it my actual form?'

Their mouths were left open, as they got an inkling of where Anirudh was headed. They shook their heads slowly.

Purusha continued, 'You couldn't pay attention to me when I was in my true, formless self. Your senses were confused at some level. And I expected that of you. I am formless, and so are ideas in general. Concepts and ideas are given form since they are easier to read using the senses, and it becomes easier to comprehend for the mind. When I was formless, you couldn't focus on my words entirely as your eyes sought me, and your ears were getting accustomed to varying sound sources. But when I am here, in this friendly form, you can understand me well. So the gods and goddesses are given forms to correspond to the ideas they represent. These ideas are explained further in the form of stories and other imagery. These divine beings represent truths about human life and principles. The object of worship should be these teachings and ideas that these gods represent, and not the gods themselves.

'Coming to the fact that your senses are seeking forms to understand ideas,' Anirudh continued, 'the goal of human life is to rise above these senses and become one with the nature around them.'

Anirudh concluded by saying, 'Well, this is all I have to say for now. The more you think about it, the more information

will emerge in your mind, and then eventually you will arrive
at the truth.'

SIXTY

Standing in the waters a couple of feet from the shore, Safeed looked at his feet submerged in the clear blue of the ocean. Then, he looked up at his companion, Anirudh, whose eyes were fixed on the horizon.

Safeed said, 'I am surprised that you are meeting me.'

The words brought forth a curious dip of Anirudh's brows, and an involuntary smile followed.

'Why is that?'

'Well . . .' Safeed started but paused to find the right words. He cleared his throat to buy some time to choose his words. 'Well . . . You . . . are Purusha, aren't you? And you are . . . well, Hindu. And I am . . .'

Before he could complete the statement, Anirudh cut in, 'Let me stop you right there. There is a misconception in your mind, and I want to clear that. And after that's resolved, you won't be surprised anymore.'

Safeed looked curiously at the speaker.

Anirudh asked him, 'I am Purusha, yes. It is one of the names that has been given to me. But it's just a name. Does the word "Purusha" belong to any religion? Doesn't it just mean "man", in plain terms? Does the word "man" itself belong to any religion?'

Safeed shook his head.

Purusha continued, 'Just like the word is secular, I am too. What am I? I am the singularity, which is present in all beings. I am consciousness, I am the soul, I am everything. I am the strand that connects everything, the force that holds it all together. I am the seed from which everything springs. So if everything comes from me, then how can I be confined to a particular religion? I am above all religions. Religions are created by mankind, and where does mankind come from? So it is impossible for me to be confined to any particular set of people.'

With an indulgent smile, he asked Safeed, 'Tell me this— to which religion does the air that you breathe belong? To which religion does your body belong? To which religion does your soul belong?'

'Ummm . . . To no one?'

'I see the doubt in your answer, but what you say is correct. The air doesn't belong to any religion, neither do the rains, oceans, trees. Your body belongs to no one—you can spend it in the service of the goals you choose, but eventually, everybody turns to dust. Your soul is never confined to any ideals or beliefs. When you are truly spiritually enlightened, you will see that the light shines the same in everyone, and that all the man-made divisions are just that, man-made divisions. I don't differentiate between people of different religions, and neither does Mother Nature. Birth comes to everyone equally, and so does death.'

Concluding his words, Anirudh said, 'So don't be surprised that you are here. You are here because you helped people during the catastrophe regardless of their gender, caste, creed or faith. You truly acted as selfless individuals, and what you felt when helping those people, that's what I am.'

'Well, I agree with you, Anirudh. I am not sure if I would be incorrect in saying that man-made divisions are the worst catastrophe. Everyone should first be educated to be better human beings, and then the topic of religion should be broached.'

Anirudh simply smiled.

Safeed added, 'Speaking of catastrophes, Mother Nature is the supreme equalizer.'

'You said it! All the conflicts, the struggles, the deceptions, the twisted ways of selfish people . . . All is pointless when She plays her card.'

Safeed smiled and whispered audibly, 'I wonder when mankind will realize that while they've been dealt the best hand, the trump cards are always held by Mother Nature. No one can best Her.'

'Well, that's one way of putting it.'

After a brief pause, Anirudh said, 'Thank you, Safeed. I really appreciate your selfless help during the unrest.'

Safeed waved his words away, saying, 'I don't think you need to be thanking me, Anirudh. I just did what's expected of a human being. I didn't do anything special. There were many others who joined hands and took care of things.'

'Well, that's true, and I will be thanking them all. Another reason you are here is because you are one of the people I have been able to establish a close connect with when I was Anirudh. It's only fair to bid you adieu in person.'

Safeed nodded.

Anirudh looked into the horizon, and whispered, 'All that humanity needed was one simple thought—live your life freely, and try not to consciously hurt people.'

'Is it possible to live life without hurting anyone?'

'Well, when do you feel hurt? When something happens that goes against your expectations? Can a person who has no expectations ever be disappointed or hurt?'

Safeed chipped in, 'Ah. And while it is possible to unconsciously hurt someone, I guess if we actually communicate and clear the misunderstandings, things will be good. The hurt will be gone.'

'True. But that would require the "hurt" person to keep their ego aside,' Anirudh said with a smile.

After a pause, the Supreme Being spoke, 'Going back to your earlier notion—you thought that I wouldn't meet you because of your religious beliefs. Your words made me realize something about the human mindset. Humans have divided themselves into religions and followers of various gods. But come to think of it, when the time comes, their gods are going to be looking for just one answer—have they been good human beings? None of the gods are going to even bother wondering whether the person has been a good follower of theirs.'

Safeed, considering his words, spoke, 'Well, it is true. Regardless of the existence of gods, every human being can at least decide at the start of the day that they would try to be a good person that day. And at the end of the day, they can ask themselves if they succeeded in that goal.'

Anirudh smiled and nodded. 'That would definitely make a lot of difference, and it would change so many things for the better.'

SIXTY-ONE

'You really aren't Anirudh,' Avyay said in a dejected manner, ending her statement with a sigh. She was walking on the sandy beach, softly tossing the granular mud with her feet as she walked.

Walking beside her, Purusha looked at her and understood her grievance.

'No, I am not the Anirudh you loved, or love.'

'Is that why you have been distant ever since you returned?'

'I haven't returned, I have taken form now. So, technically, I can't be distant.'

'I know, I am sorry. I just can't get over the fact that you look just like Anirudh.'

'Well, I chose this form because I had been this, and it was convenient.'

'Are you planning to meet your parents?' she asked.

The listener raised an eyebrow, and answered after a pause, 'I am assuming you are referring to Anirudh's parents. No, I am not meeting them.'

Avyay stared at him for some time, and he explained further.

'If it were Anirudh who had returned from the dead, then he would have. But I am not Anirudh. You know it well. And even his parents would realize the same. So why should I aggravate their pain? They aren't going to be any happier to see Anirudh's physical form once they realize that it is not actually their Anirudh. Just like you are feeling torn at the moment.'

Avyay nodded softly.

'It's not our body that defines us, it's our soul—our inner essence—isn't it?' she asked, pondering out loud.

'Indeed,' he replied.

After a pause, she asked, 'What happened to Kali? How did you kill him?'

Purusha smiled and told her, 'When did I ever say that I killed him? Killing Kali was Kalki's mission, not mine.'

'You said he's gone for good, so I assumed that he was dead, that you ended him.'

Clicking his tongue, Purusha said, 'Nah. I never intended to kill him. Instead, I gave him all that he wanted—riches, gold, power, everything. However, having understood that they are all but illusory pleasures to the senses, and that they didn't give him the happiness his soul craved, he gave them all up and turned over a new leaf. He changed for good, and I left him to find his own path and calling.'

Avyay stopped walking and looked at him, wide-mouthed. 'Are you telling me Kali, the personification of evil, *the evilest soul*, has changed into a good being, and he is still alive?'

The Supreme Being stepped beside her and answered, 'It's been twenty-four years, I don't know if he is still alive. I haven't checked on him since that day. But yes, he changed into a good being. And he is not the evilest soul, he never was.'

Avyay considered the words and resumed walking. 'Ahhh . . . I see. Humans are worse than Kali, aren't they?'

'Yes, they are indeed.'

Avyay stopped walking again as a thought struck her. Almost apologetically, she said, 'I am sorry. I failed Bhoomidevi. I couldn't protect her. Humankind has failed her, and I haven't been able to prevent it. I couldn't restore the balance between man and nature.'

'Well, in your defence, you tried your best to make things better. So, *you* haven't failed Bhoomidevi. Human beings have failed Bhoomidevi.'

'Still, maybe if I had put in a bit more effort, you may not have considered this extreme action of cleansing the world.'

'True, a bit more effort from mankind, and I may not have been here in the first place. But what's mankind doing today? Where are they placing their efforts at the moment?'

Avyay knew what he was hinting at, but she remained quiet.

Purusha spoke in a tone of severity, 'A month from now, people are going to start flying off to Mars and other distant planets, since Earth has become inhospitable. The seas are filled with waste, the air is filled with toxicity, the earth has become poisonous. So off they sail to other planets, having damaged their home beyond repair! And they are going to keep doing this . . . They will make every planet a dumping yard and keep moving to other planets. But no, they won't pause and reflect on their actions. If their efforts today are on making other planets hospitable, why aren't they directing their efforts and resources towards making their home a better place? Why not look after and nurture and heal Mother Nature, who has been selflessly providing them with everything?'

Avyay remained quiet, for she had no counter argument.

'And to be honest,' Purusha hissed, 'I haven't taken the extreme action of cleansing the world. It's not up to me. Bhoomidevi will take the decision.'

Avyay nodded. Then, suddenly, she smiled. Purusha gave her a questioning glance.

'Well, the reason for two Kalkis was because the decision of the fate of the world was too heavy a burden to rest on a single person's shoulders. And Anirudh once told me that maybe we'd never have to make the decision. He said that Krishna might have been wrong. I guess I now know why Anirudh said that. Perhaps he always knew that Bhoomidevi should be taking the decision.'

'True,' the Brahman said with a smile. 'But you wanted to make the world a better place, and you tried your best. So it's not for nothing. At least, you can be at peace knowing that you gave it a shot.'

Avyay nodded ruefully.

'If Anirudh came back, do you think he would have spent his time saving the world?'

The young man smiled softly. 'Wouldn't you both have discussed and reached an agreement?'

'That's true . . . I still can't help but wonder. Maybe he would have come up with better ways to remedy things.'

'Well, I know this for sure . . . if the decision to end things was taken, then he would have chosen you to end it all.'

Curious, with furrowed brows, she asked, 'Why me?'

'Avyay, the one in whom the universe merges—another meaning of your name.'

Avyay smiled softly.

After taking a deep breath, she sat down on the sand, her eyes fixed on the blue sea in front of her. The young man just stood by, taking in the fresh air.

'So, if Bhoomidevi decided to end things, then wouldn't the innocent perish as well?'

'Yes, they will. It's not like they are prospering under the dominion of mankind. The relentless pursuit of progress by man, at every cost, is already threatening their existence. How much forest cover is left now? It's down to the single digits. Along with it, many native tribes, exotic animals and plant species have vanished. The average temperature has jumped by at least five units. The thing is, humankind knows the cost of their advancement. But they are ready to pay it, since it is not *their wallet* it is coming out of. They are ready to damage the ecosystems of others for their selfish benefits. Of course, there won't be any damage to their personal ecosystems, for humans will adapt to all the reactions of nature and consequences. And if humankind can be dispassionate towards their surroundings, to their blessings, to other living beings, then I can be dispassionate towards every single human being. I can be dispassionate about the whole world, for I care about only one person.'

Avyay sighed. After a moment's consideration, 'Did you know that this is how things would unfold with mankind's presence?'

'No.'

'Aren't you all-knowing?'

'I know everything about the past and present, but this . . . If I had known the future, then I could have told you for sure what's going to happen regarding the fate of the universe.'

'Ummm, so you mean to say you never could know that humankind was going to take a certain path, or possible paths, which could lead to the devastation of Prakriti and the beings in it?'

The Brahman sat down next to her and conjured a sandy chessboard, with all the pieces ready for a game. Avyay looked at it curiously and then back at him.

'Do you know how many possible moves the first player can make here?'

Avyay counted the possible moves of the pawns and the knights, and she answered, 'Twenty. And even the second player would have the same number of moves available.'

'True. Now, after both the players make their moves,' he asked, pointing to the board, 'how many possible moves exist?'

Avyay pursed her lips.

'400,' said Purusha, saving her the effort of calculating the moves. 'After the second round of moves, there are 19,000 more plays possible. After three moves, 120 million plays are possible. Can you imagine?'

Avyay stared at the speaker, wide-mouthed. She gasped, 'You have got to be kidding me!'

He spoke, 'No, I am not. And all this is possible with just thirty-two pieces on a sixty-four-square board.'

He waved his hand at the chessboard made of sand, and it reshaped itself into a ball—the globe.

The Supreme Soul spoke, pointing at the earth, 'Now, picture one billion people spread across the globe. Imagine the number of possible actions the whole race can take at a given point—changing the course of their fate, changing the universe's destiny . . . The sheer amount of power and force that humankind wields! If they set their hearts to do a good deed, then can it be impossible?'

Waving his hand again, Anirudh dissolved the globe, and said, 'If they collectively decide to make Earth the best place to live, to uplift all humans and make everyone live decent lives, to nourish nature and other beings in it, wouldn't this world be the best place to live? But, sadly, the powerful and blessed humans do not care about their surroundings or their fellows. They are looking to make other planets their home, abandoning their original home.'

'You really don't like them going to other planets, do you?'

'If you are asking me if I'm not in favour of man exploring the universe, then you read me wrong. I am all for progress and space exploration for knowledge. What I don't like is that they are escaping to other planets, leaving their home in disarray. No one is trying to clean up the mess they made. They have just given up on Earth. The humans will go to another planet, but what about the broken ecosystem they are leaving behind? How can any other life survive here? They are escaping because Earth is not habitable anymore, and life will not be sustainable in a few years. Man is leaving Earth, but the plants, trees, animals and birds will still be here, won't they? And how will they survive?! The air is polluted, so is the water and soil. They are going to die a slow death, and humankind doesn't even care about it. And I am not in favour of that apathy.'

He finally concluded, saying, 'To answer your earlier question, I could never predict that humankind and their actions would lead to the devastation of Prakriti. There are just so many things that humans could have done to make the world a better place, but they never took those paths. And now that humankind has taken a considerable number of actions against Prakriti, I know that I have to support Her and help Her survive.'

SIXTY-TWO

'That decision of Bhoomidevi's isn't easy to make, is it?' Dweepa asked, as the two of them walked on the cool, sandy beach by the ocean.

Purusha stopped and turned to look at the sage. The mentor paused and turned towards the man, who looked at the sage keenly. Many years had passed since he'd seen the sage. Dweepa was old now but still fit, with a few grey strands of hair here and there.

'Tell me this, sage: why do you think Krishna told your ancestor that he should watch the submergence of Dwarka? What was the lesson to be learnt from that event? What is the lesson that *you* learnt from that event?'

The sage looked at Purusha curiously and then scratched his chin. 'What is the lesson?'

The Brahman resumed walking and Dweepa walked alongside.

'The lesson, Sage Dweepa, is that everything that has been created will be destroyed. Some of them in few days; some, in a few years; some, in a few centuries; and some, in a few aeons. Everything that is born, dies. That's the law of nature. And Dwarka had its end coming. Tell me this, dear sage. Krishna was all-knowing, correct? And all-powerful too?'

Dweepa nodded.

'So, please correct me if I am wrong, Krishna knew how his race would end, he knew the submergence of Dwarka would happen and yet, he didn't change the course of the fate of his people, nor of the city he created for his people. He let things happen as they would, right?'

The sage nodded again, his eyes slowly widening in recognition of the thought process of the speaker.

Anirudh continued speaking, 'Krishna didn't change the destiny of his people because it had to happen. His own folk had become *adharmi*, immoral. He tried his best to prevent internal conflicts, but it was all in vain. So Krishna went along with the fate written for his people, and he was aware of it. He knew the ultimate truth—all that is created will be destroyed.'

Sage Dweepa pursed his lips. The swirl of questions that had risen in his mind after hearing Purusha's words settled down after he asked just two questions, 'But can't one change destiny? If everything is pre-written, then what's the purpose of a human being's life?'

The Brahman smiled. 'Very good questions, Sage Dweepa. I will answer them each, and I will start with the first one. Before I answer that, tell me this. What is destiny, Sage? How is it written, or determined? In simpler words, what determines a person's destiny?'

'Well, a person's actions—past and present. They determine their destiny, don't they?'

'Correct. In other words, what goes around comes around. So destiny isn't written in stone. Some parts of a person's life are written in stone, like birth and death. But those are the same for all living beings. Only humans possess the power to change their destiny through their actions. Based on the past, their destiny is already written. While the past remains unchangeable, the present action can be changed to influence a better future. Meaning, you can change your destiny with your actions. But if your present course of action is along the same lines as that of your past, then the pre-written destiny, or a worse one, will be realized. So humankind has the ability to change their fate with their actions, and they can change it for good or bad.'

Dweepa bowed in acknowledgement of his words.

'Now, coming to your second question, the question of the purpose of a human being's life. Well . . . Tell me this, Sage, what's the difference between humankind and the rest of the nature, like plants, trees, animals? Is a human special in the eyes of Mother Nature for some reason?'

'Well, humankind can think, decide, act and influence their surroundings, while other beings in the nature can't really do all this. So yes, I guess this makes them special in the eyes of Mother Nature.'

The Brahman smiled and said, 'Well, Sage Dweepa, I am afraid you are mistaken about the second part. Man, woman, child—no human being is special in the eyes of Mother Nature. Everything and everyone is equal in the eyes of Prakriti. The sun shines the same on everyone, the rain showers the same on everyone, birth and death are written for everyone . . . everything is same for everyone. So, it is *humans* who think they are special, because of their ego. But the truth is that Prakriti treats everyone the same.'

Dweepa pursed his lips apologetically.

'However,' Purusha continued, 'you are correct about the difference between humankind and nature. Of all the creatures in the nature, only humans have the ability to think, create, imagine and control, amongst other things. Humankind is blessed with a mind, but that's their shackle as well.'

Dweepa looked quizzically at the Brahman.

His companion noticed this and explained, 'Your mind, while helping you be creative, is also producing your ego, your desires, your attachments. It is letting you grow but it is also limiting you. It is locking your true nature. And what's the key to unlocking it and setting yourself free? It is you, yourself. Like I said, everyone is the same to Prakriti. But men think that they are special, that they are superior, and that's leading them to harm Prakriti, intentionally or unintentionally. They cast an inferior eye on all the other aspects of nature around them, and that's because their ego has inflated to the extent that they *believe* they are the special creations of nature. But the truth is, they aren't. A tsunami that strikes this instant will wipe out everyone and everything alike—be it human, plant, tree, flower, animal, car or building. No one is special to Mother Nature. But humans are different from all the others because they are blessed with a mind. Using their mind, they can understand, expand their knowledge, control their senses and desires, and help take care of their fellow humans and other living beings in nature. In order to do all this, you would have to let go of attachments, destroy desires and ego, and become selfless. In other words, break free from the shackles of your mind. Rise above your mind and body, and then, and only then, will you become one with your soul.'

'And thereby become one with God . . . So the purpose of mankind is to attain godhood?' Dweepa asked.

'If the highest version of one's self is God, then yes, godhood.'

'Well, aren't you the highest version? Aren't you *the* God?'

Purusha smiled softly, and then took in a deep breath. Turning to the sage, he said, 'Sage Dweepa, please know this, I am not *the* God, and I am not any god. Gods are the creation of the human mind. I am formless, I am that which is everything. A single strand connecting everything. The universe is Prakriti, and I am the soul in it, the consciousness. The energy. The seed. The gods, the religions and the castes are a construct of the human mind.'

After a pause, he continued, 'To be honest, when you mention gods and goddesses, various religions come to mind. In the world around you, in Mother Nature, everything and everyone is equal. There are birds, animals, trees, fish, but there are no religions among them. It is humans, who with their mind, have created the manacles of religion. Why do you need religions and castes when all they do is divide people and pit them against each other? I understand, and I also agree that it's all right to follow a different set of principles and commandments and ideologies, but it should not lead to conflict among humans. Consider it this way, if X likes apple juice, and meets Y, who likes carrot juice, they are not going to tear each other apart, are they? They are not going to judge each other, or bear any animosity because of it, are they?'

Dweepa shook his head, understanding the words of the Supreme Being.

The Brahman continued, 'If people sitting on the upper echelons of society use this as a tool to divide people, then humans are blessed with enough intelligence and power to see through the schemes. And they can collectively choose to eradicate religion and caste, everyone can be united. Can this be done, Sage?'

Dweepa shrugged his shoulders and said, doubtfully, 'I guess so.'

'No. It cannot be,' Purusha answered sharply. 'At least not given the current circumstances. And that's because the people in charge, be it of religion or of state, love the power they wield. They are shackled by their minds. How hard is it for all the leaders, or all the humans, to get together and decide to forgo all the divisions that have sprung from the human mind? They can choose to follow a common set of principles or commandments, instead of religious doctrines. Deal with things at a spiritual level, not at a mental or an emotional level.'

The sage nodded as Anirudh continued speaking, 'The benefits of not having religious, caste or gender divides outweigh the benefits of having them. There wouldn't be any honour killings, people could start focusing on their spiritual grown, there wouldn't be hatred and people will finally be free to live in peace and brotherhood.'

Purusha looked at the sage, and the sage saw a question looming in his eyes. 'Are you a Hindu, Sage Dweepa?'

Sage Dweepa smiled, 'I am a man who follows certain principles and ethics. And they happen to be a part of the Hindu religion. If they are a part of Sikh, Muslim, Christian cultures as well, then I am a Sikh, Muslim and Christian too.'

'Well, I am glad to hear your answer. You have truly grasped what religion means. And that shows your spiritual maturity too.'

After a moment's consideration of his own words, Purusha spoke, 'People confuse religious faith with spiritual growth. Spiritual growth is getting in touch with, and realizing, your spirit. Religion can only guide you to be a good human, and up to a certain extent, help you control your mind and body. It can prove to be a tool to help you focus. But it is not necessary. An atheist can be a spiritually realized individual as well. But faith—that's something else altogether. It doesn't stem from the need for spiritual growth, it stems from the need to feel protected, to feel loved, to feel cared for. And religion today has become a tool. The way the concept of god and religion has been ingrained, it is leading towards spiritual dependency, rather than towards spiritual freedom. People are being divided and cast away on the basis of their faith and following. Spiritual growth helps you love and appreciate people on a formless level, whereas religion leads to prejudices and barriers and hatred. People depend on gods and goddesses to a degree that it chains them and prevents them from realizing their true potential. Oh, I really wish that the religions were banned, Sage.'

Dweepa's jaw fell open. 'What?' he gasped.

The Supreme Brahman, his voice bearing frustration, said, 'You heard me, Dweepa. I said that I wish humankind would forget the idea of religion. Well, not just that, I also wish they'd discard all the ideas that are divisive—caste, gender, race, status . . . Does it sound like blasphemy? But that's the thing. It isn't blasphemy! Blasphemy and sacredness are creations of the human mind, Sage.'

Taking a deep breath, he continued, 'Every single human being is composed of the same five elements. Everyone and everything has a fragment of me in them, and when they perish, they all turn to dust. So tell me, Sage, why are humans who are naturally the same in every aspect, divide themselves in such a despicable manner? Why don't they unite and live peacefully? Why should humans in blessed nature live in fear or hatred of each other based on prejudices of an artificial label that does nothing but help the upper echelon drive their propaganda. The horrors created by these barriers are far more, and worse than anything else. When Prakriti unleashes the *pralaya*, the all-conquering flood, on this earth, every human is going to be swallowed by the waters, regardless of their religion, caste, creed, sex or any other category they've divided themselves into.'

Considering these words, Dweepa asked, 'Why don't you give us another chance?'

Purusha shot back, 'And what do you hope to achieve?'

'Unification of mankind.'

The Supreme Soul smirked, 'Even if I give you a thousand chances, that won't happen.'

Dweepa responded, 'You are being unfair. You seem to have already given up on humanity.'

In a chilling voice, the Supreme Being replied, '*Seem to?* I *have* already given up on humanity. Twenty-four years, Dweepa. I waited for twenty-four years for humanity to rise above their shackles and make this earth a better place, but they have failed me. Twenty-four years is a really long time, Sage! That's twenty-four years of Mother Nature suffering silently. And I really can't be unfair to her now.'

EPILOGUE

The Brahman walked on the sandy beach, alone. The cool breeze caressed his skin and the sound of playful sea waves filled his ears. His strides were determined, he knew where he was headed. A curving path came up, and he traversed the turn. Then, he saw his destination.

At a distance, there was a large stone cliff, uniting the beach and the sea. A stony pathway snaked out from the shore and went up to the large, flat plain atop the mountain. The mountaintop stretched over and above the deep waters, like a beak. The grey stone cliff was adorned with green shrubs, plants and colourful flowers. The yellow sun glimmered palely on the rock. The blue waters created a serene ambience.

Atop the mountain, on its plain surface, there was a large throne-like structure made of stone.

Purusha smiled and quickened his steps. However, his pace slowed to a cautious tread when he saw a figure lying on the sand. As soon as he realized who it was, he started running towards the figure.

He was here to meet her. This was her abode. Her home. It had been about twenty-four years since he'd met her.

He had last met her when he had first arrived at this esoteric place. When he saw her disintegrated health that day, he had decided that he would give humankind one last chance to mend their ways.

Reaching the immobile figure in a couple of moments, he sat down on the sand and cradled her head in his lap.

'Bhoomidevi,' Purusha whispered.

Seeing her heart-rending condition, tears started escaping his eyes. He held the crippled figure of Prakriti in his arms, holding her close. Her eyes were closed, tired and worn out. All over her body were patches burnt down to her skeleton. Her face had hollowed in deep, and the burnt skin clung to her skull.

Upon seeing her immobile body and her closed eyes, Anirudh realized that she had collapsed on the beach. Conjuring some water in his hand, he splashed it gently on her face. When the water droplets hit her, she stirred slightly. She opened her eyes and looked at the figure holding her. He looked into her faded, grey eyes.

'Oh . . . I have been waiting for you for so long . . .' she whispered.

'What has happened to you, Devi?' he asked, amid tears.

She smiled slightly through her broken lips, and spoke, her voice a bare whisper. 'You are here, that's all that matters . . .'

Purusha clasped her hand softly, and she clasped his palm.

'How did this happen, Devi?' he asked.

'We knew that the poison mankind infected me with was bound to do this to me one day . . .'

Anirudh looked down at the sad condition of Prakriti. Her green saree was burnt and gone, for the most part. Some patches of the fabric remained burnt on her skin. Her arms and legs were bone-thin and at some places, he could see the bones as well. Her stomach had sunk in and her skin was broken and burnt all over. There was no inch of her skin that was intact. Her head was bare, except for a few strands of white hair.

Swallowing his tears, the Supreme Being asked, 'When did this happen? When did you collapse?'

'A few minutes . . . Meaning a few years in Earth time.'

'Then why didn't you call me right that very moment, Prakriti?' he asked in a tone full of agony and sorrow.

Seeing Bhoomidevi's horrific condition, he silently regretted giving humankind a chance they hadn't deserved.

'I knew you would come when the time was right, Purusha. You always have.'

He softly ran his thumb down her cheek and she closed her eyes to his touch.

In the haze of the comfort she got from his touch, she whispered, 'Help me up the mountain, please?'

Purusha looked up at the mountain top, at the stone throne. *Bhoomidevi's seat!*

He nodded and picked her up in his arms and carried her up the hill.

He rested her on the throne. After ensuring that she was comfortable, Purusha stepped back and looked at her seat. Her stone throne was large and had intricate carvings on it. There were two broad armrests and the seat rested on a giant rock cube. There were no legs to her regal chair. The backrest was large and tall, and its top was adorned with flowers and grass. Taking a deep breath, he turned and looked at the surroundings. The ground was covered in soft, green grass. The edges of the plain were covered in flowers of various hues. The fragrance of those flowers filled his senses. The sun, yellow like a ripe mango, glimmered softly in the sky.

The golden luminescence fell on the ground and the plants around him. He walked over to one of the edges and the sight of the gentle sea greeted him. He turned and walked to the queen of the esoteric place. Bhoomidevi was barely alive, and this place would have reflected her decay if it hadn't been for the Brahman's energy, which infused the whole area.

'You know why I have come, right?' he asked her.

With a strain, she nodded. 'I don't know what my answer is, my lord.'

'Don't call me "lord", Bhoomidevi,' he reminded her, with that dimpled smile of his. 'And as far as the answer is concerned, I think it is plain enough. You know what to do. Your current condition is evidence enough to help you decide the next course of action. However, I shall await your answer, Devi.'

She replied in a struggling whisper, 'I don't know if I will be able to do it.'

Purusha looked at her quietly. He didn't speak a word. And Prakriti understood the meaning of his silence. He would support her in whatever choice she made. But it was up to her to make the choice. He wouldn't make the choice *for* her.

She rested her back on the throne and looked at the Supreme Being. 'You were telling Avyay, using the analogy of a chess game, that humans kept making the wrong choices despite the number of choices available to them.'

He nodded, curious about where the conversation was headed. And he wasn't surprised that she knew about his conversation with Avyay. She was all-knowing too.

'So, then,' she continued, 'what would have happened if humans had made the right choices?'

'They would have become spiritually realized people. They would have understood the true nature of their soul and become one single organism.'

'And then? What would they have done after that?'

'After they grow spiritually, they would have been like the gods they imagined—filled with compassion and love for everyone and everything alike. They would have nurtured life on this earth and made it green and healthy. They would have nourished this planet and made it the best place to live.'

'That sounds like a beautiful dream, an ideal one. What would have happened after that?'

'Well, the dream becomes more beautiful and more ideal than you imagine. Since they are already on the precipice of space exploration, they would roam and inhabit various planets. They would take care of all the planets and nurture them. You would have been livelier and healthier than you ever had been, Prakriti Devi.'

'Are you serious? This is way too fantastic, Deva.'

'Of all the creations, only humankind has the ability to do this. So even though it sounds fantastic, I can assure you that it is not impossible.'

She nodded softly. 'What happens after that? After they become the nourisher of galaxies?'

Purusha's eyes narrowed and he asked her, 'What are you trying to get at, Devi?'

Clearing her throat, she explained, whispering, 'I am trying to understand the purpose of man's life. If, after a point, there is no work left for man to do, then what's the use of their existence? They are questioning it now, and they will question it even then.'

'True. To answer your question, after they become the caretaker of galaxies, humankind has to sustain the nourishment, until it all comes to an end.'

'What?'

'Why are you shocked, Devi? Everything that begins has to end as well. That's the unbreakable rule. And sustaining isn't an easy task, you know it better than anyone.'

She nodded, considering his words. 'The unbreakable rule, like you said. All that is born has to die . . . The end is always present. Perhaps that's why humans are of the mindset to live in the moment and take all the pleasures available to them in their lifetime. They make the wrong choices and stray from the path of righteousness because they are trying to make the best use of the finite.'

Anirudh took a deep breath and shook his head softly. Then he spoke, 'Tell me this, Devi. Despite all of man's wrongdoings, why haven't you taken the decision to end things? Why are you not living in the moment? Why are you absorbing all of man's torture and bearing all of the torment silently?'

'Because they are immature. They don't understand what's wrong and right. They are innocent, Purusha.'

'Devi, don't turn a blind eye to their wrongdoings! Mankind knows really well that what they are doing is wrong. They intentionally cut down forests to make space for their skyscrapers. They torture and breed animals. They treat other humans with apathy. They treat transgender and sexual minorities as outcastes. They treat people belonging to other religions and castes with prejudice. They litter the earth and the oceans alike. And now, having realized that they have damaged the earth beyond repair, they are fleeing to another planet. But have they learnt from their past mistakes? No! This cycle will continue. With mankind's presence on just one planet, this is your condition . . . I really don't want to imagine what would happen to you if they set foot on other planets, Devi.'

Prakriti sat silently, understanding the sense in his words.

'Do you know, Devi, what the saddest thing is? At least according to me?'

Mother Nature looked up at the Supreme Being, and she found anger and sadness in his smouldering gaze.

'When living beings wish that they were dead, they curse their life because other human beings have made them regret their birth.'

Tears welled up and trickled down Bhoomidevi's eyes. She could feel the pain in his words, and she had felt it in a lot of beings throughout time. He felt it in them too.

'But coming back to your earlier question. The purpose of the 'nourisher', of humankind, will always remain the same—upliftment and sustenance of all forms of life. The spiritually realized people would understand the truth—that they are but a part of the universe and are blessed with powers to feed and nurture all life forms. They would do it without any expectations. However, given that they are not spiritually developed, humankind is obviously selfish. They are under the assumption that they are the only beings that matter and are of importance. They know that this notion is incorrect, but they are trapped by their minds and egos.'

'I don't mind humans enjoying, or living, life,' he added, 'but I do mind it when they do so at the expense of other beings. That's wrong.'

Bhoomidevi spoke in a whisper, 'And despite knowing that this is wrong, humans still behave the same way. Not all of them, but a sizeable chunk does.'

He spoke, 'Sizeable enough to deteriorate your condition beyond a point of no return . . .'

Looking into her eyes, he spoke, 'So contrary to your previous assumption, humans aren't really innocent. Their conscious decisions have brought us to this point,

Prakriti Devi. They spent unbelievable amounts of money in getting the space inhabitation set-up in place. They could have spent that money wisely in making the earth a better place, undoing their past mistakes as much as possible.'

'I know, Purusha. But still, it's not an easy decision to make. Help me, please?' she pleaded in a whisper.

Dispassionately, he replied, 'Sorry, Devi. I won't help you with the decision. You know that very well.'

She looked at him with a mixture of frustration and helplessness. And he looked back at her.

Then, with an understanding smile, he spoke, 'All right, Prakriti Devi. I will bring a couple of points to your notice. Hopefully, it aids your decision-making process.'

'Yes, please . . . Thank you . . .' she said with gratitude. Her features visibly softened.

'So you know very well that humans are not the only beings on this earth. You are the Mother of all things across the entire universe, seen and unseen. So everything and everyone matters to you. When humans leave this planet, you know the state it will be in. No life can be sustained in this polluted environment. The damage is irreversible and will lead all remaining beings to their deaths. You can choose to end everything, so that you can give the innocent a quick death. Also, if humankind were to set foot on other planets, those lands would face the same fate as Earth. And human beings might just realize the gravity of their recklessness too late to correct anything, just like they have failed with Earth. But by then, even if humankind realizes the error of their ways, many planets and beings would already have been laid to waste.'

He added, 'So, you have a choice—either end everything now or prolong the atrocities on other life forms and make them victims of human cruelty. The former choice is fair to everyone, the latter is unfair to everyone except humankind. Having said all of this, I am open to counterarguments. I will support you in whatever decision you take, Devi. You have always had the freedom to do what you want, and you always will.'

Prakriti Devi nodded. Seeing that Purusha had been standing for a long time now, she conjured a throne next to hers and motioned him to sit. He bowed in gratitude but gestured that he would sit later. She nodded, and then sat quietly in thought.

After thinking a bit about Purusha's words, she conjured a wooden cane. Holding it firm in her hand, she placed its tip on the ground and slowly got up from her throne. Using the walking stick, she dragged her delicate and disintegrated body to the edge of the cliff.

'Do you recall I had asked you once what makes the protector the destroyer?' she asked as she looked at the sun.

The Supreme Being smiled and said, 'Yes, I do.'

'Well, I know the answer now . . . But I guess you already knew it,' she whispered, her eyes still fixed on the glowing orange ball.

Her companion simply replied, 'Yes, I did.'

With tears slowly trickling down her cheeks, she whispered, 'How strange are the ways in which love works.'

He stood still, for he understood every emotion of hers, and he felt every feeling she felt.

Sniffling softly and taking a deep breath, she turned and looked at Purusha as he spoke.

'All creatures and beings, don't worry about their end. They will all dissolve into me. So it's not a bad thing after all . . . I hope?' he added with a grin.

Bhoomidevi smiled feebly, that's all she could manage with her torn skin.

'I am afraid, Anirudh,' she whispered, taking the name of his physical form.

Purusha's brows furrowed, and he asked her, 'Afraid of what?'

'Of the end, of course. You know, don't you, that the end of everything means the end of me . . .'

'I know that, Devi,' he whispered, 'but why do you think it is the end for you?'

'Of course, it is the end. Only if I die will everything else die.'

'You are not going to die, Devi.'

Prakriti looked at him with curiosity-filled eyes.

Looking at her quizzical expression, Anirudh asked her, 'In this whole universe, in all that you have created, there is just one thing that I created. What is it?'

Bhoomidevi looked at the sea behind her, and then turned back to the Brahman.

'That's correct, only this sea below us is my creation,' he confirmed to her.

He continued, 'And that's for a reason. It is the sea of creation.'

Full of earnestness, he stepped closer to her. He put his arm around her fragile waist and caressed her jawline with his thumb.

As his touch brushed against her skin, she closed her eyes, absorbing his care and love for her. They were strengthening her, and she breathed softly. She heard him speak, his soft voice consoling her.

He said, 'Everything in the world will end, it should end. For that's *your* rule. But you will never end, Devi. For that's *my* rule. Even if everything ends, you will remain. Just like I remain. Always.'

She opened her eyes and looked into his.

'You will save me, Deva? Do you promise me?'

'I will save you—I promise you, Devi.'

She saw the confidence and truth in his eyes, his assurance. She took a deep breath. Anirudh let go of her and took a step back.

She looked at him and he looked back at her.

'What's going to happen now, my lord?'

He was going to admonish her for addressing him as 'lord', but he decided against it. Instead, he just smiled and said, 'Creation. And what does creation bring about?'

His question brought forth a deep smile to her lips.

'New beginnings,' she whispered.

They both looked into each other's eyes. They could see the love they bore for each other. Even their silence had a language of its own.

She silently expressed, *I love you, Purusha.*

He replied non-verbally, *I love you, Prakriti Devi.*

'You will be with me, right?' she asked, slightly worried.

'Always, I promise you,' he told her, with his characteristic reassuring smile.

She smiled back. Then, she closed her eyes and took a deep breath.

New beginnings, she told him.

New beginnings, he replied to her.

Bhoomidevi let go off the walking stick, and it evaporated into thin air. With her eyes still closed, she took a step backwards and gracefully went off the edge, into the blue sea below.

After a couple of moments, Anirudh heard a splash. Anirudh closed his eyes. He observed that everything, and everyone, in the universe had dissolved into nothing. The Immortals, Avyay, EOK—all of them ceased being. He opened his eyes, the place around him was still intact. And that was by design.

He took a couple of long strides towards the edge, and then leapt off it, diving head first into the sea below.

Under the waves, he squinted to locate Prakriti Devi. Having not found her in the vicinity, he moved his arms and propelled himself deeper into the watery womb.

After searching for a few moments, something a few feet deeper caught his attention. He quickly dove towards it. Upon reaching it, he smiled softly. His eyes were resting on the body of a baby, curled up in a ball. Stretching his hands, he gently pulled the infant Prakriti close to him and looked at the sleeping figure.

He smiled deeply as he held her close.

New beginnings.

Purusha, having emerged from the sea, walked towards the spiral pathway that led up the stony mountain. His hands supported her neck and bottom, while her head rested on his shoulder. A couple of moments later, she started crying. He smiled and patted her gently. He sang softly to her as he carried the infant Prakriti to the top of the hill.

He reached the top and sat down on the second throne that Bhoomidevi had conjured for him. Out of thin air, he procured a green cloth and wrapped the baby in it. She had stopped crying as she listened to his song. He conjured a floral wreath and placed the crown on her tiny head. Purusha cradled her in his arms and looked down at the infant's face. Her skin was aglow in the yellow luminescence of the sun.

Anirudh patted her softly, humming to her. There was silence across the whole universe. The only sounds were his humming, Prakriti's breath and her intermittent coos. She looked at the sun, and her eyes fixated on it in wonder. The golden sun shone in her soft ocean-blue eyes.

Purusha's eyes were fixed on her, as he hummed softly. Her eyes rested on him, and she yawned softly. This made him laugh slightly, and she smiled seeing him laugh. He kissed her forehead gently and resumed humming. She closed her eyes and snuggled closer to Purusha's chest. He kept humming so that he wouldn't disrupt her sleep.

Sleep well, Prakriti. It has been a long day . . .

He looked at the sun and took in its pale-golden luminescence on the green grass and flowers. He pushed himself further back into his seat. He looked at the pleasant surroundings and smiled softly. It was all peaceful now across the whole world. The silence was comforting him, and it had already comforted Prakriti, who was deep asleep. He took in a deep breath, taking in the harmony into his essence. Purusha and Prakriti were at peace now.

He looked down at Infant Nature in his arms. Taking a deep breath, he lay his head back on the throne's headrest.

It has been a long day . . .

He closed his eyes and drifted into a restful sleep.

THE NEW BEGINNING

❦

Read More by Abhinav

THE SAGE'S SECRET

(Book 1 in The Kalki Chronicles)

What if the legend of Kalki, the tenth avatar of Vishnu, is an elaborate hoax created by Lord Krishna?

In the year 2025, twenty-year-old Anirudh starts dreaming of Krishna. But these visions that keep flashing through his mind are far from an ordinary fantasy-they are vivid episodes from the god's life. Through these scenes, as Krishna's mystifying schemes are revealed, Anirudh slowly comes to terms with his real identity . . .

He is the last avatar of Vishnu, sent to restore the balance between good and evil. But an ancient and powerful nemesis, burning with the fire of revenge, has already started assembling a clan of mighty sorcerers to finally be rid of the protector god and unleash depravity on earth.

Will Anirudh realize his potential before it's too late? Or will the enemy destroy everything in their wake before the avatar finally manifests? This gripping read is the first part in the Kalki Chronicles, which unveils the greatest legend of the Kali yuga.

Read More by Abhinav

KALI'S RETRIBUTION

(Book 2 in The Kalki Chronicles)

**A god with a powerful weapon. An immortal sorcerer.
An inevitable showdown.**

Successful in deciphering Krishna's puzzles and retrieving the Kaustubha locket, Anirudh finally accepts his destiny as Kalki--the tenth avatar of Vishnu. However, with the ever-perilous world moving too fast for him to keep up with, he is taken under the wing of an esoteric society created for his protection.

As ancient allies watch over him from the Himalayas, Anirudh moves to find the greatest weapon in the universe hidden in the fabled submerged palace of Dwarka. However, the Demon of Time, Kalarakshasa, yearns to possess it as well. In an ultimate showdown, the cloaked sorcerer faces the last avatar of Vishnu on the battlefield.

Will it be long before Kali, the Lord of Evil, takes up the reins of the mortal world? And will the darkness brought upon by the Kali yuga soon eclipse the earth?